Totally Bound Publishing books by Constance Munday:

What's her Secret?: Sweet Secrets

I0674975

What's her Secret?

SWEET SECRETS

CONSTANCE MUNDAY

Sweet Secrets
ISBN # 978-1-78430-128-6
©Copyright Constance Munday 2014
Cover Art by Posh Gosh ©Copyright June 2014
Interior text design by Claire Siemaszkiewicz
Totally Bound Publishing

Published in 2014 by Totally Bound Publishing, Newland House, The Point, Weaver Road, Lincoln, LN6 3QN, United Kingdom.

Totally Bound Publishing is an imprint of Total-E-Ntwined Limited.

SWEET SECRETS

Dedication

To Violet Rose, my grandmother who inspired in me a love of baking and whose apple pie was unsurpassed. And, love and thanks to my mother, who inspired in me a passion for all romance novels through her great love of reading.

Chapter One

The sun warmed Carrie Ann Jude's face as she glanced through the large plate glass windows of the airport. Planes rose into the sky like silver birds, their metal bodies transporting people all over the world on adventures. She tightened her grip on the straps of her handbag. She had been one of those people embarking on an adventure only two weeks ago, except her journey had not started just with feelings of excitement, but trepidation. She pushed her sunglasses up over her head and took out her paperback to flip through. It was hard to concentrate with so many thoughts dancing in her head.

Carrie Ann was so deep in thought she hadn't noticed the stunning youth about to sit down beside her. Wanting to be alone and not have anyone invading her space, she'd put her large bag on the chair next to her. Before she could say anything, he'd had his hand on it and, much to her consternation, had dropped it unceremoniously onto the floor. Then, not giving her time to move out of the way, he dumped a considerably weighty backpack on her foot.

"Ouch. Watch it!" she cried out, as he bumped against her, slopping his coffee over her hand. "That was hot." She angrily snapped her book closed, noticing spots of coffee marking the pages.

"Oh, my God, I'm so sorry. Hi." He had an American accent. "I ought to have asked if you minded if I sat here, but that's me."

She looked up to make a rude retort and found herself glaring into an impossibly green pair of eyes. She flushed. It was so embarrassing to be trapped by his compelling gaze.

"I'm so clumsy, everyone says it." He held out his hand. "I'm truly sorry. My name's Dominic, and you are...?"

How could she resist those eyes and his flirtatious expression? Carrie Ann took hold of his proffered hand and shook it unenthusiastically. "Carrie Ann." What she could only describe as an electrical charge danced up her legs and ended with a pleasant fizz in the tips of her fingers and toes. He was very good-looking and his mop of shaggy blond hair that flopped into his face seemed to remind her of...

"Great." He flashed her a grin. "I'm sorry. Let me get you another coffee."

"No thanks, I don't want one." She was attempting to be more assertive, but it was harder than she'd thought. Actually, everything was so much harder out in the big wide world as she tried to cut ties to her past. Rommy, her father, so named because when he was younger he'd looked devilishly like a true Romany gypsy, had often criticized her for her submissive stance, which was ridiculous since that was what he'd wanted from her. The thought of him sent a creepy crawly shiver down her spine. No one should feel like that about their father, but she did and she couldn't help it. On occasion, she wondered if she would ever be able to get over him, shake loose all the hang-ups and phobias he had given her. It had not been abuse, but he had been good at keeping her under. She realized now she shouldn't have put up with it for so long, she should have fought more for her independence when she'd had a chance to. But that was easier said than done.

The young guy hefted his bag and again knocked her. The nerve of it. She studied him angrily out of the corner of her eye. She had keen powers of observation—it was another one of the little skills she'd developed from being alone so long. Not having a lot to occupy her, she had become exceedingly observant. His arms were bare and muscular and covered in a frosting of tight blond hair. He also had strong, capable hands. Rommy would have said the man's thighs were those of a rugby player. She had a thing about blond men, she reflected. Perhaps that was why she was instantly captivated by him. That came as a surprise and an interesting one, since anger and desire had a potent effect on her newly liberated self. It would be hard to be immune to his charms and it might be fun to test her boundaries yet again. She was woefully inexperienced with men. In a way, stepping out into the world was like learning to drive, and shy girls like her had to approach it slowly and cautiously and be prepared for any sudden unexpected turns in the road or emergency stops. She smiled to herself. She might have been confined to the house for years and had no experience of love first-hand, but she was living and breathing and had the same desires other women had.

For some reason she was shamefully hot and crossed her legs. It was utterly ridiculous being affected like this since Dominic was sexy and because of that was the kind of guy who wouldn't flirt with her, well, not seriously. She tugged her skirt down over her knees. When she glanced up, he was watching her with a wry twist to his lips, as if he found her faintly amusing.

He gestured to the terminal board. "I guess you're heading back to England."

"Naturally," she said. Carrie Ann wondered if she had a sticky label on her forehead, stamped 'England'.

Nervousness made her feel hysterical. She would much prefer to be left alone with her thoughts, besides which it was distinctly embarrassing to have a man's leg pressed against hers. He kept staring at her and she self-consciously stroked her lip. Why did he keep peering at her, like that? Besides the invisible label, there was nothing else that could make her seem even remotely interesting...was there?

At that moment a stunning girl strolled by and Dominic sized her up with interest, his gaze rippling up and down her from the tips of the high heels she was tottering in, to her layer-cut, multi-toned hair. Carrie Ann's spirits sank further. She only had to dissect some of the women around her to realize she was at a distinct disadvantage where flirting was concerned. Let's face it, she wasn't even dressed for seduction. She was draped in her shabby comfortable skirt and she hadn't even bothered with her appearance. As for what Rommy would have rather rudely termed 'slap'—that was like attempting a recipe that was way out of her comfort zone. She'd only recently ventured down the makeup trail and she still didn't like wearing it, although that might soon have to change, if her career plans took off. Makeup was weird stuff. It never looked right on her—the eyeshadow she'd tried made her dark brown eyes seem to retreat backwards so they seemed far too small, her freckles overwhelmed her complexion and her riotous mousy curls defied brushes, combs and tongs.

Any makeup she had used, she'd mistakenly plastered on to cover the freckles, and red lipstick — as Myra, the girl she had met at the ranch had pointed out — made her appear garish. Myra had given her a stick of lipstick termed nude and that did help, teamed with a tinted moisturizer. Myra was a brick, she thought grimly, pity she lived halfway across the world in Australia. She was also into baking, which had been a plus. It had been great to actually have a kindred spirit to talk with, to enthuse about her dreams to. Her heart soared and dipped. If anything was guaranteed to lift her spirits, it was the prospect of the new plans waiting for her when she got home.

"I don't bite." He touched her.

She jumped. He was smiling at her and trying to be funny by dipping his head and making puppy dog eyes at her.

She laughed, she couldn't help it. "No, I guess not."

He stretched out his long legs, settling back in his chair. "Did you enjoy it?"

"Enjoy what?"

"Your stay over here in the States. What were you doing? Was it business or pleasure?"

She was still guilty that she'd splurged a considerable amount of Rommy's nestegg on the short holiday. It was the kind of thing her father, with his thrifty ways, would have termed profligate.

"All pleasure. Something trivial actually. I just had the Arlem experience." She stared him in the eye, seeing if he got it or not. Most people knew about Arlem or they didn't.

He broke into a grin. "Wow! You're kidding. The Arlem experience, that's way cool. I read about it in a Sunday supplement." Brow creased, he seemed to be thinking. "But that's where the weird people go isn't it? You a teacher? You don't strike me as weird."

She felt a short sharp violent stab of indignation. "The people at Arlem are lovely. They specialize in helping people. People with problems."

"Yeah, but it's mostly mental problems isn't it?"

"Not always," she snapped. Goodness, he had no tact whatsoever. "And no. I'm not a teacher, I was a visitor."

He shrugged and looked away. It was as if he hadn't noticed her sharp tone. "I've just been to visit my mother," he explained. "She lives in California and he—my dad—still lives in England. After that ordeal, there were a few things I wanted to stop off and see here before I headed back. I don't know why I come back to see her because it winds me up so much. Dad's worse though, so it's the lesser of two evils. In case you wondered. They're divorced although it's a sham since neither of them abide by the rules. They frequently visit one another to have passionate interludes."

"Really." Carrie Ann was intrigued, as in her estimation, romantic folk like that only seemed to exist between the pages of novels. "How modern of them. They must like it and be very much in love to be like that. To want the continual spice."

He didn't seem to have heard her. "It's not like a divorce. It's like playing at a divorce. In fact, I reckon you're right. They rather like it. It seems to add something to their love life."

"I think it's romantic. Fancy still loving a person when you're half a world apart."

"Yes. Quaint. A grown-up kind of game. My father's version of Viagra. I often wonder if that's why I'm so messed up. It would be hard not to be, with two parents like that."

Carrie Ann fell silent. Dominic didn't look messed up. He seemed the most confident and together person she'd met. Besides being wickedly good-looking. *Come on. You deserve a slap on the wrist. He's so young for one thing. Let's face it, there's no way on earth a guy like him would ever want to date you.*

"Let's get back to a much more interesting subject. Let's get back to you. So, why Arlem?"

It was then that it happened and to this day she would never understand what came over her. It was as if she was possessed by another power and it was the power of lies. A glitch in the software of her mind said, *He's so tasty, so let's do something naughty Carrie Ann. It's like everyone told you. You're free of that shadow now, free of your domineering father and you have to begin to learn how to drive that metaphorical car. How to put this sex thing into gear and pull away from the curb. Sure, the traffic's going to be tricky, but even women of eighty manage to drive.*

It was a clever notion and she felt a wild urge to see how far she could push it by letting her hair down. Then another thought crowded in and it was one of the familiar dark ones. But there was no way on earth she could tell the truth, he would think she was such an immature dork. She would have to tell a few white lies. Lies, shit, what was happening to her? When she'd left England on her holiday she would never even have considered another lie. They were too much trouble.

"No, well I... I don't like talking about myself that much. I had a messy divorce and afterwards I was shattered. Not damaged as such, but...Rommy was the only man I ever knew, I didn't have much experience with men, so I suppose I was blinded by romance and didn't see the pitfalls. He also wasn't in the best of health. Do we have to talk about it?"

He peered at her with interest. "Hey, you had a bad relationship. Some kind of psycho was he? Wow, you don't seem the type to be divorced."

"Don't I? How does a divorced person seem?" With each word and his evident interest in her, her confidence grew, swelling and enforcing her sense of excitement. She'd never thought lying could cause such a pulse of adrenaline and the feel-good factor spurred her on. She was making up for lost time, giving herself a bit of a kick with a few white lies, and what was the harm in that? She wouldn't ever see him again anyway, would she? As soon as they got on the plane that would be it.

"He was very controlling," she continued. "He wasn't like that in the beginning. It simply happened." That wasn't that far from the truth. She'd just swapped Rommy in her mind, for a husband. She stared at the strap of her handbag. When she mustered up the courage to look at Dominic, he was sympathetic.

"I'm sorry. I shouldn't have forced you to talk about it. I realize how that personal stuff messes with your head."

"Yes, yes it does. But I'm okay. For a while I had trouble holding things together. But they're good at putting people back together at Arlem. It's not like you think. It's not full of crazy people. It's a haven, a haven where you get to mend yourself." She smiled as she recollected the trip. "I got to ride western style. It was something I'd always wanted to do." She was aware she was babbling. It was hard to stop. "I'd developed panic attacks." She wanted to clamp her hand instantly over her mouth. Why had she said that? Why tell him something that personal, something that would make lots of men run a mile. "I'm not that good with people or cities or anything like that. Plus I'd never had the chance of a holiday before."

"You'd never been on holiday?" He seemed surprised.

"No never. My husband traveled with his work, but I didn't get to go, and then when he got back from being away, he always said he'd had enough, that his life was one long holiday and he didn't want another."

"So, you don't have kids?"

"No." She elaborated, "He wasn't into kids either. He hated them." As if it wasn't bad enough giving the lie a name with Rommy, the lie's identity grew as she fleshed the beast of her imagination into a living, breathing lover. She could hardly believe her propensity for this lying business. It was like constantly topping up a potent drink with more and more alcohol. "I think I'm too old for kids now."

He glanced out of the window. "I know I shouldn't say this and I'm out of line. But you look the kind of woman who'd be good with kids." He nudged her gently.

She thought it was rather personal doing something like that to a stranger. But he was so young.

"Tell me your age then?"

"You do realize you shouldn't ask a woman that?" What was happening to her? Was that an edge of flirtation in her voice? She'd never flirted in her life.

Maybe, and she was surprised to admit it, it was because she felt comfortable with Dominic.

Then, with a pang, something hit her and it was the reason why she was warm all over. It wasn't a case of just being comfortable. She was attracted to him. And not just ordinary friendly attraction, sexual attraction. Yes, she fancied him in the same way she fancied her idol, pâtissier extraordinaire and cake-maker to the stars, Latham, but differently to Latham because here there were real possibilities. She clamped her knees together as a powerful frisson surfed up her spine, the same feeling she'd had had when she had first seen Casper, healer and director of Arlem ranch. She wasn't that naïve. She chewed her lip. She was familiar with this deeper, tantalizing sensation. It was being turned-on and she was well aware of what that was. Isolation and never having had a lover or boyfriend, had forced her to explore her circumscribed world and make her own diversions, partly as a result of Nina's intervention. Nina, her best friend at the bakery, was all for personal pleasure.

Carrie Ann's hands were clammy and she sat on them. Yes, to preserve her sanity she'd done naughty things. They'd started off as fairly innocuous and soon become the keystones of her existence as she'd toppled into absolute sin and erotic diversions and attempted to hide them from her father. It had all started when she'd discovered her creativity and brilliance at crafting pâtisserie. Until then, her sexy side had been defused by day to day concerns.

Her sick father had largely contributed to her secretive personality by curbing any outward experience, watching her every move and stopping her doing anything. He had made her hide who she was and put all her feelings on a back burner, as she'd devoted her life to him.

Savage emotions twisted her stomach into knots. She preferred not to think about the massive steps she had taken since he'd died. By that time, she'd become so paranoid that even walking out of the front gate had been like a trial by fire, as she'd battled aggressive panic attacks that made her breathless and panicky. When she was in the cottage or walking down the lane to the village she was fine. It was places like the town with its bustling people and hooting cars that did it. The only thing she had to hang onto and keep herself from going crazy with, were loose coping strategies such as centering her thoughts on Latham.

"Not ask you about your age, why?" Dominic echoed.

Carrie Ann stiffened as she shook her head to clear her fuzzy memories. Her mind was always drifting here and there as she tried to make sense of her life past and present.

"I'm sorry. You have that expression, the 'I just stood on your toes', one. You're right, I shouldn't have asked you about it. You only look young, anyway."

He was being kind, she knew he was. As a rule, solitude and lack of experience made her feel uneasy with men and on the few occasions she'd actually gotten into conversation with a guy, they had generally withdrawn from her, but at least, he wasn't doing that. He smelled nice too—a tang of virile man mingled with a cologne with notes of lemon and oak moss. She knew a lot about essential oils as she used so many of them in her cookery. That had been another thing she had hidden from Rommy. Her burgeoning secret collection of cake essences.

"It doesn't matter. I'm not that easy a person to know. Years of being shut away from the world have made me a bad communicator."

"You seem a fantastic communicator to me."

She flicked him a glance. Not once had his gaze wandered away from her. He seemed to genuinely like her. *Come on, you're kidding yourself. He can't possibly like you, Carrie Ann. He seems so young. But then again, it would be fun to play along wouldn't it?* She felt good and his attitude was shoring up her low self-esteem. She knew she could pull this game off, and it was making her feel better, stronger. She realized now what a fool she'd made of herself over Casper. Over those few days at Arlem, she had fallen in love with another guy like Latham, who was the perfect template of the romantic hero she'd feasted on in her stash of books. With no experience and let loose, she had acted like a teenager and Casper had been in the firing line, offering her what she most needed, namely an ear to listen and a human being sufficiently interested to try to help heal her. She'd failed to see that despite it being his job, it was second nature to him to soothe and nurture the visitors to Arlem that were also his clients. This was who he was and what he did. He might have been a cowboy, but furthermore he was a trained counsellor and he liked to make everybody feel better with his unique healing abilities.

Her head swam and her toes curled in a gesture of sheer agony. How foolish she'd been. Thank goodness she'd been rational enough to realize she had shifted her notions of romance onto him and that they didn't belong there. She supposed he was used to crazy, unstable women going gaga over him. He had been great about it even after the accidental kiss in the stables when she'd burst into tears and he'd soothed her, telling her she was healing now and any time soon she'd find a partner of her own — that at last she was in control of her destiny and could have anything she wanted, if she worked at it.

"I'm twenty-eight actually," Carrie Ann blurted out, as she snapped back to the present.

"Wow! Twenty-eight?" Dominic winked at her. "You don't look anywhere near that."

"Funny, someone else said that." Carrie Ann swallowed nervously. She was older than twenty-eight, but that felt like a good compromise on her real age of thirty-two which was far too old to be a virtual hermit with a grave lack of experience.

"Yes. Maybe it's the lack of makeup. I hate women who wear makeup."

She lapsed into silence as a sense of triumph stole over her. She had actually succeeded in getting one thing right. Things weren't quite as they seemed though. Any situation like this and panic would normally steal over her. Then she would have to go onto automatic pilot, breathing deeply and regularly to prevent the sick, whirling sensation. Sure enough here it came, but this time, it was different to a normal attack. This time it was more like a naughty thrill, setting into motion a wet, prohibited rush that could mean only one thing.

"Hey, are you okay?"

She stared confounded, as his hand moved onto her wrist. This would be just the thing to happen. Now her silly panic attacks or whatever this was, was about to spoil things, when she was savoring the dizzy whirl of a wild flirtatious interlude. *Try to think of a diversion, Carrie Ann, the last thing you want to mention again is the panic. Say something.*

"No, actually. I hate flying. I'm okay if I can get to the airport and get on-board without thinking about it. It's this hanging about that makes me edgy. It seems to be taking ages for them to call our flight. I take it you're on the same one?"

"Yeah, the one to Heathrow." He glanced at his watch.

It was, she noted with some degree of interest, a Mickey Mouse watch. It made him seem very young. Everything about him was young. From his T-shirt to the baseball cap that he wore turned trendily back to front.

"It probably has a technical problem," he explained. "Planes are always getting them and they never tell you the truth about what they are either. The trouble is they come in and turn them around without looking at them. It makes you wonder if they might miss something."

"Great, that makes me feel loads better."

He burst out laughing. "If you could see your face. Hey, I could let you have loads of statistics about how safe flying is. Better than that, I could hold your hand all the time from now until we land at Heathrow."

She pulled a funny face. "You really do have a corny chat up line do you know that?" She wished they'd call the flight. On the one hand, she wanted the distraction of boarding to take her mind off the terrifying melange of sensations he was causing, on the other, she wanted to prolong just sitting here, talking to a guy who seemed to be attracting a lot of attention. Yes, her heart dipped. Trendy young women were flashing Dominic covert glances and worse than that giggling as their gazes greedily consumed him.

Amazingly, right at that second, the screen began to shuffle, and up popped a message. He leaned forward, hands between his legs. "See I told you, delayed due to technical problems."

Carrie Ann sighed.

"Don't worry. It's better to be safe than sorry isn't it?"

She wondered if her bravery was slowly evaporating. She would have been okay if she could have gotten on with it. But the delay made her feel shaky.

"Say I know what we'll do. Let's go and have a coffee, there's a place over there. It would pass some time and stop you thinking about it."

It was as if he'd read her mind.

"Coffee?" She said it with a question in her voice, as if coffee was something she never did. Then she qualified it quickly. "Yes, that would be nice."

"Come on then." Before she knew what was happening, he'd grabbed her arm and was grinning down at her. "Come along, it'll be more comfortable over there."

Chapter Two

It made Carrie Ann breathless when she thought about how large a decision she had made taking this trip, and she reckoned she deserved a pat on the back. She'd had one major triumph and a flirtation. No, correction — what now looked like two flirtations, so it had been worth it. She'd come so far in a few days and while she knew she wasn't yet cured, at least she was well on the path to recovery.

Her lips lifted in pleasure as she followed Dominic across to the café. As she glanced at her reflection in the window, she saw that happiness made her round face with its smattering of freckles light up. No one could say she was a raving beauty, but she realized now she was pretty, or that was what Casper had said.

Initially petrified of taking such a huge step as a holiday to America, she had done remarkably well and couldn't have made a better choice of location. Arlem — the name for the healing center and ranch — was isolated. They had sent a minibus to collect the tiny group at the airport. That was what had attracted her to this kind of trip in the first place. There were none of the complications of making decisions and finding her way into a city teeming with people—the kind of situation that was sure to trigger one of her anxiety attacks.

It had turned out there were eight travelers in her group—a manageable enough number to cope with since bigger numbers sent her into a blind panic. It was weird, more like a dream to suddenly find herself in a place she had dreamt about for so many years when she'd been under her father's thumb. Then the nearest she had gotten to the American dream of wide open spaces had been quelling her thirst for foreign places with stolen travel brochures that she'd hidden under her bed and taken out to stare at when she'd been on her own. Yes, travel brochures and not forgetting—she smiled to herself—the odd vivid romance to hit the erotica shelves and something even sexier to Carrie Ann—cookbooks. She realized now, she would have gone crazy without these diversions. They had been the only way she'd managed to survive the long years spent closeted away with Rommy and his slowly deteriorating state of mind. She gnawed her lip as she fought down the mingling of emotions. There was no point dwelling on the past, it was over and done with and she knew Rommy would have loved to have destroyed her future by making her feel guilty. He was in all likelihood looking down on her, silently fulminating at the fact she had at last found her feet.

There was no getting away from it, she was in turmoil. She still didn't understand herself very well, probably because she'd had little time over the years to concentrate on her feelings and emotions. One thing she did know was that she was ordinary and not super-human. It was astounding how much time had sped by looking after her father and catering to his every whim. Her only indulgence cooking and hot romances—a prisoner in an inner world fueled by unachievable fantasy. She supposed now she ought to feel grateful to him in a way because he had done her a favor, forcing her to marry together her two greatest passions into a potent recipe for what she hoped was soon going to be sweet success. Carrie Ann had long been a satellite revolving around two large planets with exceptionally strong gravitational pulls—namely erotica and bakery—fused, she was sure they could create a huge bang.

The familiar black cloud spread a shadow over her. Searching in her inside pocket, she groped around, her hand closing on the familiar touchstone. Now what would people think if they knew about this? She fingered Clyde. She knew it was ridiculous having a good luck charm and especially one like this. Clyde was made of royal icing, not that he looked like it. Latham Crosswick's genius meant anything he modeled out of icing sugar seemed so lifelike it was scary.

And how had she come by Clyde? Well that was another story. Carrie Ann could only say that on that particular occasion, she'd been possessed. It was the first time she had ever really gone against Rommy and defied him by making an excuse and going to the international cake fair. Over the years she'd nursed him, she'd learnt it was much better not to fight his dictatorial nature but to look for cunning cracks in the edifice that she could use to her advantage. She realized now that her father's cruelty had not been intended but it had seemed like it at the time. He had been exceedingly clever at manipulating her and using the force of his strong personality to make her feel guilty over almost anything. On the few occasions she had rebelled, she'd spent weeks having to make it up to him.

Rommy had been paranoid about money, and the house was run on a shoestring, with heating and every other necessity rationed. The only area of non-rationing had been his choice of food. The weekly budget had been frittered away as he'd fed his insatiable appetite for sweet things.

She didn't like to think of what Rommy had become because it was too painful. Things had been fine until Mary, her mother and the love of his life, had passed away, changing Rommy from an extraordinary man into a bad-tempered replica.

How had he been extraordinary? Well, when she'd been a little girl, he'd had an interesting sideline. Rommy, the king of jam, had had his produce stocked in fancy delis and had been known over three counties for his knack of marrying together daring combinations of spice and flavors.

One thing was for sure. Rommy had thought he'd won a victory as he'd later forced Carrie Ann into slavery over the stove, when, he had in fact conceded one. She took more pleasure from baking and icing than anything else. Bakery was the panacea that soothed a soul devoid of romance and titillating objectives like sex.

She was ashamed to admit that at times she'd had hated him, yes, *hated* her own father. It was good that Arlem had managed to put all of that into perspective. She would miss the gang at the ranch who had embraced her like extended family. They had released her, made her stronger and given her enough confidence to carry through on her dream. The ranch itself was fantastic and like something out of a Wild

West picture. It took parties of people from all walks of life. What marked them out as similar was that they were recovering from major issues in their life. Arlem was unique in that things were largely left up to the guests and they were not pressured into any of the activities, but could take part or chat with a counsellor, whatever they wanted.

"Fancy having a hard icing man as a mascot." Martha, who they called matron of the ranch, had chuckled, thinking any kind of fetish was kinky. The icing man, that was a perfect self-portrait, had precious connotations, but was not half as sexy as famous Latham Crosswick, the man he was modeled on.

Carrie Ann slipped Clyde out of her pocket and looked at him again. She better make sure Dominic didn't see him. It was a bit like voodoo the way she carried the little man around and chattered to him about all her worries.

Her attention was captured by Dominic. He was striding ahead of her and as she studied his scuffed trainers. Her gaze drifted up to settle on his pert behind, clad in skin-tight jeans. Mmm.

"Hey."

Dominic shocked her out of her reverie as he turned his baseball cap around the right way, so it shaded his eyes. "Don't worry about it, I know you're miles away surfing on your nerves, but a good strong coffee will sort you out."

"I thought that was a good strong whiskey?" Carrie Ann quipped as she snapped out of her recollections and sat down at a quiet table in the corner of the café.

"Yeah, whatever." Rocking back on his heels, he considered. "Yeah, come to think of it, you look like a cappuccino girl. A nice frosting of sweet or maybe bitter on top, then when you get past the froth something hot and steamy underneath."

What makes him think that? She blushed furiously and it wasn't just because of Dominic. It was at the recollection of what she'd done all those months ago. She hadn't been able to help it. She'd stolen Clyde from off the top of a cake at the fair because she hadn't been able to leave without a memento fashioned by the master of cake craft's hands.

Latham Crosswick was her hero, her fantasy lover, and she knew everything about him, even down to his best kept secret—that his middle name was Clyde and he hated it. She was pleased about picking that snippet up. She'd had the good fortune at the fair, to be standing near a reporter with a loose tongue and he'd dropped one or two very interesting snippets that had filled her with such orgasmic delight she'd thought she was going to burst.

Latham had all the ingredients of her dream man. She worshiped his genius—the ability he had to model objects and people that were so incredibly lifelike a TV company had gotten him to construct their Plasticine models. More than that, he wielded a paintbrush with such sensitivity, each detail was unmatched. He was the only chef to have appeared on the cover of *International Cake Maker* four times, and occupied a lofty position up with the most famous in the cookery world. Grâce à the fair she also now had a first-hand recollection of his silky, smooth tones to file away in her memory banks and make her all hot and bothered. Who would believe she'd actually gotten to talk to Latham and had heard that husky voice dripping with promise.

Carrie Ann lived in hope of one day sharing more than the memory of his voice as she clung to her fantasies like a drowning woman clung to a life-raft. She plunged into reverie. Latham had the allure of a debauched aristocrat. His blond hair hung to his collar in a curtain that provoked tempting dreams of finger teasing. As for his reputation—he thrived on adrenaline, was hot stuff and known for his womanizing, acerbic wit and dangerous hobbies— snowboarding, three-day eventing and impossibly deep bungee jumps.

The adventurous escape to the fair where she'd at last met her idol had been worth every second of the hassle that had occurred later on. It was the first time she'd really lied and it was easier than she'd imagined. The trouble with lies, though, was they were like a ball of string and the longer they got, the more knots they created. Rommy had been tremendously suspicious, and his mind had run overtime where Carrie Ann was concerned. It had been a mixture of fear and selfishness, she supposed now. Selfishness because he'd wanted her there to replace her mother, and fear she would walk out and leave him.

He had gotten worse and worse as time had gone on and had resorted to watching her continually from his chair in the sitting room. Men had been his largest bugbear. She'd only had to talk to the postman or a delivery guy and like a vulture, he'd been ready to squawk about it afterwards. It was as if he'd suspected she was plotting a dirty weekend or something.

A dirty weekend with Latham. Her heart did a little skip and jump. Chance would be a fine thing. Carrie Ann would do anything to get close to him as she languished in delayed adolescence.

She still wondered how she'd managed to find the courage to escape to the fair. She supposed fate had given her a nudge. Rommy's old army mate, Bennie, who now lived in Adelaide, had phoned out of the blue asking if he could come and stay for a few days, during his visit to see his new grandson. This had caused a mammoth stir as delirious with pleasure, Rommy had been sent down the path of enthusiastic musings.

She had shuddered, fought hard to keep her excitement in check as the fantastic opportunity to visit the fair had fallen into her hands. A diverted Rommy had presented an incredible prize and presented her with the perfect opportunity to plan her escape.

Her father, employing emotional blackmail, had by now carefully crafted her lack of confidence to his advantage by drip-feeding her a devious concoction of stories and getting so upset when she said she wanted to go out on her own, that she didn't bother anymore. House arrest was only ever relaxed if she had to take an unavoidable trip into town for shopping or a walk to the corner shop to get his newspaper, rarely anything further afield.

Indeed the only occasion she could recall using the mothballed car was for a rare trip to the hospital. The car had been bought second-hand and to Carrie Ann had seemed pristine, being hardly ever used. Rommy had always been thrifty and her mother had suffered at the hands of the thrift by only enjoying a ride out when Rommy had thought it warranted it. That puzzled her, how her mother could have so loved him, when he had been a stingy beggar.

As her heart had thumped and bumped in anticipation of freedom, she hadn't considered what would happen if she achieved her objective.

As she had set out on the journey to the fair, a strange feeling of otherworldliness had closed in on her and the familiar fist had squeezed the air out of her. However, miraculously, having fielded the harrowing journey, she had been so dead set on impressing Latham, any panic had been consumed by dogged determination.

She'd wondered if her age was in part responsible for the recent changes and the long awaited spark of needing to challenge Rommy's authority. When she had hit thirty, something had happened and she'd begun to feel uneasy. Life seemed to have passed her by somehow. The hours, days, months and years swallowed up by a selfish man had denied her what she knew she wanted more than anything—contact with men and some kind of love life.

"He's a bully," Nina at the bakery had said, when Carrie Ann had explained about the possible escape plan. "You ought to tell him you're going out for the day. He's not a jailer, he can't stop you."

"I couldn't." She'd sat on a chair in the café attached to Oh Crumbs! and had stared into her coffee. "You don't know Rommy."

"I do actually. The irascible toad." Nina had kicked back from the table, folding her hands over her stomach. "He manages to come in here to see how the cakes are selling, so I can't understand this illness."

Carrie Ann had looked at her sharply. "It's not the kind of thing you can see, silly."

"No, well, I understand the type. He's a frightened man and he plays on your nature. You're such a lovely woman, he's learnt how to dominate you. He's worse than the meanest, most controlling husband."

Carrie Ann had blinked at her. Nina was forever chiding her over her devotion to her father.

Latham had been visiting the fair as he did a number of events, every year, but things had been kicked into overdrive when, for the first time ever, she'd found out he was descending from the lofty heights of *God Latham* to judge the sugar craft classes and hand out the prizes.

Despite shaking in her boots, she'd known she had to somehow conquer her nerves. This would be a good test of the self-help book Nina had bought her and was almost like a powerful aphrodisiac. She would attempt to force herself out of her shell by not just managing to get to London but being brave enough to enter the craft class. How she'd managed it she didn't know, but conjuring up images of her paramour on the train had powered her footsteps on and off various modes of transport and into the exhibition hall.

Once inside and having caught a glimpse of a blond head and chef's whites from afar, Carrie Ann had then switched onto erotic automatic pilot as she'd filled out her application form.

As the competition had started, she had stood at her work station dazed, spending a full fifteen minutes staring at Latham Crosswick, who'd strutted around flashing disparaging looks at the motley contestants. About to start the class, she ought to have been inspecting her work bench because they were against the clock. Instead she had been mesmerized by the apparition in whites and trademark stylish pointed boots, who strutted about the room, his gaze more often than not settling on her. After feeling what she thought was his breath on her neck, her fuse had burst into life and she'd flared into action, her motive to impress. It was amazing what came over her once she lifted a whisk, or manipulated a bowl of icing.

As Latham had flounced between the tables with his hands laced behind his back, she had had plenty of time to study him again and speculate about love potential. He was very tall, and had a habit of deftly flicking back his long blond locks with sexy impertinence. On the cover of *Kitchen News* he'd subdued them in a ponytail and she wasn't sure which she liked the best. The floppy hair was sexy, but the ponytail meant you could see his cheekbones, more of his crooked nose and a small scar that raised one side of his lip. The damaged nose and scar had been the result of a tumble at the ditch at the Badminton horse trials, when Latham wanting to be best at everything, had taken the jump at too sharp an angle. It was his lips that did it for Carrie Ann though. They were very sexy and the notion of what they could do rang deep messages of eroticism.

Odd to see him up close like that. By the time she'd finished staring at him for the second time in a row she had wasted another five minutes and had had to rouse herself so she could get to work.

Memories, memories, they were coming thick and fast as if talking to Dominic had released them. She stifled a smile, he was so nice and funny and he seemed dead keen on her. The least she could do was focus her attention more on him and less on her fantasy man, Latham.

"You're so cute, it's this kind of dreamy way you have about you." Resting his chin on his fist, Dominic peered at her.

It was vaguely unnerving but nice.

"I'm not half as cute as you think," Carrie Ann replied. "And my father used to say it was dead irritating the way I'd go off on a daydream."

"Now, you're making yourself sound even cuter." He made a funny face at her. "I can't wait to hear more about you." He took off the baseball cap and combed his fingers through his hair.

Carrie Ann experienced a weird feeling in the pit of her stomach. He also had such kissable lips—even more kissable than Latham's—and a nice dusting of designer stubble.

After reaching in his jeans pocket, he produced a packet of chocolate then, tearing off the wrapper handed her half. "Here you can get started on that and I'll go and see about that coffee. What do you want, or shall I surprise you?"

"Surprise me," she flirted.

Left alone her thoughts drifted back in time. Maybe all this constant introspection was what the healing process was all about. For the first time she was feeling comfortable about dwelling on memories that before Arlem had been painful.

Thank heavens for Oh Crumbs! or she might have gone mad. That was one lining to the silver cloud and another mystery in her life. How fate conspired to take her cakes. Initially Rommy had moaned over even that, since he'd seen it as a form of competition, the cakes diverting her attention from the more important one of caring for him. However, the lure of income from an unexpected source had made his eyes glitter with avarice. Where money was concerned he'd been as sharp as a pin and they had always been low on funds. God knows why, since he had a pension and never spent anything.

Carrie Ann lived in a village called Puddleford. It was perfectly poised on the tourist route into the valleys. There was a crooked little street, peppered with quaint houses with Tudor-style beams that made everybody get their cameras out, a scattering of interesting shops, a fabulous oldy-worldy inn called The Angel and Oh Crumbs!, the bakery. Oh Crumbs!'s cakes and pastries were esteemed far and wide, and the little shop owed its success to the fact that Carrie Ann's bakes were now enjoyed by Michelin starred restaurant, The Manor, just over the ford in Weston.

Despite her amazingly desperate situation, Carrie Ann seemed prone to experience twists of fate that worked in her favor. She was thankful for the day the supply van had failed to get through to the village due to the snow, and having gotten wind of it, she'd trudged down to Oh Crumbs! with a basket of offerings. Ms Bunting hadn't believed she'd baked them, although her father's legendary Jude's Jams fiasco and the many times he had upset the women at the WI still lingered in everyone's minds. After a queue had materialized that spread right down the high street, though, Ms Bunting had been quick to order three batches a week and diversify into Carrie Ann's experimental cakes.

Her gift at cookery was the diamond glittering amongst the dull pebbles. Rommy might have blown the wind out of her sails, but she possessed her mother's feisty streak and this glimmer of triumph, blew embers into life. Given license to literally, 'get her teeth into something', Carrie Ann had rapidly immersed herself in the satisfying world of creativity. She had inherited her grandmother's gift for cookery, her lightness of touch and attention to detail. Her father may have been the mastermind behind small business operation Jude's Jams, but her grandmother was the wizard of pastry and icing.

Using the recipe books bequeathed to her by her grandmother, Carrie Ann's love of baking had grown exponentially. It had also become her passion, an escape route and the passport for small successes. The woodland walks Rommy had tried to stifle had become work related forays in cookery experimentation that he hadn't been able to object to. The importance of foraged supplies was an essential addition to the delights provided by his pride and joy, the garden, which was full of rare old-fashioned varieties of plum and apple trees, an old stand of raspberry and gooseberries, together with blackcurrants that occupied a large slice of garden down by the sheds.

She had come so far in such a short space of time, she reflected. The taking on of her bakes had expanded rapidly when she'd decided to use her father's recipe for lemon and elderflower blackcurrant jam in her grandmother's bakewell fancy recipe. Marcus at The Manor had tasted one and said it was good enough to be used on his restaurant's afternoon tea menu.

It was at that point Ms Bunting had offered Carrie Ann a proper job. Needless to say, Rommy wouldn't allow it. It had led to a massive argument with Carrie Ann, for the first time in her life standing her ground but eventually, as had always happened in the end, losing.

Catapulted back to the present, Carrie Ann jiggled her feet and crossed her arms. She wished she could get on the plane because all this hanging about was filling her with trepidation. A lump stuck in her throat as her ebullience vanished like a snuffed out match. Only an hour or so ago, Casper had dropped her at the airport and she had had to say her goodbyes and face up to a huge hurdle. She was going home, back to real life, Puddleford and all the drama and hassles that would bring with it. More than that, going home meant having to face the painful memories of her father's death. He might have been a tyrant and ruined her life, but she'd still loved him and had occasionally caught a glimmer of the man he used to be. It hadn't all been his fault, he'd just been needy, that was all.

She oughtn't to feel sad for him. Martha at the ranch had pointed that out. Her father was one of life's victims. He was needy and wanted her to himself and that was cruel. She hadn't had any life of her own—no friends, no hobbies—Rommy had snuffed them out before they'd even had a chance to grow. It was the same argument Nina used and it was true. However, Carrie Ann still felt guilty.

She hunched deeper into her seat, glancing at the clock. They were late boarding, but it couldn't be much longer, could it? A pity she wasn't traveling back with anyone she'd met. Most of them had come with partners except her, how desperate. Her fellow travelers had caught other flights. Two of them had been French, a wonderful couple called Martine and Pierre, who had given her their address in Paris and forced her to promise to go and visit them. *Wow!* She would like that and she'd been seriously considering it. Especially since the prize she had won at the fair with Latham had been a weekend at an esteemed Parisian cookery school.

Taking a moment to reflect, she stared morosely through the airport window at the bright sky and her body began to tighten. This was what the panic attacks were like. They were hard to control and she had to fight for every breath. The only difference was that she felt that now she could control them a little bit better. A smile danced over her lips. The short holiday had done her the world of good despite how she was feeling. She would be sorry to wave goodbye to the United States — she had loved everything about it, but returning to England wasn't all bleak, there would be many more adventures. *Come on, face it, Carrie Ann. It isn't that bad. You'll be happy to get home, even though it means hours on the plane.*

"Do you always have your head in the clouds?"

Dominic shocked her out of her reverie and she sat bolt upright. "Oh, hi."

"Sorry I took so long, the guy at the counter seemed to have vanished." He put the coffee on the table and pulled a chair up so close their knees knocked together. "Not still worrying about the flight are you? I thought I might have distracted you with my considerable charms."

Shit, she blushed again. "Well, I, uh."

"Forget it. If we have to bail out somewhere over the Atlantic, I'll save you. I got my lifeguard's certificate."

"Is that meant to make me feel better?"

"It should do."

Carrie Ann felt as if her skin was fizzing all over. This was the first time she had actually flirted with a man who was single. Damn, why couldn't there have been a single guy in the party at the ranch? Why had she had to focus her attentions on Casper? Why did this have to happen now and with a man who looked half her age? *Stop it. But I fancy him. I fancy him like hell.*

Dominic pressed his leg harder against hers and a pulse shot up her legs and settled with a dull throb in her belly.

He certainly had a sweet tooth, she thought as she watched him open one sugar sachet after another and empty it into his mug. "You want to watch it."

He glanced up, a look of surprise on his face. "Watch it? Why should I? Are you afraid that the sugar high might turn me into a beast?" He bared his teeth and growled at her.

She giggled. "Don't be silly." She stirred her drink. Every time she looked at him, her heart did a funny little flip and her stomach rolled over. Really, she ought to have more control because she was acting like a teenager.

"So, what do you do, Carrie Ann? You must do something?"

That was unexpected. She grasped at the lies that floated around like clouds in her mind. It was easy to grasp one, pluck it down and tether it in place. "I'm between jobs. You see I didn't work when I was married. Rommy didn't believe in it. He liked his wife to be at home all the time. Although, I did have a pastime. We used to entertain so I became great at cookery." That was a masterstroke, she had included an element of truth to shore up the shaky foundation of deceit.

He nodded at her sympathetically. "Shit, what a tyrant. What was he doing, living in the Middle Ages?"

"I realize it sounds funny for a woman to put up with it, but I was young when I got married and, well, I was in love."

He twirled an empty sugar sachet around in his fingers. "Yeah, I get it. Something like that happened to me. Better not talked about though, huh?"

She nodded in relief. "What about you?"

Dominic yawned, kicking back in his chair. "That's a long story." He turned his baseball cap around. "I just finished uni. Graduated with a 2:1 in finance, I suppose this means I begin the treadmill, if Dad gets his way. I don't know if I can stand the thought of working in an office."

There was something there, something he wasn't telling her, she was sure of it. A warmth filled her, a powerful feeling of kinship. Maybe he had secrets too, either that or he was just a loser out to fool her. This was different to how she'd felt about Casper, but then again, Casper had been totally unavailable if she'd been honest with herself. *Come on, Carrie Ann,* her mind trundled out the usual warnings. *Whatever way you look at it, he's way out of your league. Guys like him don't go for plain, shy women like you.* "Look will you excuse me for a moment? I have to go to the ladies."

"Ah, I get it. You're going to try and make a getaway," he joked, springing up.

She was on her feet, slipping her bag over her shoulder.

Taking her by surprise, he caught hold of her hand. "Now I've found you, I don't want to let you go."

"Don't be silly."

"Who said anything about being silly?"

God, she wished he wouldn't flirt like this.

"What if I never see you again?"

She laughed. "That's mad. You don't know me. You only met me a while ago. Besides, I can't get very far. I'm trapped in the airport."

He pulled her closer so she was pressed up against him. It was a blatantly provocative move. She was light-headed as she peered at him.

"I feel a connection with you that I don't want to lose until I've explored it, Carrie Ann. Why don't you give me a chance of getting to know you? You're single aren't you? Or at least you make out you are. And you're grown up, you're not a kid?" His gaze searched her face.

She sat back down with a bump. She couldn't deny the attraction that was fizzing and popping between them.

And so it happened. Time sped by and before she knew what was happening she was talking to Dominic and more lies were tripping off her tongue. Lies, lies, lies. Well, even if this was going nowhere, it was important to create a smokescreen to veil the dull boring Carrie Ann and make her appear more exciting. That was when she told him about her cookery plans, her dreams for her own company, Sweet Secrets.

Bored with the bakewells, she had begun to experiment with intricate piping and spun sugar, and that was not all. Her imagination had roamed and before she'd known what she was doing, she'd pinched and manipulated a firm pair of muscles into shape and realized she had come up with something quite extraordinary, the idea for a daring venture. This had led to further experimentation, the endeavors becoming naughtier and naughtier and giving her a secret kick as she'd hid them from her father or stuffed them in her mouth and enjoyed eating them before he caught her. Creative cake decorating, she realized, was her thing. It was easy for her, it was what she wanted to do.

These days she carried a notebook with her. It was amazing where her latest inspiration could come from and it could strike at any time. Erotica, sensuality, it was everywhere and right now...well right now that book was burning a hole through the leather in her handbag as she juggled with her thoughts.

"Oh my, look, the lounge is almost empty," Carrie Ann exclaimed, as she noticed the last few people heading toward the departure gate.

He laughed. "I didn't notice. It must be your magical powers of enchantment."

They were really flirting now and she was getting used to his easy charm and banter. She was amazed how she felt with him. She'd never imagined, not for a second, that it would be this easy to fall under a man's thrall. "Guess we ought to board then?" She was reluctant, but it was best to be practical. This was it then. All too soon she had to sever the connection and it was probably just as well. If by chance she got to sit next to Dominic on the flight, which, of course, she wouldn't, they'd simply get closer and that would make the wrench harder when it came. Games had a habit of getting out of control, she'd read about it often enough in her novels and this was going nowhere wasn't it? Even if it had come at the tail end, this was still a holiday romance.

"Pity we couldn't sit together." He smiled as they stood in the queue. "I expect I'll be next to some horrible kid or failing that, a miserable git who doesn't want to talk and tries to take up half my chair."

She held out her hand. "It was nice meeting you. Really nice."

"Yeah." He shook it, and his expression was loaded with meaning. "It certainly was."

Carrie Ann felt as if she could float down the airplane aisle as they shuffled forward. For the first time she was smiling spontaneously. The trip, Casper and now Dominic. It had done wonders for her self-confidence.

"Well, I think I'm back down this way." He thumbed over his shoulder. "Maybe I'll try and move up during the flight so we can have a chat."

She couldn't see that. The plane was packed to capacity, but she flashed him a regretful smile as she glanced at her boarding pass and noticed it was a window seat. "Yep, who knows."

He caught her by surprise, grabbing her arm and briefly kissing her cheek as a woman bumped into her. Before she had time to respond, a portly man and his three children had crowded the aisle so she lost sight of him.

Here was her seat. She secured her bag in the overhead locker then took out the in-flight magazine as she tried to take her mind off the imminent roar of the engines signaling the coming fear and the ultimate stomach churning lurch as they lifted into the sky. It was a relief to be away from him. The easy manner and the fabrications that had slipped off her tongue had terrified her. Maybe she ought not to have lied because with hindsight it seemed ridiculous, but what else could she have done? If she were truthful with herself, she had been terrified. She wasn't ready for a relationship, it was way too soon and silly to even consider it. She needed more time, needed to work her way into this dating scene like easing on a shoe — wear it in a bit until it softened up and didn't rub at her. This situation was exactly the same, she needed to wear herself in until she felt comfortable — move forward one step at a time. The trouble was her sense of romance had already gotten a grip on her.

She consoled herself, she had had to lie. For one thing she didn't even know how to go about explaining her situation to a stranger. How would ordinary people view her anyway? What woman would care for her father and put up with what she'd had put up with? Inevitably if she got drawn into conversation she would be quizzed about it and she didn't have any answers. To a bystander she would look feeble and weak. It was different with Ms

Bunting and Nina at the shop, she had known them forever. At least she'd proved one thing. She was better at life's events and more able to cope than she'd thought. God, she was tired. Stretching her arms and letting her head loll back against the headrest, she yawned.

Right that second, there was a bit of a commotion and the next thing she knew she'd been hit with a resounding thwack from a knapsack. "Ooh." She put her hands over her face. The blow had jarred her and for a moment she was stunned.

"I'm so sorry. How wild's this? I managed to swap seats." Dominic grinned down at her having stowed the offending article away. "Do you think we have a kind of fatal attraction?"

"I should have known. There's only one person that would hit me three times in one day." The funny thing was she couldn't help it. Her heart was doing skips and jumps and she couldn't keep the excitement out of her voice. "You rigged this?"

"Of course, I did. I'd be crazy to pass up the opportunity to trap you for hours. I do seem to have inherited a fair degree of charm off Dad and I've just used it to my advantage." He slid into the seat beside her. "It's what my father would call divine intervention. A twist of events that's pushed us together and made that air hostess back there a bit of a sucker. You're the most interesting girl I've met in ages."

Her heart beat faster as his bare elbow brushed her arm. Being pressed into a seat beside him was perversely exciting. As always when she needed some Dutch courage, she reached in her pocket to find Clyde. It was empty. Her heart stopped and the color must have drained from her face because he noticed.

"What is it? I'm not that bad am I? Do I smell or something?" He mimed smelling under his armpit which at any other time would have had her in fits.

"It's nothing, nothing…" she stuttered trying to look on the floor. "I think I dropped something that's all. It might have been when you bumped me."

"What, what did you drop? Let me help you look." Unbuckling his seat belt, he got down on his hands and knees, searching on the floor. "Christ, it couldn't be this could it?" He held up Clyde, turning the icing man—now minus an arm—in his fingers.

"Oh." She wailed in relief, snatching it out of his fingers. "He's broken. He's lost his arm."

"You pervert. Is this some kind of voodoo fetish?"

"No it isn't. Hands off." She felt an astounding sense of despair. It had always been her and Clyde. He was her good luck charm and helped her through her panic attacks.

He bent back down and began searching around again. "Here is this what you're looking for?"

Her hand shook as she took the arm and tried to fit it back on. She was dangerously close to tears. "Yes, thanks."

There was a gleam in Dominic's eye. "Well you're certainly a woman of many secrets. Hey, I'm sorry, I'm being insensitive. I know how touchy you girls can be about things like this. I once had a girlfriend who had this imaginary friend. I used to poke fun at her until she finished with me. That was how serious she was. Say." He blinked at her. "You're not that bad are you?"

"No, I'm not. It's a mascot. Latham Crosswick gave it to me."

He snorted like an angry horse. "Come on, you're pulling my leg. Not *the* Latham Crosswick?"

"Why not? Don't sound so alarmed." Her cheeks flushed again. How embarrassing. She'd been holding it together so well.

"What's he to you, if you don't mind my asking?"

She might just as well give in. She took out a tissue and after carefully wrapping Clyde, put him safely in the inside pocket of her handbag. "I told you, I decorate cakes and Latham's a great cake maker. Well, he's the god of cake art."

He didn't look as startled as she'd thought he would. "Well, surprises and secrets. Do you realize how hard that world is to break into though?"

"My, you can be patronizing." Where had that come from? She hadn't been that brave before.

"I'm sorry. You could be famous for all I know." Dominic looked genuinely contrite. "I can put my foot in it sometimes. That's what comes from being a damaged child."

Carrie Ann ignored this. She was getting used to him by now. "I was always fab at cakes, but I was stifled when I was married. I used to idolize Latham, still do. It's great coming out of the closet and thinking of baking as a job. I'm doing rather well at it, actually." She was amazed at how prideful she sounded. That was what Arlem had taught her. She had to be proud of her achievements, no matter how small. "I had to get some kind of job with the bills mounting up and cake making, in particular fancy icing, was something I was good at."

"Sure, but it takes a degree of talent to become a cake decorator like Latham, the competition's fierce. Cookery, baking, it's become gigantic over the last few years. It's all over the TV." He stared out of the window.

She thought he'd looked intense as she'd studied him, as if he were about to say something but didn't know whether to or not. It was then it struck her. No wonder she was attracted to him because he was like a very young-looking Latham.

"You're young to be thinking about a high-flying cake business aren't you?"

"No," she said, catching a glimpse of herself in the window. There was an uncustomary glint to her eye. "Anyway, I don't want to talk about it. It's not happened yet. It's early days."

"God, you're quite a lady, do you realize that?" He lowered his voice to a whisper, "I could get off on your kinks and fetishes." Then he bent forward so his breath tickled her ear. "I have you captive, Carrie Ann, aren't you afraid?"

"You're nuts, do you know that?" She made a face at him and opened the in-flight magazine again, pretending to scan the pages.

"Yes I am. But you have to admit you haven't even thought about taking off have you? I'm doing a great job of keeping you occupied. Look, we're already taxiing."

If only he knew the truth about the figure. Of course, Latham hadn't given it to her. Actually, she had done a very bad thing, a very bad thing indeed. She'd stolen it off Latham's pride and joy — the demonstration cake on the exhibition table. It had been wildly exhilarating to do something so naughty. Her only excuse was the frustration of Latham being so close.

Chapter Three

Cookery Fair

It had been the greatest day of her life when—
possessed by the desire to be close to the man she
lusted over—she entered the competition. Latham was
so close she could smell his male scent mingled with
sexy aftershave and see that wry smile that was all the
more overwhelming in the flesh. What's more, she
was sure those square manly hands caressed hers
when he handed her her prize, a ticket for a
weekend's cookery course at the *école Roumaise
Culinaire* in the heart of Paris.

It was a dream come true. No one could get into the
école for training, although she would have settled for
the caress of that hand as a prize. Latham simmered
with a variety of emotional undercurrents, most of
them sexual, his gaze roving everywhere as he saw
women—all women—as easy prey. Despite his
dismissive attitude and over-inflated ego, it seemed
every female in the hall was enamored by him and
there was no shortage of flustered faces and preening

as his tidal wave of charisma and charm swept them away in currents and eddies of excitement.

Standing in line for the presentations, Carrie Ann couldn't resist ogling Latham's latest culinary triumph. She noticed as someone brushed against it though, that he hadn't fixed the models on top very securely and they wobbled precariously.

Latham's fabulous multi-tiered icing superstructure — a segment of the Great Wall of China done for an important charity function, was breathtaking. Each stone had been carefully crafted and the people walking across the top were all identifiable personalities from politics. Not forgetting Latham's egotistical trademark twist of incorporating a model of himself. It was that one she wanted. Her heart swelled with triumph and pleasure. It was so easy. As the table shuddered, Latham started wobbling on the Great Wall steps and she whipped the figure into her large overall pocket. She could have told Latham a thing or two about how important it was to make sure he firmly cemented his figures with royal icing.

She rippled with an orgasmic satisfaction at her coup.

"Carrie Ann, we're going to need your address and details because we'll maybe want to do a follow up." After the competition, a woman with a glowing smile and impeccable makeup had come up to her brandishing a clipboard.

Carrie Ann shuddered and blushed so hotly she had to grasp the edge of the table. God, what if someone had seen her? What if they'd grabbed her, searched in her pockets and found out she had this weird fetish for pinching models off cakes? *Don't be silly, Carrie Ann. If someone had noticed they would have questioned you before now.* She pushed Clyde deeper into her pocket. Easy, he was not that big.

"What kind of follow up?" She hadn't bargained on a silly competition for cake crafting having such far-reaching ripples.

"Oh." The woman smiled. "You know the kind of thing. A picture and maybe an interview saying how you got into cake craft."

Carrie Ann experienced a wave of consternation.

"Don't worry, you're probably shy like me. It's only the usual thing. Most people jump at the chance. If Latham thinks you're good, it could get you on and I would imagine with your talent you'd want to get on, wouldn't you?"

Carrie Ann did, but she couldn't possibly give her correct address. Although it broke her heart, Rommy cast such a shadow over her she had to make one up, a slightly different one. Well, she couldn't have anyone turn up on the doorstep could she?

Right when she was about to leave the hall, all hell broke loose. She could hear Latham's shrieks and he was famous for those, each word peppered with French and German phrases, even over by the refreshment tents. Funny how it filled her with a sense of wanton danger, almost sexual in intensity.

She felt hot and excited on the journey home. One thing was for sure it had given her a huge amount of material with which to feed her fantasies, and she had a great many of those—enough to fill a book in fact—not having a boyfriend of her own to dote on. Her favorite one was imagining Latham in cake judging mode, walking up and down a row of competition entries. Stopping at hers, he would flash her his seductive trademark look. How could he not be impressed by a Sweet Secrets cake with one of its fabulous sexy twists? She had in mind many naughty, scintillating creations. Most of them were merely suggestive, but she did have a rude sideline if requested, that was a humorous twist on a theme.

Her body tingled as she imagined the famous chef's artistic hand with his famous long fingers darting out to caress a cake model. In her fantasy the man next to her at the competition was crying. Latham would have done that, he had been known to reduce grown men to tears as he was quick to praise or kill a dream. In fact, Latham had flattened many a career before it had even started. When he'd done that, the victim would probably be so shattered they'd never want to pick up a piping bag again. In this instance, he glanced at Carrie Ann pinning her to the spot. "My, what do we have here? Something different, something out of the box, a cook not afraid to try and impress me."

Ripples surfed up and down her spine even though it was only a dream.

Latham was impressed by her talent. Instead of knocking her down, he asked her a bit about her training. Carrie Ann told him she owed it to her parents, and Latham, being a natural born genius himself, applauded her, so everyone else stared at her hard, jealousy gleaming in their eyes. Her burgeoning sense of accomplishment smacked a bit of ego, but she would allow herself this one transgression, because it was all about her art. As he walked away leaving her in a swoon, her gaze rippled over his upright back and she pictured just what Latham might look like stripped. She would later find out in this particular fantasy. Occasionally her thoughts were so powerful they seemed real. Casper said it was great, the way she visualized positively. Apparently, you could make great things happen with that approach, and she desperately wanted for her new career to be a success. She'd never had anything of her own in her life.

She was perplexed by the feeling of success that day at the fair, and the ecstatic sense of accomplishment. Already she was fashioning a new fantasy based on it, of being close to Latham.

"And the winner is Carrie Ann of Sweet Secrets." The actual competition dulled in the face of her most powerful fantasy yet.

The feeling, well, she now knew you couldn't put it into words. In her fantasy Carrie Ann accepted the trophy and the prize—the biggest and best prize of them all, the one thing she coveted. A training position with one of the best modern pastry chefs. What was more exciting though was Latham who handed her her prize. He leaned forward, saying to her in his husky, go to bed voice, "Carrie Ann, meet me. I want to talk to you, see you. Your talent is amazing, it excites me."

It was such a stupid dream, but she supposed many women had them—mostly young women, and especially ones who felt they'd missed the boat. How many times had she seduced Latham? A great many times and in lots of different ways although the scenario generally followed more or less the same formula. Latham, not wanting anyone to know, invited her to his plush suite. When he opened the door he was a different man because Latham would be different with her wouldn't he? She was all he had ever wanted and she would be the one to change him. Yes, Latham had had his fill of superficial women. He was continually in this and that gossip magazine, and dated loads of glamorous females across the globe—fellow cooks, pop stars, you name it. But all his life he had been seeking that most elusive of things—a woman with more to her than a pretty face — and he told her so as he stroked her hair out of her face and ran his finger around her lips.

She had made an effort for this date. She wore what she would most like to wear but had always been afraid to. A nice short black dress that showed off her curves, finishing this off with stockings and heels. As she got to know Latham, he would release her from her inhibitions even more and she would metamorphose into the woman she had always wanted to be. Latham was the man with the magic touch as he coaxed her into things that were bright and daring, things she would never have considered. It wasn't that Rommy had forbidden clothes like this, it was just that her life had been so dull and uninteresting she hadn't bothered. What was the point, when she didn't go anywhere?

In reality, she'd only ever bought one nice dress in her life. The one she had snuck to the real show and that Nina had helped her hide. Lord knows how she'd had the courage to wear it. No wonder her heart had been pounding nineteen to the dozen. Red was meant to be stimulating wasn't it? She'd had to find out a great deal about the science of color for Sweet Secrets. The red dress had done the trick and even covered with the competition apron, Latham seemed to have noticed her and singled her out.

* * * *

Carrie Ann pondered, lost in fantasy, as they turned to meet the runway.

In her fantasy, she slips off her coat. Underneath she has on the short black dress and she realizes she looks amazingly good in it. Of course, in her reverie she is not half as plain as she thinks. She has had one of those miraculous transformations through love. Latham has made her metamorphose like the ugly duckling, and when she glances in the mirror, she thinks she is glowing. With this outer transformation comes a transformation in her mind and soul too. It is as if Latham has lit a fuse and that fuse is slowly traveling up her and igniting every inch of her. The feelings that race through her are not surprising because she knows what's lurking inside. The emotions, buried deep, needed a man like Latham to start the snowball effect. Latham is speechless. He steps back, amazed she can scrub up so well, when she doesn't have icing smudges on her nose and spun sugar stuck in her hair. That's good, because he'll have even more of a shock when he knows what other secrets she's hiding. She runs her tongue over her lips in invitation. It seems the natural thing to do as she thinks how much she would like to eat him. He looks super cool. He's dressed in designer jeans and a white shirt, stylishly undone by about three buttons. His shaggy hair is a neat frame for his sexy face.

"You look amazing. Kind of different to how I imagined."

"Thanks." She brushes past him, giving him a teasing look.

Latham does not hang back when it comes to seduction, he grabs her waist and Carrie Ann explodes, the sensations shoot right the way through her like a pulse of electricity. He stands there and nuzzles her neck and she fizzes and pops, tilting her head so he can run his tongue over her bare neck.

Beneath her dress amazing things are going on. Her body seems to have become one vibrating note of pleasure. Sometimes the vibrations are slow, sometimes fast. Every time he runs his tongue behind her ear, she experiences a corresponding tug between her legs as if his tongue has somehow moved down and is nestling between her dips and folds and is playing there. Latham is an expert with her zipper. He lifts her dress away and lets it drop to the floor. She stands with him drawing her back against his erection. She is wearing only a small pair of lace briefs and a bra.

His hands moved in staccato, teasing movements over her skin. She is not a waif, she is aware of her bulges, but she has tried to make the best of them. Latham squeezes her hips. "I like you, Carrie Ann. Dining out on those stick thin women gets so wearing. I've been searching for a real woman like you all my life. Besides which..." He cups her breast, her nipples springing nicely erect. "I always had a thing for a woman with brains and you certainly have those. You're bloody amazing."

That is all that it takes, all that she needs to hear. She leans her head back against Latham and a moan escapes her lips as he fondles her breast a bit roughly, but just how she wants. He pinches and rolls it between his thumb and finger before turning his attention to the other. She is drifting now on a pleasant sea of promise. She is moist between her legs, and her clitoris is twanging with a stridency that makes her want more. Latham seems to intuit what she craves. She craves slow seduction. But hold on. Dare she spring the secret on him? Yes, she will. His hand comes down and he plays between her legs, cupping her mound and sliding his hand through the lace to feel her, rubbing the fabric gently back and forward over her by now, rock hard nub. She gasps as the ripples of orgasm become too strong to resist. She will have this moment, she thinks with triumph. She grabs his hand, unable to hold back as she seizes the moment. In her fantasy she is a whore, directing him to each pulse point, so eventually, she gets what she wants — waves of hot washing satisfaction, so intense they almost drown her as she comes against him with a cry.

Latham laughs in her ear. "Oh, Carrie Ann. You look so demure and you're not are you? Orgasms, dearie me. You're so easy to ignite aren't you?"

He turns her around. She stands in front of him in her underwear and the nice pair of sheer black stockings and suspenders she bought specifically for just such an encounter. With a sigh, she thinks. Here goes. *"Latham, I'm afraid you might not like what I have to say."*

He raises an eyebrow. "What, what might I not like?"

"I'm a virgin. Yes, I realize it seems unlikely at my age and it might put you off, but you ought to know." In her fantasy she isn't at all afraid. She doesn't buy into all the notions about virginity and how much it hurts your first time. Besides, she's as good as already had sex with Latham. Her vibrator has become her best friend over the past two years and she is sure all that personal fucking has given her enough experience for it not to be unpleasant, but rather something to be savored.

"A virgin? Hell, are you kidding me, delicious girl." He isn't turned off, in fact, he's even more turned on. "Come here." He grabs her hips and stares into her face. Then he cups her head and kisses her hard on the lips – not a chaste kiss, but a tangle of tongues and hungry jousting. "I love it, you're fucking amazing." He picks her up, carries her through into his suite then places her on the bed.

She is driven on as if another Carrie Ann has taken her over. She is concentrating on the lust that is eating her up. She watches him as he unzips his jeans and peels out of the fabric in a sexy strip tease. Her body quivers. There's not much time to think about her inhibitions as his shirt pools on the ground. She has seen Latham practically naked since he did a semi-naked series of calendar shots for a charity and she still has it pinned to the wall. Latham loves making an exhibition of himself and he's good at it. He has even been approached to do a TV film deal, but he says his heart is only in his cooking. That raises him even higher in her estimation since he is a man close to her heart, who shares her passion of only putting his brilliance in cookery first.

*A sigh, no it's a moan, she just moaned, in shock,
pleasure? He has taut, muscular thighs and a washboard
flat stomach. What draws her attention though is his cock,
dare she say that. Yes, penis, cock, whatever. Of course, his
prowess is legendary but you hear all sorts of stories. Carrie
Ann was ready to have her dreams trampled on, but feels a
frisson that her expectations have not been dashed. It gives
her immense satisfaction to see his thick cock lengthen and
strengthen under the caress of her gaze, jutting forward
from what is the perfectly shaved huddle of his balls. Her
throat is dry and her heart pounds so loudly she thinks she
might pass out. He is actually touching it, holding it. It
would seem quite funny if she didn't want that huge thing
buried deep inside her.*

*Latham flops down beside her on the bed, teasing her hair
with his fingers, as his penis grazes her naked flesh. "You're
something, Carrie Ann. I'm fascinated by your talent and
your hidden twisted personality. It is twisted isn't it? Or
you wouldn't be able to dream up such lurid ideas for your
art. Shit, that's hot, hot, hot."*

*These are the things she wants to hear. But this is a
fabrication and fantasies are perfect. She smiles because
what can you say to the object of your desires? Then he
kisses her again and she dissolves. It is hard to say how she
feels, but her arms, legs and insides are liquid as if the
energy has been sucked out of her. Latham could do
whatever he wanted and she wouldn't object. She spreads
out languorously on the Egyptian cotton sheets. Pressed to
her, his body is warm, hard and powerful. She teasingly
rubs her thighs against his thick ones and Latham licks her
ear, then runs his tongue around her face and lips. Her
mouth opens involuntarily in an exclamation of wonder and
welcome. His tongue dives in and she soars higher and
higher, into infinity. It is like a drug this love, this lust.
Latham's cock feathers her leg, and reaching down, she
brushes it with her finger, surprised at how firm it is. There*

are lots of things she would like to do, but she isn't sure and she wants him to lead the way.

He grabs her hands holding them mock hard. "Don't worry, I'll show you. Just follow my lead and tell me if you don't like it. Course, I would like to go with some handcuffs, but it might scare you?"

Scare me, I don't think so. *Her breasts in her black lace bra rise and fall as Latham's thumb makes circuits and creates trails across her body. Wherever he touches, he leaves licks of fire. She thinks that after this her body will be a map of footpaths created by Latham, which the next time around they will be able to follow, concentrating on their favorite routes. And that map will not be followed by anyone else because it is a secret only she and Latham share. This thought fills her with a warm sense of wonder as she stretches up to cradle his head and kiss his eyes and cheeks.*

* * * *

In the beginning this was where her fantasy would end as if she was afraid to go any further. But after that meeting with Latham at the competition, new scenarios had emerged and she was not ashamed to admit they had become very hot and inventive indeed.

The engines were now whining as they picked up momentum. Carrie Ann felt a curious mixture of emotions, both fear and excitement. Her mind was bubbling over with projects. That was another thing she had to thank Arlem for. Casper had helped her see her plan clearly. When she'd left England, she'd set the framework in place for her new life, but it was difficult to see the future and push away the dark clouds then. There was still so much to think about. She realized that her father's nest egg—accumulated through so much scrimping and saving—wouldn't go that far. For one thing, the cottage needed so many repairs. Besides that, if she wanted to start her own business, there were so many costs to work out.

Even though she'd now taken on a more permanent job at Oh Crumbs! it was still part-time and would nowhere near pay the bills. She could attempt to get a job farther afield, but she didn't think that idea was very practical. There were hardly any buses through Puddleford and she didn't drive. She supposed that some way down the line that would be another must have. She would have to take driving lessons. Then she could maybe get the car out of the garage. She would have to be able to drive if Sweet Secrets was going to expand.

It was naïve to think that her clients would be local, she'd already found that out. Besides which, she'd need to be able to fetch supplies. It was terrifying. Was she ready to enter the bustling world beyond Puddleford yet? This short trip was one thing, but it was like heading out into enemy territory to consider regular trips to the city and especially to consider driving with all that honking and road rage. Her hands were clammy. She didn't know which emotion was the stronger, excitement or terror, especially now her dream was closer than she'd ever believed possible.

Marcus had helped. Amazing how the chef from The Manor seemed to show such an interest in her. He had egged her on, saying she had talent and he should know, having gained a Michelin star for the second year running and that was some accomplishment. Ms Bunting had been overwhelmed at Carrie Ann taking Marcus' eye. It was her mille-feuille that had sealed her fate. A mille-feuille was notoriously difficult to pull off successfully but she had felt braver about trying even more daring things after the competition. For one thing, the pastry layers had to be many and super light and it required quite a bit of skill to mix the détrempe and beurrage dough's together, besides all the turning and folding. It seemed whatever she touched with pastry or icing, though, just turned out right or better than right, fantastic. The elderberry and blackcurrant twist secretly hidden within the crème pâtisserie was bound to be a winner, it having gone down like hotcakes in the bakewells as Nina had kept pointing out, when she'd tried to be funny. Home baking and comfortable old favorites—even fancy bakewells had not been the pinnacle of achievement that Carrie Ann strived for though. She excelled at detail and the fancier the better. This was where the twist of fate with the mille-feuille had come in as she'd expanded operations into delicate French techniques.

Marcus seemed to visit Oh Crumbs! more often now that she was there providing regular contributions and Ms Bunting and Nina were continually going on about it.

"I think Marcus fancies you," Nina had laughed one day. "I think he wants to get you over the table and cover you in icing or put his nozzle where he shouldn't."

"You're mind's so filthy, Nina, it's like a sewer." Carrie Ann found her friend's comments amusing.

Personally, she didn't fancy Marcus because he wasn't her type in so many ways. But she liked him. Surprising since he was egocentric like Latham, although not quite as bad. Marcus liked to source his supplies locally if possible. When he'd pulled up outside the shop in his yellow sports car, Carrie Ann had been leaning on the counter and there had been nowhere to hide. It had to be divine providence that she'd brought the mille-feuille down to the shop to see if Ms Bunting would trial a new idea. They were wonderful, even if she said so herself. Each thin crisp layer had been filled with lemon infused cream and thin layers of either elderberry and blackcurrant or raspberry and mint jam, finished off with icing. She had had the notion to put names on top so that people could use them as an alternative to a birthday cake. Ms Bunting was raving over the genius of such a novel idea, since no one else seemed to have thought of it.

She was always surprised when she saw him. Marcus looked very tall when he was cooking on the TV, but in real life he was tiny and a buzzing energy unit. Gone was the impeccable grooming that saw his sixties quiff presented to perfection, his hair having been blown about by the open top car was standing on end, like he'd had an electric shock.

"Eh." She'd flushed. It was no secret that Marcus and Latham had once appeared on television together.

"*Parfait.*" He'd grinned as he'd come through the door pushing his sunglasses up over his head. "Here is the Miss Cake Perfection." He spoke in broken English despite a good many years living in the UK.

She'd blushed. "What are you calling me that for?"

"I think it suits you. You still haven't changed your mind then?"

"Marcus. I have my mind set on, well..." she'd stammered.

"*Certainement, certainement.*" His French accent was so sexy. "In one way to ask you to train with me is how do you say...shooting me in the foot. It is the gamble to take on a new pastry chef. But chefs with your skills and dedication are few. It is a conspiracy that the cake making god who fashioned Carrie Ann gave her angel fingers."

She had wished the ground would open up and swallow her.

"Anyway, I'm so glad to see you as it is about the multi-seed with Chia seed."

Her head had reeled. She didn't consider herself an artisan baker, but good hands and a way with the dough meant she was good at that as well, and did a pretty tasty loaf.

His gaze had landed on the mille-feuille that had been resting on the counter. "Your art as usual, *hein*?" Out dove a hand and up went the mille-feuille toward his lips before she'd been able to stop him.

For a man who had judged many of the best, it had made her heart flip. Marcus' black eyes fixed on her. "It looks good but does it taste good? I have seen most excellent chef prepare food that looks and is presented..." He'd stared at the ceiling. "I can't find a good English word for it, but in French you say...*formidable*, and yet it tastes like cardboard."

Nina had stood in the doorway and Ms Bunting behind her, hands folded over her apron. Marcus had bit into the silky soft pastry and flakes like confetti had fluttered to the floor. "Do you know something, *petit-chou*, you amaze me. I offer you job, you crazy not to take it."

She'd burst into giggles. It had been only moments later she'd realized he was serious. The truth of the matter was, she would have loved a job up at The Manor being tutored by Marcus, but if she did that, she knew what would happen. She would put her secret plans on the back burner.

"Carrie Ann has dreams." Ms Bunting had said.

"What kind of dreams? You'll have to tell me about them."

"It's a secret," Nina had said, winking at her.

Marcus had nodded. "It is a conspiracy of women. How can one man win? So fine, I will find out soon enough. Now, Carrie Ann. The bakewells were *superbe*. However, at The Manor, we pride ourselves on changing the menu regularly. So, do you think you could do a regular order of these? But dainty, maybe half the size. I could see them going well on the desert menu for 'The Summer Kitchen'."

"The Summer Kitchen." She'd wobbled and had had to clutch the counter. Marcus' innovative summer menu was the talk of the town. It was too good to be true. "That would be great." All this had happened quite a while ago now and she'd pushed the logistics of things to the back of her mind, like she had a tendency to do. It would have meant providing a sizeable amount for Friday's special menu, but she was sure she could cope when the time came.

Her experimental flavors had not gone unnoticed by Marcus. "What a palate you have, *chérie*. I am amazed at this, Cinderella."

She had inherited the Jude gift of having a super-sensitive palate that understood flavors. Years ago when her father had been who she thought of as the likeable, bouncy person he had said to her, "Darling, I think you have inherited the Jude gift." Personally, she thought Rommy had the Jude gift, but he dismissed his ability, saying the jam was a lucky discovery. Rommy had also said that cookery was the closest profession to love.

"Why is that?" she had asked.

He'd tapped his nose. "Well forgive me, sweetheart. Although your mother would hate me to say it, it's sensual with all that kneading and smoothing. And then there's the delicate perfumes and the sheer delight of eating what you've created. Why do you think they say it's the way to a man's heart?"

"That's food, Dad."

"It'll be easy to fix. You want to put some super glue on that arm, or make up some more icing? It sets like cement doesn't it?" Dominic observed.

She snapped back to the present and the rumble of the engines. The plane dropped in a turbulent spiral of air and she had to grab the edge of her seat as it began a steeper ascent. "How did you learn about icing?" *Take your mind off this, Carrie Ann, don't think about the plane.*

"Oh, my mother was a stalwart of the WI, she used to judge the annual show. My family are what you might term upper middle class for their sins."

She thought he sounded rather disparaging.

Dominic was silent as if he was weighing something up. "I love my mother and she doesn't deserve Father. Father can be a monster. Very overbearing, never listening to anyone else. He's a bit of a bully."

"I see. And yet, your parents have this love hate relationship."

"You don't mention yours?" he asked clearly trying to change the subject.

She hesitated. "Mine died. A car accident when I was tiny." This was not a total lie. It was something she hated to even think about. That day, that awful day, when her mother had gone into town and, always dreaming, had not concentrated as she'd crossed the road and had been knocked down by some guy who'd shot the red lights. She stared out of the window, feeling like bursting into tears. Sometimes it was all too much. "I didn't know them very well. I can hardly remember them, if I'm truthful."

"I'm sorry." He squeezed her hand and raising it to his lips, kissed it. "There, that should make you feel better."

She couldn't take offense, she didn't want to. They lapsed into a companionable silence. Already they had similarities and that made it easier to draw closer.

Time passed remarkably quickly on the flight. At one point she escaped to the toilets and peered at herself in the mirror. There was a glow to her cheeks that hadn't been there before. She bent forward, studying herself carefully. Funny that. Funny how someone could change her. She was filled with restless anticipation and couldn't wait to get back out to talk some more. She tugged down her dress, arranging the skirt. Now she wasn't being so hard on herself, she reckoned she looked quite attractive. *Silly, Carrie Ann. Do you think anything will come of this, because you're mad if you do. It's just a silly holiday romance. He's filling in the time with you because you're so innocent and he realizes he can wind you up.* She applied a slick of her nude lipstick and brushed her hair back from her face. Why then did she feel so fantastic? Carrie Ann took a deep breath and, making her way out of the cubicle, headed back toward her seat.

By this time they were in mid-flight and they'd found out they shared heaps in common from music to films and funniest of all, Doctor Who. Conversation flowed like the course of a river, any difficult moments moving around the boulders in its path, before racing on its way toward its destination. What destination? A smile quirked her lips as she wondered what an embrace or a kiss from him would feel like.

The possibility of real romance was only a hair's breadth away and that was intriguing.

Filled with childish enthusiasm, she couldn't resist getting out her phone and showing him her cake portfolio. The only person who actually knew anything up to now about her detailed plans for her bespoke cake company was Nina. Sweet Secrets was just that at present, a secret. She could tell he was impressed.

"They're fantastic, Carrie Ann."

"Yes, so I've been told. But there's more." She tapped her nose. She was feeling daring. "I don't intend my business to be an orthodox one. I'm going to call it Sweet Secrets, and it's going to be a cake company with a twist."

"Mmm." He teased, "Now I wonder what twist that could possibly be?"

Needless to say, no one would believe she could be so daring. After the kind of life she'd led, they wouldn't think she had it in her. But she now knew the devilish side to her personality couldn't be repressed any longer. Sweet Secrets was the perfect vessel for her creativity. It would portray every aspect of who she was. She'd done her homework assiduously and there seemed to be a gap in the market as regards to erotic cake art. She had lots of ideas regarding icing art, so many she could fill a book with them.

Besides saucy little models based on old fashioned risqué postcards, she was going to do a romance, historical and contemporary series, all of them alluring. And yes there was going to be a rude series as well. They would go down a treat for adult birthday, hen and stag parties.

She had already set about testing the market for private commissions and had placed an advertisement in Cake Modellers Monthly. She had been shocked when she'd had a telephone call for a birthday cake with a Betty Boop twist. It had been a triumph. Her client had been amazed and delighted at the sexy Betty result and it was surprising how quickly word of mouth traveled. Before long she'd been making two cakes a week. It was then she'd discovered things had to change. Yes, life was hotting up for her, in more ways than one. The real Sweet Secrets was about to be born.

"It's been wonderful meeting you, Carrie Ann." Dominic stared at her intently.

She felt silly, but she wondered if he was going to kiss her, he was leaning so close. *Yes, kiss me, kiss me please.* When, as a matter of fact, he did, cupping her head and gently pressing his mouth to hers, she gasped it was such a surprise.

"Well, at least you didn't hit me with Clyde."

She smiled.

"I really like you. How about we exchange addresses and when we get back, we could meet up again?" he pressed.

"Dominic, don't be silly, we just met, didn't we? You have your life and I have mine."

"I don't think it's silly."

They were approaching land. Out of the window she could see the jagged coastline through veils of tattered clouds. In no time they would be following their descent path.

"I could get my best friend, Dave, to drive you back. He always picks me up."

"I know we live fairly close, but it's over thirty miles away. Puddleford is so out in the sticks," Carrie Ann objected.

"So what?"

She was tempted, so tempted to take it further. But romances like this only happened in stories. She was deflated. She was attracted to him, but it was unrealistic. He was so much younger and she didn't think she could cope with the emotions of a rocky romance. Those kinds of emotional dramas happened to other women, stronger, more together women.

"I'd like to take you out. We could have great fun. We could go to a nice restaurant and you could size up the opposition. I'd treat you to the whole dessert menu. I know a restaurant that does great fancy pâtisserie. Come on, you're clever and we have heaps in common. I thought we were getting along so well and I thought...well that you might want to, you know...go out on a proper date."

"Dominic, you are funny. I mean you seem so genuine and I really think you're on the level, but nothing could come of this. There are dozens of gorgeous women around, I've noticed them and they're all slathering over you."

"Are they? I didn't notice. You have all my attention."

She swallowed. It was like a thrilling rollercoaster ride. She'd bumped into a man and now he wanted to date her. But why couldn't it have been simpler? "I'm being realistic. After Rommy, I couldn't take another emotional battle."

"No, no, of course you couldn't." It was then he cupped her chin, forcing her to look at him. "But I wouldn't do that to you. The last thing I'd do is hurt you. I'm not on about a fling or a one-night stand. I'm on about dating you."

"It wouldn't work."

"I think it would. Give that here." He snatched her mobile phone off her and keyed in his number. "Now you have this. I have a hunch you'll call me."

It was right at that second that the plane began to bank. They were making their final descent to Heathrow. Rather than being nervous like she'd thought she'd be, she was flying high.

He held her hand and, leaning closer, he winked at her then whispered in her ear, "I'll find you, Carrie Ann. You won't get away."

He seemed reluctant when at last the plane taxied to a stop and, giving her a whimsical look, he got his rucksack down from the locker. "So, guess if I can't give you a lift, this is it until you give me a call."

"Dominic" — she searched for an excuse — "I've had a fantastic time, but you're not serious. You can't be."

They stood in the aisle being jostled as everybody finished getting their bags down from the lockers and pushed toward the front to be the first off.

"I am. Very serious. Why wouldn't I be? We're both available." He squeezed her hips, his fingers circling. Now that was daring, and she liked it.

She shook her head and shuffled her feet. He made her feel hot under the collar. Every time she moved she seemed to brush against him and it was doing weird things to her. Why wouldn't he take no for an answer? She sighed inwardly. There was nothing she could do. She had to say no. It was ridiculous. Come on. Carrie Ann Jude dating a younger guy? That didn't happen. At least in her world it didn't and it wasn't likely too.

As they walked off the plane, he grabbed her hand. "It's okay. From what you told me you've been through a rough time. But I could show you us guys are not all the same."

"Cheesy," she said, blinking at him as he drew her close into his hips.

Before she could move, he kissed her on the lips in full view of the passengers.

"Is that cheesy enough for you?"

Cheeks flaming, she was glued to the spot.

"I know what you think. I picked you up because I was bored and wanted a bit of in-flight entertainment. But it's not like that. This is the best thing ever. I end up next to a girl I fancy like hell." His glance raked her face. "Come on, Carrie Ann, give me something. Even if you just say you'll call me when you've had time to think about it."

She was lost in a mist of euphoria. Despite the ramifications, this chance encounter had done her a world of good. What an end to her holiday.

Chapter Four

She wondered if she was one of those pitiful sex-starved women. After all, she seemed to have the knack of picking unattainable men. On the bus ride home, she thought back over the holiday. She'd reckoned it would be so hard leaving Casper and Martha, but meeting Dominic had put things into perspective. She'd been stupid, she realized that. She'd thought Casper liked her, when in actual fact she'd gotten the signals wrong. It had been a case of being overcome by the warmth of the homestead and Casper and Martha's welcome. She had quickly grown close to Martha, the mother hen of the whole operation. She was always bustling around and worked a lot of the time in the kitchen and serving the home-cooked meals. She'd told Carrie Ann that most women fell wildly in love with Casper and couldn't help swooning over the six-foot-four cowboy and it wasn't surprising.

Carrie Ann hadn't been able to hide her surprise at how stunning he was when Casper, who was in charge of activities, had walked into the room to address the group on the first night of their arrival. Tall and tanned, he was the first man after Latham that she'd fancied. Over the days ahead she realized she must have made it evident how madly in love she was with him as she'd stumbled over her words and blushed all the time.

Martha had joked about it before gently trying to divert her in that way she had. Carrie Ann remembered one day in particular.

* * * *

Arlem

Carrie Ann was in the kitchen when Martha walked by and tousled her hair.

"You want to be careful, honey. You can't trust these cowboy types. A girl in every town or on the back of every horse and all that." Then, seeing Carrie Ann's look of consternation, she burst out laughing. "Don't look so sad, I'm only kidding. He seems to have a real soft spot for you. You'll soon see he isn't the guy for you though. Casper's married to his work and he has" — she winked at Carrie Ann — "got tendencies in another direction. He's in love with a rodeo guy, Carl."

"Oh." Carrie Ann didn't know how to take that. She couldn't believe it, the way he joked and fooled with the women. Anyway, whether he was gay or not, she still fancied him like hell.

Arlem began to work its magic on her almost immediately and it was a wild, wild feeling. Her first attempt at freedom was working out better than she'd thought and at liberty to indulge, she reveled in the stirrings of her body. She had read enough about bondage, having gleaned a rather smutty collection of ideas from her reading collection. Well, she felt like she had been in a certain kind of bondage over the past few years and now the shackles and chains had dropped away, she was left scared on the one hand, and wildly exhilarated on the other.

In a warm haze, she allowed her fantasies to take full flight and much to her surprise she found that involved a degree of voyeurism. Her room looked out onto the paddock and she had plenty of opportunity to ogle Casper, who got up before the others at the crack of dawn. She would set her alarm last thing at night, then in the morning, drawing aside her drapes, watch him wander out to the paddocks or bring the horses out of the stable for a groom. *God, how sad.* She had a massive crush on a cowboy and she realized there was no future in it. How could there be? At the same time it gave her an opportunity to indulge burgeoning sexual feelings.

She must be getting better because somehow she was holding it together through her crush. Normally, her emotions would go overboard, leading to full blown panic attacks. Moreover, she'd been hugely self-critical, now though she felt more level—able to indulge her feelings and face reality while still flying high with her imagination. She smiled as she recalled ambling along on the daily rides, behind him, drinking in the sight of his slim hips and the way his thick black hair curled over the collar of his check-patterned shirt.

Every so often he'd turned around and flashed her a grin. "Hey, Carrie Ann. Keep up will you."

Sometimes he talked to her like she was a little kid. In a way it was irritating and like her father had treated her on occasion, but she couldn't take offense with Casper because he meant it in a lighthearted way. Rommy's way of talking to her and his constant criticisms, on the other hand, had changed daily to suit his circumstances and the way he was feeling. She had been his little girl when he'd wanted to keep her in check, but she could quickly become his nurse, his secretary, his cook. Anything he wanted.

The day before she came home, she opened up to Martha. The ranch was quiet and she watched from the kitchen door as Martha layered pecans on the top of a pie.

"Come on in here, kid. Didn't you want to go out for the last ride? Casper's taking everyone out to the painted bluffs."

She shook her head. "It was an all day thing. I wanted to get some rest and then go out and see the horses, say goodbye to them, you know."

"You've taken a shine to your horse Buster, haven't you? Yes, it sometimes gets folk like that when it's about time to leave. It's hard to say *au revoir* but of course you can start planning to come and see us again. Maybe next year?"

Carrie Ann wandered over to the table. Icing and food colorings exerted the same kind of effect on her that shoes and cosmetics did with other women. She didn't understand why that should be. Although her father, in one of his softer moments, had spoken about her grandmother being creative and an artist and never being able to leave her paintbrushes and sketchpad alone. That was something she'd have to do. Research her family tree one day. There had also been murmurs of her grandmother's family having a tearoom somewhere in the Midlands. Her grandmother had done something to upset Rommy and Mary, but Rommy hadn't liked to talk about it.

That was her father all over. He'd fashioned the chains of bondage by rationing any information. It was like he'd thought if he'd given her too much to go on, she would have just upped and left. Information was power.

"You being a baker, how do you like my good old home cooking, Carrie Ann?"

"Can I pinch a recipe or two?" She sat down, stealing a pecan out of the bowl on the table.

"Sure you can, kid. I'll give you a handful of my recipe cards." She pushed the mixing bowl across the table. "Here, don't tell anyone."

Carrie Ann licked the spoon, a childish habit she couldn't get out of. She realized she'd developed a liking for Martha's particular twist to American frosting and was already wondering how to include it in her recipes.

"Say why don't you help me ice some cookies? I thought about making up a little presentation bag for everybody to take with them on the ride to the airport."

She leaped to her feet. She couldn't wait to show off her skills. "Wow! That sounds like a great idea."

It was as they iced the biscuits that she told Martha. Told her how cookery had given her an escape route, stopped her from hiding away in her room, been a way for her to express herself.

"He was a bit of a control freak, your father then?"

"Yes. Cooking had to be done, though, and he was fond of cakes."

Martha left her in charge of the cookies while she finished the spread for the goodbye feast. On this occasion there looked like there was enough to feed an army—pumpkin and pecan pie, muffins and flapjacks. Besides the farewell barbecue.

She iced a little picture onto each cookie, her interpretation of how she saw each visitor. Martha glanced over her shoulder. "Hey, kid, you didn't say you were *that* good?"

Carrie Ann shook her head and blushed. She was a closet artist with the same creative desires most artists had—the urge to create and keep on creating. This was the one good thing to come out of her relationship with Rommy. He had unwittingly done her a favor. Continually at his beck and call, the kitchen had been the one place she hadn't been bothered.

For a second she paused, icing bag raised. He had brainwashed her, drip-feeding his poison so it had seeped into her consciousness. She couldn't recall quite when the bonds had become so tight though. Once she'd had a bit of liberty, she could certainly remember that. She had been allowed out into the pretty front garden to look after the fruit and vegetables, would even help Rommy stumble slowly down the rows so he could fawn over the fruit and berries. There had been daily visits down the lane into the village and general store where she'd bought her father's cigarettes. It was hard to pinpoint when it had become so bad.

Of course, having recently discovered the truth about Rommy, she felt it was easier to forgive him. He had kept his cards close to his chest and had never told her he'd had Alzheimer's. Following his funeral, the doctor had approached her, said that Rommy had in a way wanted to protect her, hadn't wanted her to worry. She would have liked to have known the truth, but that was Rommy. Immediately everything began to make sense. Over the last few years, her father had become progressively meaner and obsessed with what he saw as unwanted intervention. Outsiders had been seen as invaders and not to be trusted. This embraced anyone that tried to help him—social services, doctors, nurses and psychiatrists, all of whom he'd seen as trying to inveigle their way into his life. Rommy's paranoia had taken a turn for the worst after her Aunt Caroline, who lived in Spain and rarely came to England, had decided to pay them an impromptu visit. She had been the one person Rommy hadn't been able to bully.

Carrie Ann's vision blossomed with tears. Stupidly this was what baking did, it released something inside her—made her reflect on things so deeply that she often cried into the pastry and dough. Martha put an arm around her shoulder.

"What is it, poppet? Why are you crying? Yeah, yeah I realize it's the last day. But there's a bit more to it than that, isn't there?"

"I didn't come here for therapy. I came here for a holiday and because it's a nice quiet place to get myself together," she said, as Martha pressed her back down in her chair and brought her a glass of iced tea.

"I'm not a shrink, I'm your friend," Martha said. "Come on, kid, spill the beans. What was the real reason you didn't go out with everyone else today? That last ride. You wanted to go, didn't you?"

"Yes," she said, then felt stupid. The major reason she hadn't wanted to go was her crush on Casper. The last ride together seemed so final and meant she had to face the prospect of going home. Home, if she could call it that. The cottage needed so much doing to it. Yes, Rommy had left her that nest egg, but by the time she'd had the sheds out the back repaired and ready for her business, she doubted there would be very much left over, and as for Oh Crumbs! that didn't pay much. She was almost afraid to admit she was thirty-two and what did she have to show for it?

"I know you didn't come here as a patient, Carrie Ann. People come here for lots of different reasons. There are so many facets to what we do at the ranch. As you know, we're also a retreat, a place for people to find themselves."

Carrie Ann blinked at her. Out of everybody, she wondered if Martha — mother hen — wasn't the best therapist of them all. "I think you're a fraud," she said with a weak smile.

"Mmm, that I am." Martha held her hand so tightly it was like wringing out a cloth and squeezing out Carrie Ann's emotions.

Before she knew what she was doing, she'd told Martha every detail. As she talked, it seemed so clear, the events playing back like scenes from a film with just as much poignancy and clarity. Her time at the cottage, her life. Her vivid imagination conjured up the sensation of the earth beneath her knees as she knelt digging over the vegetable patch. It had been the last frontier before her father had ordered her inside and metaphorically slammed the prison cell door. She recollected Rommy leaning over the front gate gossiping to everyone who went by, then becoming so strange he didn't even venture out of the door. Things had become awful after that, with the garden going wild.

Her worst recollection, though, was Aunt Caroline's visit. She recalled the raised voices as her aunt and father had engaged in what was to turn out to be their last battle. What made it worse, was that it was over her, with words like — repression, young woman, hermits and freedom bandied about. Carrie Ann had dug her trowel into the thick, soft earth turning it over carefully because of the earthworms that deftly yielded themselves up for inspection and proceeded to vanish again. Her tears had dripped into the flower bed, nicely watering the French marigolds she'd planted to keep the bugs off the lettuces. Her aunt had eventually come to the door, tugging down her jacket and looking disheveled.

"Aren't you staying for tea, Aunty?"

"No, dear. If I have to spend another second in the company of that man I'll explode." She'd stroked Carrie Ann's hair. "You ought to stand up to him more. Although, I realize that's very hard. One thing I will say is this. I was half tempted to take you away from here and I would. Except that we're not living in feudal times and you wouldn't come anyway, would you? Not with your kind heart. I know how close you and Rommy once were."

"Of course not." She stood up with the trowel in her hands. "Did you see the cake I made you? Do you want to take it? Let me go inside and put it in that old biscuit tin before Rommy consumes it. He might have lost his craving for most things, but cake isn't one of them." She had brushed by her aunt into the kitchen. There had been no sound. She'd gathered Rommy would be sitting in his favorite haunt in the front parlor—a room trapped in time—gloating over the battle. She'd slid the carefully decorated cake into the tin.

"You have a real talent with the cakes, Carrie Ann. You shouldn't let him crush it out of you and he will. He hates competitiveness and he'll even see baking as competition."

Carrie Ann had stood in front of her aunt holding the tin.

Her aunt, who was diminutive, had looked fierce with the set of her mouth and hostile gaze. "I realize what he's like and I saw it coming. He had this thing about authority. Then something happened after Mary didn't it? Like a faulty piece of machinery, he finally broke down."

Carrie Ann hadn't been sure she'd wanted to hear this. It frightened her and when it came down to it, despite things, she'd still loved Rommy. It had been the two of them for as long as she could remember and in the beginning there had been some very good times. Times when she could recollect taking the train down to the coast and long windswept walks along the beach. It had been fantastic stumbling through the rock pools. Then later Rommy would lie on his back in the sand, and using her bucket and spade she'd bury him. He had been handsome and carefree, if at times guarded. But never this bad.

"He adored your mother. There was no one else like her, but she was a free spirit and she was strong. Too strong for Rommy to manhandle. That's perhaps why he fears you, you know, because he sees that strength, is afraid to stir it up too much in case you up and leave."

"What *me*? Come on." She had been astonished at this revelation because she could barely remember her mother. This was the most her aunt had ever revealed and she was not about to say more. She thought she got the general drift though. It had been a love hate relationship between her mother and Rommy.

She'd held out the biscuit tin, but her aunt had not finished. "In case you're wondering, I told him what I thought. I said 'She's not a child, she's a grownup, you monster. You should cut her some slack. We're not in the Middle Ages'. Anyway." She patted Carrie Ann's hand. "You have a talent like your mother and grandmother had. If you had been allowed, I think you would have gone to university. But there's no point thinking about things that'll never happen. One thing I will say, you're a lovely young woman and you've got a good heart, Carrie Ann."

Carrie Ann blinked.

Martha squeezed her hand. "That's some story. But I'm glad you told me, now you can begin healing."

Carrie Ann smiled as realization dawned. "Yeah, I can, can't I, because I just made that big step that Casper's always talking about? The step that means telling my story, so I can begin to deal with it and move on."

Chapter Five

It was two weeks since she had returned from America, and Carrie Ann was at last facing up to facts. There was so much to do. Already she had set to work in her spare time painting the cottage in vibrant colors, but life was strange without Rommy and she missed him. As horrible as it sounded, there was a bright side to the depressing subject of Rommy's death. He had passed away before he had gotten any worse and she was relieved about that. She knew Rommy had already been angry at himself over his deteriorating mental state and that was why he'd been so unbearable and taken things out on her. Heaven knows what he would have felt like if his memory had worsened even more.

"Horrible old bugger," Nina had said when she'd called round. "He was a tyrant. I don't know why you waste your life feeling sorry."

"He was still my father."

"Yeah, and you were his daughter, but that didn't stop him from victimizing you, did it?"

The cottage looked like a new pin. Besides which she had had a local builder and electrician in to look at the sheds. It wasn't as bad as she had expected, but it was still going to cost a lot of money. Nothing came cheap these days. She fought hard to hold herself together. Nina was right. In the end, her father had become unbearable. Anyway he was with Mary now and Carrie Ann was swept up in her ideas and trying to move on. Getting everything in order and being busy was therapeutic, meaning that she didn't have time to think as she divided her attention between Oh Crumbs! on the one hand and Sweet Secrets on the other.

However, the pressures were piling up and if she wanted to be successful she had to face up to her demons. It was no good, she wasn't able to put it off any longer. It wouldn't be easy, but the trip she had been putting off for ages would be a good start. Her father's solicitor had called her about an important matter he wouldn't discuss over the phone, so she had to take the train to the city. It would dovetail with an opportunity to eye up potential suppliers and visit a kitchen equipment show because she needed to make her final decision over equipping the sheds.

The thought of going into the city filled her with trepidation as she stared in the mirror and pulled her curls up into two combs at the side of her head. At least she looked good and that gave her some courage. A tinted moisturizer and a new eye shadow teamed with a slick of coral lipstick made her look like a new woman. The transformation was incredible but now was the hard part. Her stomach tied up in knots at the thought of once again stepping outside the door, but at least she had a better understanding of her panic attacks. They'd explained at Arlem that they were difficult to get over and took time, so she mustn't fight it and had to take it slowly.

She'd been so much better at Arlem, but then she'd had the wide open spaces and the long rides with Casper to look forward to. Now she was back on her own again. She took a deep breath and placed her hand on her heart in the healing way Martha had taught her. It helped in calming her down and centering her. She wouldn't let this beat her. She was determined and this was the first real step in proving if being away and the Arlem experience was working. Besides, nothing could go wrong. She had her map and details worked out, so if she stuck to that she'd be fine. First the solicitors, then a shop or two, and if she had enough time, a quick look in at the show. How simple was that? All she had to do was concentrate on getting from A to B. It wasn't that hard, she thought smugly. She'd just managed to get to America and back.

She'd forgotten how busy the city was though and instantly she was overwhelmed when she arrived at the station and got off the train. There were people everywhere and they were so impatient. Carrie Ann squealed as a woman's heel stabbed her foot like a dagger and she was jostled by impatient commuters. As soon as she had negotiated the platform, she was then assailed by dirty exhaust-filled air that made her struggle for breath. Could she do this? She was still such a mess. Yes, she had to do it.

She sank down on a bench in the station lobby, her heart pounding as she searched in her handbag. She mustn't make it obvious. She didn't want everybody to see that she was falling apart. What could she do? Find a café, that was what. Casper had told her if she ever felt an attack coming on she needed to sit down somewhere quiet and have some sugar and that might be enough to sort it out. She headed out of the station, her attention darting here and there. Over the crossroads there was a narrow road and from the sight of the awnings it looked like there could be a café or two up there. She headed off determinedly, her hair bouncing on her shoulders. A couple of men glanced at her, but that was probably because she looked such an idiot. She breathed a sigh of relief as she spotted exactly the kind of place she wanted, a quaint Italian trattoria with a little café attached.

It seemed almost empty. The door was open and she strolled in, glancing at her watch. She'd given herself plenty of time and she was early, just like she'd wanted. She sank down on a chair at a table in the corner. It was the perfect hiding place. She ordered a coffee and tried a few deep breathing exercises. She was just managing to slow up her rapid heartbeat when a voice interrupted her.

"Shit, I thought it was you and then I thought no it can't be, my mind's playing tricks on me because I fancied her so much."

She glanced up. At first she thought she'd been mistaken. But there was no mistaking Dominic's mellow tones. It couldn't possibly be, could it?

She experienced a weird mixture of emotions. Disbelief, joy. "Dominic. I don't believe it."

Staring down at her, he looked even more handsome than before and the look in his eyes... Surely she wasn't imagining that look. "My God. This kind of thing doesn't happen does it? Well, only in books?"

"It looks like it just did. Where's your sense of romance?" After pulling out a chair he sat down, running his hand through his hair.

She closed her mouth that had seemed to be hanging open. He looked so different in a smart pinstripe suit and blue tie.

"Actually, I was getting off a train and I thought I saw you. I hope you don't mind, but I followed you. I wasn't certain at first, you looked different. Just as delicious, even more so." His stare lingered on her ruffled blouse and pencil skirt. "You look amazing."

"Thanks." She sipped her coffee as she tried to stop her hands shaking.

"I still can't believe it, but the world is such a tiny place sometimes it can be freaky. The other year I was backpacking in India and I bumped into a guy I used to go to school with. I'd call that a one in a million chance wouldn't you?"

"Yes, I guess so."

He leaned forward, clasping her hands across the table. "But this is fantastic and I'm elated. I'm so glad I bumped into you. Guess why?"

"Why?"

"Because, Carrie Ann, as corny as it sounds. After I met you, I couldn't get you out of my head. I kept hoping and hoping you'd ring me and that you felt the same way. I was devastated when you didn't— ring me that is."

She didn't know whether to burst out laughing or not. It couldn't be true of course. Her gaze shifted over his face suspiciously as she tried to detect a lie. Nothing could alter the fact that she hadn't stopped thinking about him either. Her battle had started when she'd gotten home. She'd mistakenly believed with so many projects, she could push the memory of him out of her head, but she hadn't been able to. In the fourteen hours they had spent together, they had talked more about each other than they might have done to a partner in a lifetime and she felt a connection, a real connection.

"I wish you wouldn't keep pulling my leg. I mean, I realize how this looks and it would be easy to believe in fairytales, but I think we have to face facts, this is one of those massively coincidental events. You told me you come into the city all the time anyway."

"Who said anything about pulling your leg? My, you don't have much of a sense of romance do you?" His fingers tightened on hers. "The more I chatted to you. Well, you can guess. You grew on me."

She peered more intently into his face as if by so doing she would be able to see the truth betrayed in his expression. The trouble was he did seem genuine. It was then she was struck once more by the demon. The demon who had made her lie in the first place. What harm was she doing anyone? If she wanted to chat and flirt with him, she could do. She was single, a grown up and she had no one to answer to. Besides, it made her feel miles better. Already her panic attack was forgotten.

"I'm not a crazy or a stalker. We happened to have a chance meeting and I think we ought to make the most of it."

"Yes, you're right."

The seconds ticked by. She ought to have been on her way to the solicitors by now. She didn't have long because she wanted to get everything done and be back by dark.

"Well, what are you here for? You're a long way from home."

"It's a long story. I have something legal to sort out and then I was going to the expo at Earl's Court." Meeting Dominic again made her feel as if she was in a dream.

He raised an eyebrow. "No kidding. I could come with you?"

"Come on, Dominic. Don't you have something better to do? What interest is a kitchen equipment expo to you?"

"Actually, I'm done with what I had to do but I don't want to get into all that now. Maybe I have a secret too. Maybe I'm a chef in my spare time," he quipped. "Come on I'll get us a taxi to this solicitors and wait for you. Then we'll go on. I won't take no for an answer. You'll see I can be very determined when I want something."

She wanted to go into the solicitor's alone so he waited for her in the park across the road. The office would have inspired awe in her before, because she wasn't used to visiting such plush surroundings, but not today. She must be getting better, she reflected as she looked around with interest. The carpet was so thick it muffled any sound and people buzzed about with calm efficiency working in hushed tones from behind computer consoles, while she sat behind a potted palm with her hands crossed over her handbag and waited. Outside the enormous chrome windows, a fountain splashed, the droplets catching the light like diamonds, and intelligent, well-dressed people moved through the carefully trimmed pathways like robots.

She jumped when the girl called her name.

"Miss Jude. Mr Willis will see you now."

She found the room on the first floor quite easily. Mr Willis was in his fifties and had the look most legal people seemed to have—a mixture of polish and brusque efficiency. It was another one of her observational games to squeeze people into compartments. Stereotyping them was fun. Now, Mr

Legal perfectly fitted the remit in his gray suit and silk
tie, his steel gray hair giving him the look of a
trustworthy father figure. He leafed through the
papers on his desk.

"You don't remember me, do you?"

"No." She smiled at him. "Sorry to be obtuse. Who
are you?"

"It was an awfully long time ago." He seemed to
have not heard her.

She nervously opened and closed the clasp on her
handbag. It was a strange pattern in her life that she
had come to accept oncoming drama with a stoic
heart. So many years of fielding it had given her a
tough hide.

"Do you remember your mother?"

She shook her head. This was not technically true.
She did remember her a bit, but it was like a hazy
shadow.

"Carrie Ann, may I speak frankly without hurting
you?"

"Nothing much hurts me. If you'd lived with
Rommy as long as I did..." Her voice trailed off.

"Yes, yes of course. It wasn't easy. You looked after
him, didn't you?"

"As a matter of fact, yes. I did everything for him."
This man had no idea of the burden she'd carried
around for so long, the burden of mentally carrying a
parent disconnected from reality. For the first time,
though, she didn't feel like crying.

Mr Willis smiled back, his face breaking up into soft
patterns that made her like him.

"I am not the enemy, Carrie Ann, I'm working for
you. Would you like a cup of coffee, before I tell you
the good news?"

She nodded. Good news, that was a first. She had been sure it would be yet more hassle, but she had decided to face up to it. "A coffee would be lovely." What an innocent she must seem. The hushed office at least gave her a breathing space before the next onslaught of having to face Dominic again, and she dared not think of that.

She sipped her coffee while Mr Willis shuffled papers and finally looked up at her. "Did you enjoy your trip to the States?"

"It was terrific, thanks."

His smile broadened. "Good, perhaps things are changing for you, because, as I mentioned, I have some good news. Your mother left you a small amount in trust. Rommy was meant to tell you about it when you were twenty-six. Evidently in his state of mind he forgot."

She looked up sharply, almost spilling her coffee.

"I think we can forgive him, can't we? The thing is, his death brought forth a few legal issues to be tidied up and this was lodged with another solicitor, the one he and Mary used to deal with years ago."

"Mmm." She tapped her handbag. There were so many questions buzzing around in her head.

"It's not riches, but a tidy sum. Enough to help you fix that leaky roof and get your business off the ground."

She swallowed past the lump in her throat. Mr Willis pushed a piece of paper across the table. For a second things faded in and out and she thought she was seeing things. "But it's almost twenty-five thousand pounds?"

"Yes, Carrie Ann. A lot of money."

She smiled weakly and was still smiling as she came downstairs and crossed the road.

When she joined Dominic on the park bench, her hands were still shaking.

"Are you okay? You look like you've seen a ghost."

"It seems like I just came into a sum of money. My mother left it for me ages ago and what with one thing and another... It seems Rommy forgot about it. He was so ill, things were always slipping his mind toward the end."

"Well, that's good news isn't it?"

"Yes, it's terrific news." She jumped to her feet. "So, are we going?"

She slid her hand into his. He walked close to her, their bodies brushing, sparking delicious sensations. For once she felt ten feet tall. Soon she caught sight of Earl's Court. The streets were thronging. It appeared kitchen equipment attracted a lot of attention.

"So you're going to be this hot shot cake artist are you?" He flicked her a look as they wandered inside.

"Actually. You know I am."

Her attention shifted about as she took everything in. The hall was packed. Around them were various stalls advertising products as diverse as baking tins to organic food colorings and high-tech ovens. He squeezed her hand as she was struck by the magnitude of what she was about to do.

"This must be so boring for you, Dom. It's nothing like the enormous one in November. At least they have seminars and cake classes there."

"On the contrary, whatever interests you, interests me."

"And that's plain corny." She nudged him playfully.

He stuck close by her side and every time she bought something or acquired a sample, he would carry her bags, leaving her hands free for more exploring. Moreover, he did on occasion seem rather interested in her opinion and kept stopping to exclaim over a new make of Japanese knives and a range of electric woks, but that might just have been politeness.

Eventually, after two and a half hours she thought she'd done just about everything and had checked off all the items on her list.

Tugging at Dominic's arm, she led him toward the exit. She had already spent more time enthusing over all the gadgets and buying things than she had intended. Now, she wanted to get home so she could set to work on Miranda's cake. It was her first substantial order, something stylish, and as usual wanted in a hurry.

The trouble was Dominic was hanging back. They strolled along. The sun was sinking, it was later than she'd thought. He stopped her with his hand on her arm. "You don't have to rush back that quickly, do you, Carrie Ann? You could stay and have something to eat, even if it's takeout chips down by the bridge."

She looked at her watch. "No, I don't think so. I have to get back to the station, it'll take ages in the rush-hour."

"Well, sit the rush-hour out."

She extricated herself. "I don't think that's a good idea." She stated.

"I do." Before she could avoid him, he caught hold of her shoulder, turned her to face him and kissed her hard on the lips.

This was not the soft kiss she remembered. It was a kiss of pure physical longing. She was so surprised she simply stood with her hands on his shoulders and let him continue. The feel of his lips and tongue softly investigating started warm stirrings that rapidly turned into powerful surges of emotion as her body began to betray her. What was most troubling was that Dominic seemed skilled at it. Maybe he did this all the time? Perhaps he was a serial chaser of older women? Perhaps he had loads of girlfriends? Dozens of questions whizzed through her mind.

She stepped back, touching her lips experimentally. His kisses had been so greedy, so hungry, he had bruised her, but in a stunning way.

"Well like I said before, you didn't hit me. So, that's something," he murmured.

It was as if her whole world had shifted.

"Look, at least give me a call."

"Dominic have you looked at yourself in a mirror, you're way out of my league."

"I would rather of thought you were out of my league."

She shook her head. She wasn't going to win her argument that easily.

"Stop putting up silly obstacles. I get the picture. You got married and don't have that much experience. So what. Furthermore, this monster Rommy damaged you in some way. Well, let me put you back together again. Let me show you what love is."

"Dominic, you're being unrealistic."

"No, I'm not and call me Dom for God's sake. You sound like my father when you keep calling me Dominic."

"All right. Dom." She bit her lip as she stared at the pavement. She knew what she ought to do. Stop it properly and perhaps she would. She had hesitated several times over deleting his phone number. Maybe she should have done, but having it there made her feel, well…it was hard to put into words how it made her feel exactly. Hopeful, excited, flattered?

He stroked her cheek, and she turned her face into his palm in a gesture she had seen in the movies.

Now, it seemed so natural as he stroked her face, smoothed her shoulders with his hand. His touch moved sensually, flickering across her skin, arousing her. She opened her mouth to object, then closed it again as he outlined her lips and kissed her again, slipping his hands around her waist and gathering her to him in a sweet, welcoming embrace. Perfect!

She loved running her hands over his suit and feeling him. They fitted together as easily as pieces of a jigsaw puzzle—her hips to his, his erection just to the front of her, his firm muscles pressing against her breasts. She was breathless, but this time for another reason. As he curled his hands through her hair, he seduced her with his tongue, while the sounds around her seemed to fade away. He could have done anything and she doubted she would have stopped him.

"I know you like me. That's why you'll call me, won't you? I'll come and meet you anywhere. Why won't you embrace life like I decided to do today? Yes, today I made a few important decisions too."

Frowning she slipped her hand back into his as they headed back toward the station. "What decisions, tell me? You didn't really explain why you were here?"

"I had a few job interviews lined up."

He seemed in her view to be engaging in avoidance tactics.

"There's a lot you have to learn about me. Just let's say all my life I've been doing what my father wanted. Today, I decided to face up to him. Tell him what I really want to do, you realize something…?" Dominic hesitated.

They were entering the main hall of the station.

"You did that for me, Carrie Ann. When you told me about your husband and how he'd repressed you, and

I saw how strong you were, how together. It made me realize I had to make certain changes too."

"Dom," she went to object. His story sounded so remarkably familiar. So much like her and Rommy's. He put his finger over her lips.

"All right, I don't want to scare you off if you're not ready. How about, I wait until you do feel ready. How's that?"

"I don't know, I don't know when I'll feel ready."

"That's fine. I'll keep reminding you and then…one day. One day you'll be there." He kissed her quickly on the lips. "There now, you'll have to run to catch your train, you only have five minutes. Hey, your hands are wandering."

Were they? How had that happened? She stepped back—flushing. She glanced up at the board and when she looked back, Dominic had gone, just vanished into thin air. Shaking her head, Carrie Ann, with a new spring in her step, found her train and settled down with her bags spread out on the seat next to her.

Her mind worked overtime. He had filled her head with conflicting questions and emotions. She wanted to see him again, couldn't get him out of her head. But how could she? The distance for one thing, then there was the age difference. It was dark as she watched the stations speeding by in brief snatches of newsreel light. It was amazing how far she'd come in such a short space of time but this…

She glanced up at a fellow passenger, a man holding a newspaper, who smiled at her pleasantly. She had always walked with her head down staring at the ground, never engaged people's interest because she'd been afraid. Afraid of what? Afraid of life, pain, involvement? Why had she ever put up with Rommy? In a way she was glad she had. She hadn't realized how bad the Alzheimer's had been. Still, as Nina had said, there was no excuse for him sealing her off from the world like a Puritan, barring the door to her world with the effectiveness of a real lock and key.

She pressed her thumb to the glass of the railway carriage window. It was steamed up and she did the foolish thing she had seen a woman do once on a favorite episode of one of her soaps. She drew a heart and wrote the name Dominic underneath. She glanced around at her fellow travelers. Once people had stared at her with an open sense of curiosity as she'd looked so dated, so scared. Now, they barely flicked her a glance. She settled back in her seat. For the first time she was free and it filled her with a sense of personal achievement that she had at least come this far. On a wild goose chase probably, but...but what about Dominic?

It was late when she got back home, and she couldn't rest even when she got to bed. Pulling the duvet up to her chin, she couldn't shake off the powerful sensations in her body that he'd sparked. Shrugging off the bedclothes, she stumbled to her feet then wandered to the window. Outside a silver moon spilled its light over the rows of neatly planted bushes. Things were coming along. She had never worked so hard as she had when she'd gotten back from her holiday. Whenever she'd needed a break between the detailed work of baking and decorating, she'd spent hours on the garden that would be her future investment. She thought of the tight buds forming into the rich ripe fruit. It would go into candied fruits, peels and jams. She felt a burgeoning sense of satisfaction. In time she would have a self-sufficient business. Her heart jumped.

Chapter Six

"He likes you," Ms Bunting said. "I should know, I have a long enough history of men."

Carrie Ann wanted to laugh. It was common knowledge Ms Bunting was a spinster and anyway, she didn't think Marcus genuinely liking her was very probable. She picked up an empty cake carrier and placed it on the counter.

"You know, young lady, you've fallen on your feet." There was a gleam in Ms Bunting's eye. "Anyway, as I was saying before, Marcus popped into my mind. Let me increase your hours. Our fame's spreading, I need another pair of hands, and it would help with the bills wouldn't it, while you, you know?" She nudged Carrie Ann. "We all realize you're up to something, it doesn't take a genius. I just don't understand why you won't tell me, since you've told Nina, but the two of you are as thick as jam and I suppose you have your reasons."

"How do you know I'm up to something?"

"You have that gleam in your eye. Besides I know when Nina's keeping a secret. She's good at that." Ms

Bunting considered her carefully. "Do you know you came back with a tan, but I'm certain other things have changed about you..." She adjusted her glasses as she leaned forward over the counter. "There's something sparkly about you, if you don't mind me saying so."

"Don't be daft." Carrie Ann took some shortbread fingers out of one of the other carriers. She was deep in thought. Since she had been back, her mind had been working overtime. It was like her holiday at Arlem had blown away the cobwebs and allowed her to think clearly and she was waking up, waking up to lots of things. She shivered. Rommy's old sheds were not the most salubrious of surroundings, they were full of spiders and nests of mice. In reality, they were not sheds, but rather like two prefab garages joined together. The business had been quite successful in its time and he'd produced a lot of jam. Besides the two separate stoves, put there because Mary hadn't been able to stand the heat and mess in her own kitchen, there were all sorts of other paraphernalia to do with jam making littered all over the place. Makeshift cupboards overflowed with metal containers and old jars and papers and the sweet smell of jam seemed to have pervaded the walls.

She smiled. She had fond recollections of the sheds and watching her father stirring the great old copper pot of jam. There had been no smell like it. He would rather have spent a Saturday afternoon busy stirring away like a mad professor than going out with his mates to the football. Her family had been attached to that cottage. She couldn't envisage moving away.

When she'd gotten back from Arizona, she'd strolled out into the garden. It was a large garden, far too large for one man. Rommy had only managed a third of it, meaning there was plenty of scope for expansion—that was another problem. She wouldn't be able to manage it on her own soon and she would need some help to keep it productive. She had been pleased to see the gooseberry and blackcurrant patches were still in good shape. Farther down, past the sheds, though, the ground had gone wild. Tall straggly weeds that Bert had scythed two or three times a year and that hummed with insects, provided a ready-made jungle for the unwary.

She had pushed her way down through the parsley and ragwort. The prospect of what she was about to do and her plans for the garden was exciting. If she could get the land into shape she could probably be self-supporting with fruit even earlier than she'd estimated, which gave no end to expansion possibilities for the business. She had big plans, but that was what Casper had told her to do. Think big. She intended to get off the ground with the icing and cake decorating because she knew she could corner a niche market with that. When she was established, the sky was the limit as she'd already proved her pastry skills.

She still had the prize to Paris to take too. Now that was worth thinking about, but she'd have to take it before the business really took off. She had written to the company and they had been great when they'd heard her story and had said they would hold it over, make the amendment to her address. But they would expect the dreaded interview. That was okay, she'd cross that bridge too, when she came to it, because publicity was essential. The main thing was she could take it at a later date. She had pushed her hands into her jeans pockets. Things were looking up for her, it was just— Suddenly she had been struck by something. She had no one to share it with, in particular Dominic. It had been so good talking to him—he had such an easy way and she'd been so comfortable with him. *Better not think about that, Carrie Ann.*

She'd reached the fence at the bottom. She used to feed the ponies in the field and had been delighted to see they were still there. As she'd leaned over the fence, stroking the silky muzzles, she'd gazed up the hill toward The Manor. There were exciting possibilities ahead if she could harness them. It was like she was coming to life with ideas that had been stifled. In fact, she had never thought she'd have so many.

Her mind wandered so much lately, Carrie Ann pondered as she was spirited back to the present. Nina, who was watching her from the bakery kitchen, shared a wink. She brought Carrie Ann a coffee and forced her to sit down for their customary Oh Crumbs! tea break. "Ms Bunting's right of course, Marcus does fancy you."

Carrie Ann pulled a face. "What, the sexy Frenchman? I don't think so."

"He's very nice," Nina added.

"You can have him then." She cradled her mug. "Anyway, I've got too much on my plate to think about romance, forgive the pun. First off I need to get the sheds done. I contacted this guy Bert used to go down the pub with. He took a look and the sheds are not in that bad shape. It's health and safety though so the electrics have to be done and the new ovens put in, insulation checked. That kind of thing. I've already priced up most of the stuff I'll need." Her stomach flipped as she realized the immensity of the task.

"Bit of a shame, there's no time for romance in any of this." Nina gave her a loaded look. "You want to hurry it along, you're not exactly in the first flush of youth, are you?"

"Thanks a lot, Nina, I needed that."

Nina was right in a way. She would have liked a boyfriend. Hello, that was her phone vibrating again. She took it out of her bag thinking it might be one of the suppliers or the builder. Instead she saw it was another message from Dominic. She'd give him one thing—he was insistent and it looked like he didn't intend giving up. How many was that now? Dozens? She had to admit to feeling guilty, hardly sending any back, but she didn't know how to untangle her confused thoughts. Since he'd kissed her in the way he had, she'd felt different and she wanted to process the sensation. On the one hand she was tempted. It would be great to go into town and spend another afternoon with him. She could imagine how it would feel to walk around the shops hanging onto his arm. They'd have so much fun. But it was silly wasn't it? Once she did that he would want more and how would she be able to extricate herself, especially since she had woven such a web of deceit?

She walked back up the lane from the bakery with her basket over her arm, glancing nervously at the sky as she did so. There was so much cake decorating stuff and the kitchen in the cottage was so small—she'd had to move the cake making outfit into the least damaged of the ramshackle sheds. The builder had given it the once over and after pegging down a tarpaulin over the roof had told her it should be watertight enough for her to at least use it as an assembly point. That was a relief. This meant she could set out the things she needed in one place. She would have to bake cakes in the oven in the kitchen in batches then bring them down to the shed.

She felt a niggle of apprehension. She didn't like the look of the black clouds that were building up on the horizon. The builder had warned her that the remedial work should hold up provided they didn't have a freak downpour and that had been known to happen. Puddleford was not called Puddleford for nothing. On countless occasions the stream and ford had flooded. She thought about Miranda's cake sitting on the table. Being her largest commission yet, she didn't dare contemplate anything going wrong. It had been a complicated project to take on. In the end the sunset theme she'd decided on with Miranda meant the cake looked graduated in color around the edges and had a complimentary apricot and peach flavoring. This required a lot of work and having to paint each part by hand.

When she got back she made a light supper and carried it out to the shed, where she surveyed the job in hand. Even as she set to work, though, outside raindrops the size of pennies began to fall, hitting the tin roof with a loud pinging sound. Her heart sped up. It was a worst case scenario if the rain got in and ruined things. But it was already ominously dark and she didn't fancy a long walk back to the house with the cake. In the end she changed her mind and decided she would manhandle it back and leave the rest of her stuff. The risk was too great. She'd have to cross her fingers and hope the builder had tacked the tarpaulin down well enough.

As evening fell, she listened with trepidation as the sturdy breeze picked up into the expected high winds and the fierce lashing rain the weather forecast had warned about. Wandering to the window she hugged herself. Well, there was nothing she could do.

She sat down by the fire, and after sliding on her glasses began studying the templates for the cake decorations. She was so absorbed that at first she didn't hear the knock at the door, and the second time dismissed it as the wind. People hardly ever called on her and especially at this time of night. Yawning and stretching, she stood up. Then the knock came again followed this time by a voice. "Carrie Ann, let me in."

She switched off the light and crept into the hallway.

She gasped at the realization as it dawned on her and her mind made the connection between the voice and personality. She knew whose voice that was, it was Dominic. Quickly, she slid back the bolts. He was standing on the doorstep, his hair plastered to his head as he tried to angle himself into the porch out of the worst of the wind.

"Dominic, I don't believe it. What are you doing here?"

"Let me in, Carrie Ann. I'm soaking." He shivered, his teeth chattering.

She stood aside defensively, pulling her dressing gown around her.

"I'm sorry, I didn't know what else to do, who to go to."

Now he was inside and standing in her hallway, her heart welled up with sympathy. "You're drenched," she said, as he dripped a puddle onto the carpet.

"I must have been crazy, but I was so angry I wasn't thinking straight and I just decided to walk from the station. I didn't realize how far it was."

"What you walked from Weston? Are you crazy?"

"It looks like it. But I couldn't stand it anymore."

She led the way into the lounge where the fire still glowed in the grate. "Sit down."

He sank down on a chair, his hands between his legs. "Everything's such a mess. I had no money left for a bus or anything. I left without picking up my credit card and only had a bit of cash. I wasn't even sure how to find you. I asked this taxi driver and he said the only Mill Cottage it could be was the one over the ford and down the main street. I could hardly see where I was going."

She sucked her lip. "Well one thing's for sure, you can't sit around in those wet clothes. I don't have anything that would suit you. I'll get you a bathrobe and I'll put yours into the dryer."

"Thanks."

She pulled the door closed behind her and leaned against it, her heart tripping. She couldn't believe what was happening. What was more, she couldn't understand her reaction. She really liked him and realized now that the way she felt about him was different to her other obsessions. Why had she fooled herself she didn't want to see him again? She was overjoyed he'd turned up. She wandered upstairs to fetch the spare bathrobe. Then when she came back downstairs she put the coffee on to brew, while he changed.

He sat shivering and holding out his hands toward the glowing coals in the grate when she came back in. He looked so forlorn that something warm and maternal stirred her inside.

"It was the final straw, Carrie Ann. I thought I could hack it back home with Dad but he's unbearable. You'll never guess what he did? When he came back from Benidorm, he told me he was moving her, the girlfriend, in. Just like that. It's like he's having a midlife crisis or something. It wasn't as if he even thought about me."

She shook her head.

Dominic cupped his hands around the mug of coffee she'd brought him. "Dad's incorrigible. I left after I blurted something out. It was the last straw. She hates me you know. She sees me as standing in the way of her and Dad, I know she does. Dad's loaded and she isn't of course. He can be incorrigible. Any pretty young thing and he simply loses his head. I couldn't help it. I was rude about her and we had this blazing argument that ended up with him telling me that if that was the way I felt, I could leave. Anyway, while he cools off, I couldn't think of anywhere else to go."

"Maybe it's not like you think. I mean you told me yourself, your father's getting a divorce. Maybe at long last, your parents are cutting loose and thinking about moving on?" She sat down by the fire, cradling her knees self-consciously. A smile curved her lips. Dominic looked so funny in her spare bathrobe. Being so tall the arms only came down to his elbows.

"Whose side are you meant to be on?"

"No one's. I'm just thinking perhaps it's not what it seems and anyway your dad probably thought you were about to move out didn't he? What with the job interviews and everything?"

He frowned and again the strange expression she had noticed earlier veiled his face. He looked about to make a sour retort and sat back. "That's what I liked about you from word go, Carrie Ann. How sensible you are."

She was staring at him. She still couldn't believe he was here.

He flapped his arms at her. "Funny huh? Look that cool in this, do I?"

"Sorry, I couldn't help it." She smiled. Then the words poured out, "I won't say I'm not delighted to see you because I am."

He nodded. "Cool, I was kind of hoping how we parted that you might have..."

"Might have what? You didn't exactly attack me did you? I fancied you and you kissed me."

"I did a whole lot more than kiss you."

Her cheeks burned. "I know and the truth is I wanted you to. But we'll talk about that later."

"Great, I hope so, because I meant it."

"You have mates, don't you? All guys have mates they go to when they're in trouble don't they?" She found it odd that a friend hadn't been his first port of call.

"Not that many and I wouldn't want them laughing at me. They, eh, never mind..." His voice trailed off. "Please don't ask me so many questions."

"Sorry." It was strange having a man in the house. Strange but oddly exciting.

"I can stay, can't I? You won't turn this poor specimen out in the rain? Pretty please." He made puppy dog eyes at her.

She felt a jolt. She hadn't thought about it. "Well, I, uh..."

"I knew you'd say yes. Knew that you'd listen to me, help me sort myself out. You're a gem."

"Dominic, I don't know if that's a good idea, I mean."

"I realize what you're going to say. That you have to watch your reputation and things. That's another thing I like. How innocent you are."

"Well, I wouldn't have put it quite that way. You make me sound like a heroine out of a Victorian novel."

Grinning, he hitched the sleeves up his arms. "So? I find that rather cool. There's not many girls like you around, Carrie Ann."

He didn't give her time to reply. "I'll be discreet. In fact, you won't even know I'm here. I have to sort things out. As soon as I can, I'll get onto Chris and see if I can go down there. The trouble is he's been away backpacking. He's the guy I went on that trip to India with."

"Dom, I..."

"Come on, you have loads of bedrooms and I promise I won't pounce on you. Well, only if you want me to."

She would have to let him stay. How could she turn him out on the street? "I guess so. At least until you sort things out. I'll go and make up the spare bed." She felt like she was in a daze as she went up the stairs. Who would believe it? After that she made a cup of hot chocolate. It was three a.m. when they finally finished talking and Dominic said they ought to call it a day. Both of them were tired and Carrie Ann had a huge day ahead. It was only when she got upstairs and snuggled under her duvet that she realized she had almost completely forgotten her ideas for mapping out the final plans for the cake.

Chapter Seven

She had set her alarm for five in the morning, and Carrie Ann struggled to open her eyes. They had been awake so late talking last night that tiredness clung to her in a misty aura and was irritatingly hard to shake off. No good, when she needed to be at her most clearheaded.

Jumping out of bed, she combed her fingers through her hair, before stepping into the shower and soaping herself all over. It was only as she turned the showerhead to cold, trying to jolt herself awake, she realized she had left the bathroom door open. What if he came out of the bedroom and saw her? The shower door was broken so it wouldn't be hard. A warm flush suffused her skin. Funny how that thought didn't alarm her, actually she was excited by it and filled with a sense of daring.

Come on, Carrie Ann. You're almost middle-aged. He isn't going to find you attractive when he could have one of those trendy young girls. Biting her lip, she reached for a towel, before quickly draping it around her body. She oughtn't to be so hard on herself, but she kept coming back to the question of stepping out of her comfort zone. It seemed she kept beating herself up and going over old ground as far as her desirability was concerned and that was bad. She should be planning forward and that started with an improvement in her self-image. Even so, as exciting and kinky as the prospect of Dominic ogling her was, she would have to think about getting new locks as most of them were ancient and didn't work.

She yawned. She needed a strong coffee then she had to get to work. She wanted her client to be bowled over.

When she designed a cake, Carrie Ann gave each one a theme and a name. She was going to call this one Sweet Tequila Sunrise. The icing flowers were the hardest part. She wanted to achieve discreet beauty with rose petals graduated in color. As well as painting the sides, it meant that to get the best effect she had to hand paint as well as using a tricky spray gun. She had set herself a massive task with only three days to go until Miranda came to check on progress, and she was lagging behind.

It was only after she'd finished dressing and was brushing her hair that a thought struck her and she glanced out of the window. The garden looked like a bomb site. The ferocious gale that had developed, had blown leaves all over the place and several large branches off the old oak tree had fallen into the garden. A cold creeping feeling eased itself up her spine. There was no way the tarpaulin would have stayed in place, surely? She hardly dared look.

After opening the back door she wandered down the garden, her breath coming in stabbing gasps. It was a lot worse than she'd anticipated. The tarpaulin was ripped free of the roof and fluttering in the breeze and some of the paneling looked a bit wonky — that meant that the whole of the shed might be wet. She unlocked the door and stood on the threshold. *Shit.* The floor was saturated, meaning she certainly couldn't work in here today. Tears stung her eyes. She ought to have had more sense and moved everything into the kitchen yesterday. Except she hadn't really thought it would happen, had she? She pressed her hands over her face and gave a sob. It was no use wasting time feeling sorry for herself, she'd have to move the center of operations into the old conservatory. It wasn't very large, but the light was good. God how ridiculous. She only had herself to blame. She should have moved everything before, but it was a big job and with all the drama over the cake, she hadn't really felt like it.

Feeling downhearted she trudged back to the conservatory and set to work, making do with what would be for the moment, a temporary setup, since there was no time to waste. She was so absorbed she didn't hear Dominic walk in. He was carrying a mug of coffee and some biscuits on a plate. "Hey there. I thought you could use this." He set the mug and plate down on the table.

"What's the time?" Carrie Ann's brow furrowed, and she pushed her glasses up her nose. *It's not too late is it?* It was, it had taken her an hour to carry all the stuff back up, then after mixing the food dyes and laying out her templates, she had had to set to work without a second thought.

He glanced at his watch. "Eleven-thirty. I peeped in on you earlier, but you were so intent I didn't want to disturb you. I could see you were busy. You have to have something, you've been at it for hours. By the way, I thought you said you worked in the sheds?"

"Seen the state of them have you?" She pointed through the window. "I called the builder to come around and re-patch the roof, but there was so much damage last night, his phone's busy and he won't pick up." She stretched her limbs and pushed her hair back off her face.

He peered over her shoulder. "Wow, that's incredible. The coloring's so subtle."

"Thanks."

"From what you showed me, though, I could tell you had real talent." He pulled out a chair and sat down. "Hey, I could help you with that. I realize you probably don't trust me, but it looks like you could do with a hand and I'm pretty neat as an artist." Picking up a delicate flower he turned it in his hands. "This is exquisite. It looks real."

"Leave that alone please," she snapped, tiredness making her short-tempered. "This isn't playschool, this stuff's expensive." She knew how she sounded — curt and petty.

"Ouch, that hurt." He grinned at her good-naturedly and her heart flipped. "You can be an old dragon."

It was getting harder and harder to control her feelings, and her emotions were stirred up. "What did you say?"

"I said you can be like an old dragon."

Her lips tightened as she bit back a retort.

"You told me every cake tells a story. What does this one say?" Dominic was so good at moving the conversation around and deflecting her.

Carrie Ann carefully painted on the food coloring that she had delicately flavored. Most cake decorations were mostly hard sugar and tasted pretty bad, but she intended for hers to be miniature feasts. "It's the memory of a honeymoon. She's called

Miranda and she's in her sixties now. They're having a blessing and they want to be reminded of everything it represented years ago. The roses unfurl from a tight bud that's meant to represent the birth of romance."

"Wow, what an incredible concept." His lips raised in a doubtful smile. "Do you think we'll be that romantic in twenty years?"

"Dom, for goodness' sake. Do you never stop joking, never give up? There won't be an *us* will there? Technically we've only just met and we're just friends." She shot him a glance. She never knew when he was joking.

"Well I guess friendship is something."

It was only as she paused and sipped her coffee that it dawned on her how tired she was.

"Are you okay? You look dreadful."

"I'm fine. I'd be even better if you didn't interfere. I have to get this done and I need to concentrate. Talking of which—" She glanced at her watch and saw with horror that it was almost midday. "Look at the time, oh my Lord, I'm miles behind." She leaped to her feet. "Ooh." She grabbed at the edge of the table as she was overcome by dizziness. "I don't feel very well. I think I'm more tired than I thought." She sat back down with a bump as the room tilted.

"Don't worry." He pushed a glass of cold water between her fingers. "Here, drink this and then we'll get you up to bed."

"I don't want to go to bed, thank you." She tried to push his hand away. "Oh, Dominic, why don't you go away?"

"You don't mean that." He seemed wounded.

"Yes, yes I do mean it." She sipped the cold water then her eyes filled with tears again. It seemed crying was all she was doing lately. She had rarely cried all the time she had lived with her father. No, she'd had to be brave that was why—if she had given way to tears, she knew she would have just fallen apart.

"You know you're not good at it." He wiped at her cheeks with a napkin.

"What, what aren't I good at?" She now felt nauseous.

"Pretending to be something you're not, pretending to be Miss Tough. I'm not stupid. Come on." He took hold of her arm.

She shuddered in alarm. She had been having dreams about it for weeks. Now being this close to Dominic caused a resumption of the crazy rush he'd precipitated in her before. It was like being an infatuated teenager and it made her want to cry all the harder. It was sublime though and she would have liked to have sat there for longer just so she could dissect the unfamiliar pulsing feelings, which seemed to radiate out from her heart. She wished she wasn't so deep, so intense that she had to separate things like this. She would have given anything to be spontaneous. But Rommy had stamped the spontaneous out of her. Her lips quivered harder as she realized she had never properly processed what had gone on. Her victimization was like an invisible bruise that never went away. It was a nasty secret, very nasty indeed.

"Look, here's how I see it." He guided her toward the stairs. "You tell me what kind of a hand you need and I'll help. When you've had an hour or so rest, you'll be even better able to work. It'll pay dividends. If you're tired you'll only be careless and not at your best."

Why didn't she argue with him, as he helped her upstairs?

"My mother was always having bouts of nervous exhaustion, so I realize what they look like."

"Clever clogs." She let him pull the duvet up over her shoulders.

"Now, get some sleep."

* * * *

Carrie Ann sprang out of bed. Her clock said three p.m. — she'd lost hours. She raced downstairs. Pulse pumping. How could Dominic have let her oversleep like that? She'd kill him when she saw him. Except she couldn't see him anywhere. Her attention darted around and settled on the table, her heart juddering to a halt momentarily as she saw the cake had gone.

Right at that moment, he came through the door. "Great, you seem much better. I made you some lunch, it's in the fridge in the kitchen. I put the cake in this second fridge. I take it the one in here's for the pastry and cake stuff because there's loads of cake making ingredients in it?"

"Oh." She wailed, putting her hand to her head. "But what if I didn't want you to put it in the cooler?"

He winked at her. "But you did. It would have to be cooled. I made you up a batch of fresh icing. I didn't know how much you needed though."

"Dominic, this is a serious cake. How could you possibly understand what I want? It isn't a Blue Peter project."

He didn't have any skill, how could he presume to make icing? He seemed impervious to the caustic note in her voice as he walked through into the kitchen and, after opening the fridge door, he began laying out a salad and cold cuts on the kitchen table.

"You didn't have much food in, so I walked into the village and got some stuff from that quaint little deli. Then I had a look at your shed roof. I think you were ripped off and I'm not trying to be funny. The reason why he wasn't picking up was probably because he was dodging all his irate customers. You want to get yourself another builder. He didn't fasten it very well. I found the stepladder and had a look and you could see. He'd just tied it with some stupid thin rope. I'm not a builder and even I wouldn't be daft enough to use that. Anyway I think I got it all back into place. It should last until you find someone else. I looked in the phone book and picked out a couple of qualified guys. Ones that look reliable. You can't penny pinch with something this important."

"Dominic, I…" Her anger rapidly dissipated. "Look, I know what you're trying to do, but what do you know about cookery and icing and roofs on sheds?"

"More than you think, as a matter of fact." A shadow crossed his face. "Now sit down, stop whinging and refuel and then we can set to work."

"We?"

"Yes, we, but before that—" He went and fetched a bowl. "I want you to dip your digit into this and tell me if it's up to scratch. I'm not too crash hot on sweet stuff."

Frowning, Carrie Ann dipped her finger into a bowl of glossy icing, and, lifting it to her lips, tasted it. It was really very good, very good indeed.

Chapter Eight

Dominic seemed dreadfully good at making up most any recipe, much better than he'd made out, and she found it hard to keep him away from the kitchen. It was funny really and a bit of a mystery. She'd tried to tackle him about it, but he always changed the subject back to her. Anyway, if she had wanted an apprentice he would have been the perfect choice. There was an added bonus too. It was sexy working with a guy and having him brush against her, accidentally on purpose when they were standing together.

They had opened the back door. It was a hot day, making it hard for Carrie Ann to work the icing, which benefited from a cooler environment. Surprisingly the cake was coming together remarkably well and by tea time she had much of the hard work done as Dominic went back inside to make supper. She watched him through the door—she couldn't keep the smile off her face. It was nice and he was good to work with. He caught on quickly and didn't keep bothering her. What was more, something was happening and she wasn't too certain what it was, but it was great—no *better* than great.

She studied him covertly, letting her body and mind explore the new feelings that were growing. They filled her with an illicit longing that made her squirm and feel euphoric. As she studied him, it dawned on her she was deconstructing him to find out what it was about him that excited her so much. She was coming to the conclusion it was not any one thing, but a combination of things. His boyish charm and enthusiasm for one—the way he bopped around the room and rotated his hips in a sexy calypso dance move when he was standing at her counter. His look for another. He was extremely attractive. She was dying to slide her fingers through the golden hair that fell in loose waves to his shoulder.

She liked his hands, his back. Shaking her head and smiling, she laid down her paintbrush. She was dangerously close to falling in either love or infatuation, and she realized it was no good telling herself to back off. As stupid as it seemed, maybe Dominic was right and fate had somehow conspired to push them together. Anyway, she didn't have much time to think about it now. Miranda had called and was coming around tomorrow to take a look at the cake.

"I saw you staring at me." He leaned on the doorframe, watching her. "Do you have any idea how sexy that is for a guy? How long do you think you're going to be able to control yourself? My charms have been known to wear impervious women away."

She darted him a look. "Not this one. I told you before. I'm not in the market for a boyfriend."

"Tell me, tell me why a desirable, lovely woman like you, can't love again. Then maybe I'll understand and leave you alone."

She picked her paintbrush up. "Don't go on about it, Dominic. You're making it hard."

"Hard why? Hard to talk about that shit that tore you in two. In my opinion, things like that need lancing like a boil."

"What do you mean?" she asked.

"The pain and the resentment. You need to lance it and let the poison out so you can move on."

She swallowed. His direct questioning was doing something. It was like he was forcing a key into the lock of a firmly secured door that she wanted to remain closed because inside the room behind it was a lot of pain that she couldn't face up to. The worst part was, half of her wanted to process her pain, so she could move on.

Rommy had left an indelible stain and it was preventing her moving forward, but how could she talk about it? She had lied to Dominic and she didn't fancy having to tell him the truth. How she wished she hadn't fibbed in the first place. She bit her lip. What would he think of her? No, no she couldn't tell the truth, she couldn't even consider it. It was too much, too embarrassing. When she glanced up noticing his gaze loaded with sympathy, all the pain and anger seemed to simply bear down on her. She pressed her hands to her face, the tears washing down her cheeks as, leaping to her feet, she fled upstairs taking the steps two at a time. After slamming the door behind her, she lay on the bed, pulling the duvet up over her head as she gave vent to her frustrations. She couldn't believe it when, after a while, the bed sagged down on one side and he tried to wrestle the duvet away from her.

"Don't be silly, why did you run away like that? Running away doesn't solve anything."

"You're a fine one to talk." She rolled onto her side hugging her pillow. "Go away."

"You don't mean that. The very fact you keep on saying you want me to go away, just tells me you don't. You want to get it out of your system, that's all. It's okay, I haven't taken offense."

"You do have a tough hide don't you, and have you turned into some weird New Age counsellor?" She lay on her back staring at the ceiling. She was still dressed in her rainbow spotted apron and there were blobs of icing in her hair.

"You have to talk about whatever it is that's bothering you." Stretching out beside her, he tucked her hair behind her ear. "It's not good to keep it inside. Believe me I should know."

"I can't, I don't want to talk about it. It's too painful and it kind of makes me feel out of control. Besides it's nothing, only angst and frustration, I guess." A fresh avalanche of tears pressed against the backs of her eyes. "As it is. Some days I'm only just holding it together. I'm fine if I don't think about it too much, but if I do it's like everything comes tumbling down."

"You have to or you'll detonate. I should know. I had enough counseling over my father."

She shot him a look. "You did? You didn't say anything about that."

"Yeah, I am what you would call, a dysfunctional kid."

She wanted to tell him about her father but she was torn in two. Maybe she could twist it enough it resembled the truth. "My husband was controlling.

He had a good way of making you feel sorry for him. I suppose in a way it was my own fault. I let the ties get too strong and before I realized it I was under his thumb."

"Carry on. I realize that's only the start." Dominic punched the pillow beside her, stretching out his lean, sexy body. He had moved so close now they were touching. He slid his arm under her head and pulled it against his shoulder. "There. Now you have a life-raft to hang onto in case you sense things getting away from you. So you can fire away."

What was she doing? Her body betrayed her as she pressed even closer, enjoying the male warmth, the spreading ripples and tingles, the feeling of comforting togetherness. This wasn't how desire was meant to be, was it? That was meant to be rude and lusty, not easy and companionable.

"How long were you married?" he asked.

"A lifetime."

That much was true. Her incarceration with Rommy had seemed like a lifetime. "I got married very young. He was the only guy I ever knew. My first boyfriend. There was no one else." She darted him a glance. "A pathetic specimen, aren't I?"

He laughed. "No, I wouldn't say so. Just a normal human being."

"I let him take me over. It started with tiny things and then before I knew it he had consumed me. He controlled everything I did. I couldn't go out, have friends. I kind of forgot what the outside world was like and then when I realized it was there, I was scared of it. It had become a place that petrified me."

"It's not that unusual," Dominic soothed, gently rubbing her shoulder. "That kind of thing happens to loads of people."

"Mmm, that's so nice." She sighed as she felt the tension begin to ease away and her nipples prickled and firmed with unmistakable lust.

"So now you have to pick up the pieces and move on, right?"

"Yes."

"And you've set yourself quite a task from what you've told me, haven't you?"

"I'm going to succeed. But there's more." Her mouth was dry, but she had to somehow circle around to a story that approximated more to the truth. "Rommy was older than me. I didn't actually divorce him, although it was coming to that. Before I ever got around to it we found out he was ill. He had Alzheimer's and that was what had apparently made his personality so awful. It wasn't his fault. Poor Rommy." Again she fought back the tears, stiffening as she realized she might have said too much.

His hand stopped its gentle stroking. "My God, how much older than you was he then? Was he ancient if he had Alzheimer's?"

She felt a shaft of angry indignation at the tone of his voice. The unnecessary need to stand up for her father. "No, not that old. You can get Alzheimer's fairly young, you know?"

"Okay, okay. So, then you got the old guilt complex did you? And even though the man was a brute, you were obligated to stay and look after him?"

"Yes, something like that. In the beginning we had had a good life though, Dominic." She glanced at him. "It's true. In a manner of speaking, I was happy once. How could I not care for him, tell me that?"

"Whatever he had wrong with him, it didn't make up for him treating you like that."

It was dangerous ground and the same argument Nina kept making. She held her breath. She could see how the situation must look to him.

"Still," he said after a second, as if he had reconsidered. "It's over, it's in the past and now someone has to mend you. And... That's going to be me."

"Thanks a lot, but I think I'm doing pretty well on my own. They tell you at Arlem that's it's bad to have props."

"Everyone needs a friend to lean on, it's okay to come over tough and independent, but you have to get the balance right."

He ran his thumb across her forehead, along the tiny frown lines she had noticed often enough in the mirror.

"Fine, I'm sorry. I'm pushing you and I shouldn't. I shouldn't have said all that. I'm crossing the line. Look you don't have to tell me any more. But I really think you're going to have to take on an assistant. You can't do all this on your own. No one can who wants to run a successful business."

"But I like to keep an eye on things, Dominic. Someone else couldn't do it the way I can and the quality would begin to suffer."

"No, not if you're careful. Not if you take on a helper who shares your passion and who you can tutor in your ways. You're very suspicious aren't you?"

"Yeah, I guess I am. What a loser. The trouble is, I've been cut off from life and I suppose I'm a bit distrustful. My whole existence is this dream for my cake business, Dominic. I'm so afraid sometimes, I just don't let myself think about it. Especially those hard things, like delegation and how to manage people."

He nodded. "Okay, but that can be solved. You can go on training courses. While I'm here you could do a short course and I could help out. I might even be able to give you a few pointers. And before you say you don't want anyone changing things around here, I won't. I'll gently nudge you in the right direction."

She laughed. "You're nuts if you think I'm ready to go away on a training course, but I suppose those tips might come in handy."

He rolled over so he was looking into her face. Pressed close, she could feel her heart thundering. He traced her lips with his finger and kissed her, and for a moment she even forgot about Miranda's cake.

"In fact I have tips on a great many subjects you might find interesting, Carrie Ann." And not giving her time to mutter an objection, he kissed her again, harder this time.

Chapter Nine

"Where are you going?"

"Into town, to see a man."

"So, I should be jealous then?" Dominic watched her as she sat in front of her dressing table mirror. Then he came forward and did something amazing. He picked up a loose tendril of her hair and, taking one of her pins, pinned it into place. Her body jumped to attention like a piece of machinery. A piece of machinery it had to be said, that having been rusty for a number of years was grinding into life—each movement, each rotation becoming easier. She was tempted to put her hand over his, except she was rooted to the spot, sabotaged as it were by a tidal wave of feelings, most of them telling her how wrong this was. In the end he neatly steered the ship of her emotions into port. He stared at her in the mirror, his green eyes full of a depth and intensity she couldn't fathom. "I have to say, Carrie Ann, you look amazing. I wish you'd done it before, come out of your shell that is. It's kind of like a secret you. One you unveil from time to time. It's exciting for a young guy like me, this older woman, younger man thing."

It was the worst thing he could have said and she felt her spirits—which until that second had been buoyant—dip appreciably.

"There's not that much difference between our ages, only a few years." Why did she have to keep on about it?

Over the past few days they'd been getting on so well and she'd thought she'd gotten used to Dominic's wry turn of phrase and sense of humor. The truth was dawning though. She fancied him. He'd been here now for two weeks and there was no indication he was about to move on. The funny thing was, she didn't want him to. She picked at her fingernails and it was then she felt him. Felt him move closer. She was sure she could detect the warmth from his body as he brushed against her arm, bent down and kissed her right on her nape, very erotically it might be said and with what she was sure was the tip of his tongue. Her heart stopped.

When she glanced back in the mirror she was met with an erotic tableau. Her face, her expression full of such an emotion it was like someone had lit a match behind it. And him, bending over her shoulder, his mouth buried beneath the collar of her new best gray jacket, holding it aside so he could savor her neck, just under her ear, working at it with such application it was like a scene from a sexy movie.

It was then that something moved inside her— something secret, dangerous and powerful. Come what may, she had to have him. Had to push herself closer and closer to the borderline. She couldn't consider the implications, didn't want to, all she knew was she had to enjoy it for as long as she could.

"You look stunning. Lucky man whoever he is."

"It's another commission. I don't have high hopes because I think they need the savories catered for and I'm not equipped for that," Carrie Ann said, putting down her hairbrush. "Besides which, they want something really sexy and out of the ordinary for the top."

Miranda had called yesterday because she had been so bowled over and wanted to thank her for the attention the cake had drawn. Things were looking up since she had told at least half a dozen of her friends — and she had told Carrie Ann that the Sleights, with this possible commission, were one of them. The Sleights were an important family locally and only had the best of everything so that would be a huge coup. She put the brush down. "He's a business owner as well, they carry a lot of weight locally, it would have been a great triumph for my portfolio. A real Sweet Secrets cake that pushed the boundaries.

"Ah yes, Sweet Secrets, I'm intoxicated with the whole idea of it. But surely you could manage the top, that's your strong point and what's a few savories? You could do that in your sleep, couldn't you?"

"Are you joking again? You must be. Pastry chefs often find savories hard."

"Yeah, hey I like to see you get wound up, I like to see that secret fire. I know there's so much more to you."

He mock glared at her in the mirror. Dominic had looked strained the last few days. He had dark rings under his eyes and he seemed troubled. She'd asked him several times what the matter was, but she always got the same response, that it was nothing. And what did the journeys away mean? Occasionally he went out for the day and came back worn out and grumpy.

She recollected the other evening when she had been poring over some ideas.

"So this is Sweet Secrets." He had bent over her shoulder studying her notes. It was impossible to keep anything about Sweet Secrets secret from him.

"Yes, Dominic, but it's still a secret. No one except you and Nina knows about it. I don't want them to until I am ready. You do realize" — she had caught hold of his neck playfully — "you're party to sensitive secrets and I might have to torture you or kill you should you divulge them."

"Naughty, naughty, but I fancy the sound of that." He'd waved the notebook about above her head. "Why would you want to hide your talent though, especially when Sweet Secrets is such a hot proposition?" He'd looked at her speculatively. "For a quiet one you certainly have a melting side, don't you? It's tantalizing for a young guy like me."

"Doesn't every woman have a melting side? And I wish you wouldn't keep on teasing me about it."

He'd broken out laughing. "I think it's great. Terrific in fact. You've sold it to me. You're perfect for it, aren't you? With that mixture of demure and risqué."

It was as if he read her mind now as he locked her reflected gaze in the mirror.

"I wouldn't tease you, Carrie Ann. I mean everything I say. Actually, when you get back today, I want to talk to you about something."

"Eh." She climbed to her feet.

"Maybe I could come with you."

She shrugged into her coat. "Look I'm not trying to be funny or anything, and I don't want you to take this the wrong way. But I don't think it's a very good idea people knowing you're staying with me."

He darted in front of her, stopping her walking out of the door. "What, what are you trying to say? Are you nuts? This is a tiny village anyway. Everyone must have noticed I'm here."

She experienced a wave of nausea. This was a subject she had hoped she wouldn't have to tackle. However, she had to and he was right. She loved Ms Bunting to death, but she was a bit of a busybody and she'd noticed Dominic and kept making odd remarks.

"Why would you want to hide me away? We're friends aren't we? I haven't done anything wrong."

"It makes it awkward, that's all."

"Does it? In what way?" he persisted.

"It just does." She shook her head. "For goodness' sake. I was wondering about saying you were my nephew or the son of a friend or something."

He wore a wounded frown. "Thanks, thanks a lot. You're not ashamed of having me here are you?"

Carrie Ann picked up her bag. "Don't be daft. Look, I'm going to be late. We'll talk about it later." It was, she reflected, no one else's business if she chose to have a man stay with her, so why was she lying about it? She wasn't ready for such in depth revelations, that was why. No, as much as she had pushed the prospect away and attempted not to face up to it, at some point very soon, she would have to stomp on this friendship, put an end to it and tell Dominic to pack up and leave. She just couldn't face all that innuendo and cross-questioning.

* * * *

She called in to the bakery on her way back. Marcus wanted another order of mille-feuille, this time with a chocolate crème that she had cleverly flavored with black mint. Nina was in the kitchen and raised an eyebrow. "Wow, you look awesome."

Carrie Ann touched her hair self-consciously. She knew she was changing and it was weird, but exciting at the same time. Like shedding one skin and assuming another.

Nina wore the expression she always wore when she was dying to ask about something. "You can be infuriating, do you realize that. What's the secret?"

"Did I say I have a secret?"

"Lately, you always have a secret of one kind or another." Nina pouted as she stirred the pot of Eccles cake fruit mixture. "I thought we were friends. Why can't you share it with me? Scared Marcus will be jealous?" She wiggled her eyebrows humorously.

"Oh, come on, not that old chestnut again. You know I don't fancy Marcus."

"No, but Marcus fancies you. He keeps making excuses to come down here."

Carrie Ann smiled wanly. "I think not."

"You know the very fact you won't talk about it, makes you look all the guiltier."

She blushed, it was a dead giveaway.

Nina's face lit up as she danced around the kitchen. "I knew it, I knew it. But it's not Marcus is it? It's the golden-haired mystery boy. You met him when you were away and now he's come to stay. I knew you looked different. Love changes you, everybody said it when I fell in love."

Carrie Ann sank down on a kitchen chair, her palms to her cheeks. She should have felt buoyant. She'd just been practically offered the Sleight commission. But it was so complex. Mr and Mrs Sleight wanted the catering for the savories, desserts and cake done by the same person and she didn't have the capacity or skills yet to do such a large job. However, that didn't stop her wanting it for her portfolio. It would test her, probably get her circulating in the local horsey set and that was really hard to get into. The horsey set encompassed some of the most wealthy families around the county. She hadn't turned it down but had asked for a few days to think about it.

"Don't tell me then." Nina gave a particularly vigorous stir. "Misery guts."

"Nina. He's only a friend. I don't want anyone to know."

"They won't. I won't tell anyone, you know that. I won't even tell Ms Bunting if you don't want me to."

"No, I don't want you to tell Ms Bunting."

Nina scurried away to get a coffee and a slice of Carrie Ann's famous walnut cake. Then she sat down opposite her at the cluttered kitchen table, squeezing her hand. "Don't look so down. You look as if your world's fallen in. Whatever it is, I think it's terrific."

"My world has fallen down."

"How could it? If I had a guy like that hanging around, I'd be elated."

"Sometimes, Nina, especially for a married woman, you have a one track mind. Do you have to be thinking about men and other people's relationships all the time?"

"Love makes the world go round, babe."

"I'm saying he's my nephew."

Nina shot upright. "But he's not. He's this cool guy you met on holiday, right? Besides won't saying he's your nephew lead to even more complicated questions? You don't have a nephew, at least one I know about, unless that's a secret as well."

Carrie Ann shot her a look loaded with invective. "All right, you've made your point as usual, but I still don't want it bandied around. Honestly, Nina, I wouldn't know where to start with romance. I'm a virgin. The only ideas I've got have come from books."

"As if that needs to stop you. You're a hot cookie." Nina clapped her hand to her mouth as she realized she'd cracked a joke.

"Anyway I have more important things to think about, like this possible commission. If I took it on, I'd feel like I was hanging on with my fingernails."

"Why?"

"Don't be dumb, Nina. I'm into pâtisserie—I'm not a pastry chef. I'm only passable with savory things. They could never match up to the Sleights' or my standards."

"Um." Nina pinched her bottom lip thoughtfully. "I see what you mean, but there has to be a way around it. Anyway"—she shook her hair back from her shoulders—"come on, chicken, tell me a bit, a teeny bit. You like him right? It's written all over you."

"Okay. I like him. But I'm not mad and I wouldn't want to be a cradle snatcher. Besides I'd just be kidding myself if I thought I had a chance with him, he's gorgeous..."

"So, you do fancy him?"

"Who wouldn't fancy him? But it's the age old story. We can't always have what we want, can we?"

Nina grinned. "True. But I don't get it. What's the problem? These days loads of women have younger guys."

Shit, even Nina had noticed the age difference. Carrie Ann's heart sank further if that were possible. She felt frustrated. She didn't need this conversation, not after the day she'd just had. She felt exhausted and her head was buzzing. "Yeah, more together women.

Not ones like me with all these hang-ups. A virgin who lived with her overbearing father."

"Now, you're being silly. If you like him why not go for it? Life's too short."

"And make a fool of myself? I don't think so." Even as she said it though, Carrie Ann wasn't so certain. Yes, the thought of a love affair with Dominic scared her half to death and she wasn't even sure she knew how to go about seducing him. Then the other part of her said, why not go for it? Besides she was feeling braver now and he had kissed her hadn't he, and not the other way around? She was confused. She'd thought initially it would be hard having him in the house. In reality, though, she'd gotten used to having him around. No one could fail to notice the increasing sexual tension between them. He continually watched her, filling her with scintillating thrills, and she wanted to touch him too. Could barely concentrate when he was there.

Nina got to her feet and whispered in her ear, "For what it's worth, kid, I think you're nuts. I'd jump on him."

She knew she could trust Nina. She was the only woman she had told about Rommy and the extent of her captivity.

* * * *

When she got home, she shrugged out of her jacket and made her way upstairs. She was about to walk down the corridor, when she stopped and turned. Her cheeks burned as she put her eye to the crack. He was in the bathroom. Tantalizingly hidden by the shower screen, she could see half of him in profile, the sudsy water washing down his body. She had to pull herself together. More than that, she shouldn't be perving on a man who was technically her lodger. The sight of him that close, naked, virile, filled her with overwhelming desire. She sank down on the bed, fighting the throbbing, needy signals her body was giving out. It wasn't the first time she'd come upon him like that. He had no qualms and was a bit of a free spirit.

She tied her hair back into a ponytail, then after putting on a loose summer dress, she headed down to the shed. Immersing herself in some work was bound to kill off her growing filthy thoughts, ones that made her squirm around on her chair. She was working on a complicated garland to edge a party cake and was peering intently through her magnifying glass when he strolled in. He stood for a moment watching her from the door.

She glanced up, aware of the blobs of icing on her face. She had a habit of touching her cheeks and lips when she was deep in thought.

He laughed. "Do you have any idea how funny you look?"

"How funny do I look?" She mock glared at him, feeling self-conscious at the recollection of catching him in the shower.

"This funny." He made a gesture with his hands before coming over and beginning to rub her shoulders with slow, delicious movements.

She knew she ought to tell him to stop, but she couldn't as her body started to relax and drift. How she wished his hands would travel farther, farther, farther. She wriggled her butt against the chair cushion, biting her lip as he accidentally feathered her breast, making her jolt alarmingly to life. Tingles and a warm, insistent throbbing started in her belly and soon turned into an irritating nagging between her legs.

"You look so worried, what is it?"

"It's nothing," she said. "It's silly. But you know I went into town today."

He nodded. "Yes."

"Well I have the chance of another contract, but I don't know if I'll be able to cope with it. They want a centerpiece which I can just about handle. But they also want the buffet to match the cake and there's no way without staff that I could handle that. Although I can manage the desserts they want, I'm not good at savories."

"But you must have known you wouldn't be brilliant at every aspect of baking and that you wouldn't be able to stay a one man band for long? You're bound to need help, I told you that. And you won't stand still will you, you'll want to expand?"

"I'm not so sure. I hadn't thought that far along the line." She rested her chin on her fist. "It's stupid. But it's too late to take on anyone now anyway. They'd have to be trained up into my way of doing things and I don't have time. It's no good. I won't be able to do this contract and it would really have gotten me on, and been marvelous experience."

He sat down with that thoughtful look on his face she had become familiar with over the last few weeks. "You won't be able to do every job that comes your way, Carrie Ann, it's impossible. There will always be something you can't manage, that's outside your comfort zone."

"Yes, I realize that. But it's so important to create a good impression when you're getting off the ground."

"I could help you know. You only have to ask."

"How?" She burst out laughing. "You can't magic a catering company out of the sky, can you?"

"Fine. If that's the way you feel? I didn't know I wasn't welcome. I thought you enjoyed having me around."

She knew she'd been rude and he'd only been trying to help. "Don't be like that, Dom," she cried as he got to his feet. "You're taking it the wrong way."

"Am I?" He considered a moment, before spearing her with his gaze. "I haven't exactly been lying around sponging off you have I, so what's it to you? I've paid my way, forced some cash on you if you remember."

Stung, Carrie Ann did a double-take. "Dom, I…"

"And for your information I've been doing all I can. Where do you think I've been going off to? I've been trying to work out a way to…" He ground to a halt, looking deflated. Oh, never mind."

* * * *

She didn't see him for the rest of the day, which put her on edge. Generally, when she was working he came out with a coffee or brought her a sandwich, but there wasn't a sign of him. Perhaps he'd gone for a walk. It was a lovely day and she had the doors of the shed open. Next week a builder was coming to start work on them. Dominic had said he would keep an eye on him, make sure that the repairs were carried out properly. She turned her attention back to the plans for the cake. The Sleights had given her until the end of the week to see if she could come up with something. She rubbed her head, she was tired. Miranda's cake had taken it out of her. The pace was crazy. He was right of course, she needed help. There was no way she could do this on her own.

As usual when she was under stress, her attention drifted to Latham and the hotel scenario. Since she had been on her own, her fantasies had become even more erotic. She liked to be alone when she thought of Latham, touching and exploring her body, pretending her hands were his as they explored her dips and hollows. When she slid them inside her warm silken folds to find that fantastic trigger that made her orgasm and keep on orgasming, it was almost unbearable. Now, though, the drift of the fantasy kept being interrupted by Dominic. Where did they go from here?

Come on Carrie Ann, you're making too much of it. Yes, I realize he says he likes you, but he's flirting. She glanced out of the window. She needed to take a break, that was the best thing. She'd wander up to Oh Crumbs! and collect the empty baskets. Then she would have one last think about the catering before she admitted defeat.

Oh Crumbs! was practically empty at this time of day. The door was propped open and Nina sat on a stool behind the counter, fanning herself. Her cheeks were pink.

"What's the matter with you?" Carrie Ann asked.

Nina slithered off the stool. "Your boyfriend, that's who." She leaned against the counter. "If I wasn't married I'd have a flirt."

"I expect everyone says that."

"He's a real go-getter isn't he? If I had somebody out to help me like that, I'd be overjoyed."

"Help you how?"

"He was in here earlier, asking if we had any spare space. I thought he could have the old room at the back. The one they used to use for breadmaking."

She felt a queer, queasy sensation. Oh Crumbs! had been a bakery for as long as anyone could remember and the old bread oven and baking room was a feature of the building. They hardly ever used it now though. It was used as a place to sit and relax.

"He asked could he rent it. That he was helping you out on a job."

At the sight of her expression, Nina closed her mouth and made a zipping motion. "My God, I haven't said something I shouldn't, have I?"

"It looks like it. What else did he say?"

"That was all really. He doesn't seem short on a bob or two, rather mysterious isn't it? Anyway what's the harm? He's helping you out, isn't he?"

Carrie Ann rattled the empty baskets angrily. "He had no business mentioning anything. I don't make a song and dance over my secret life. How could he, I'll kill him."

"He didn't say anything. I think he was trying to be agreeable."

"Yeah, I bet he was." She couldn't decide whether to be angry or not. It was ludicrous of course. What did Dominic know about catering and baking? Nothing. "He's mad because he can't have that much cooking experience. He just plays around with it. It's always the same with people, they see you cooking or decorating a cake and they think it's child's play."

"Eh." Nina looked at her nails. "I'm sorry I mentioned it. Don't take on so and don't tell him I told you, will you? Maybe it's best to wait until he says something, which he's bound to."

"And what did Ms Bunting say about him using the room?"

Nina blinked at her. "It's hard to resist his charms. Ms Bunting won't know if he uses it when the shop is technically closed."

* * * *

By the time Carrie Ann wandered into the cottage, Dominic was in the kitchen. She leaned against the door watching him.

"I can feel your stare drilling a hole in my back, Carrie Ann. What's the problem?"

She lurched forward, snatching the spoon out of his hands.

"Hey!"

"You're the problem, clever clogs. I don't believe this." She was furious. "What were you doing walking into the village like that and asking to use Oh Crumbs!?"

He smiled at her, took her hands and held them tightly. "Calm down. It's simple. I realize how much this business means to you and I saw how much you want the contract. Well, now you can go back to this guy and tell him you'll do it because I'll help you."

She clapped her hands to her head. She squeezed hard as if by doing so she could make sense of things. "You are crazy, aren't you? This isn't simply a case of knocking up a few cakes and vol au vents, Dominic. It's a tad more sophisticated than the student crap you might have been used to conjuring up."

"Yes, and I could do it easily. I'm not half bad at it, you know. Mum's daily was a dab hand. I told you about my parents. Well, Mum loved it. She saw me being in the kitchen as being a way to get me out of the way. It was fun. Sure, nothing like the stuff you do, but I liked it and was pretty good at it."

Her jaw dropped. "You are mad, do you know how ridiculous this sounds. Somewhere along the line you've lost it. You're an amateur."

He was very calm in the face of her mounting anger, she'd give him that.

"Sit down and I'll make you a cup of tea. Then we'll talk about it." He pulled out a chair and pushed her down.

"We won't talk about it, because there's nothing to talk about. You have no idea what the client wants."

"Actually, yes I do. You left that little notebook on the table and I had a look. I could manage it standing on my head."

"Pull the other one. So now you've turned into a top chef, just like that. Voilà."

"No, Carrie Ann. Look, let me tell you something." He made her a mug of sweet tea then brought it to the table.

Fragrant smells of basil and tomato filled the kitchen. It was hard to think straight.

"It wasn't just the cook. I got sent away loads to my grandmother's. My grandmother was a great cook, like you told me yours was. It soon transpired I had quite a knack. I would have liked to have gone into cookery but of course, Dad being so macho, he saw cookery as a sissy profession. He wanted me to follow in his footsteps. The trouble was, I loved creating and being around a stove. I used to help Mum arrange her parties. That was the one thing she did like. She loved fiddling with food. Mum was okay with cookery, provided it wasn't difficult. I can rustle up a good high quality vol au vent in no time. I'm good. Let me show you. Give me an hour to impress."

She squeezed her palms even harder to her temples and massaged gently. "You don't have to."

"Yes, I do. Let me rustle up that recipe for the mini goat's cheese Cornish and if it's rubbish, I'll get lost." He shrugged. "If not, well…"

"You're missing the point," she wailed. "I wanted my business kept secret. Only Nina knew all the facts, because she had to, because she helped me, Dominic. I don't want Ms Bunting knowing and now you've gone marching in there."

He grinned. "Come on, Carrie Ann, don't be daft, you're over-reacting. You said yourself the secret had all but leaked out. That star turn friend of yours, Nina, said I could use it on the Sunday when the shop is closed so I don't get in the way."

Carrie Ann flushed, she knew that was true. "You'll show yourself up. You'll show us both up. Besides it'll never work. It's just too wacky to be true. Oh, Dominic, what have you done?"

This was the last thing she wanted at a time like this. She needed her wits about her to deal with the ideas for the cake. She rubbed her fingers nervously over one another.

"I won't let you down." His voice softened. "I'll do you some catering to be proud of. Look, how does this sound? You talk over the ideas you have and then I'll cook up a trial batch. You can give me a trial run and if I'm no good what have you lost? You might even like one or two of the ideas I could throw into the pot about spicing. I'm quite good at that."

"Dominic, it's a saucy afternoon tea theme. It's an incredibly hard thing to pull off with a centerpiece as well and all of it…" Her voice tailed off. "Having to dovetail."

"Yes, so what. Reserve judgment until you see what I can come up with. Come on, what have you got to lose?"

"It's twenty-five guests. I know it doesn't sound like a lot, but it is."

"Between us we could do it easily. You only need to do say, three savories and four pastries."

She shrugged. "Well, I suppose so." Why was she giving in like this? What was the matter with her? What he was suggesting was ludicrous. But she felt so exhausted and when she looked at it from the angle of his argument...

He winked at her and, coming over, curled his fists into her hair. There was a dangerous glint in his eyes. "How about a wager?"

"What kind of wager?"

"A win, win situation for you. If I'm a complete failure I promise never to stick my nose into your business again. Should I completely floor you with the brilliance of my baking, though, you'll give in and let me seduce you properly."

She stifled a snort of laughter. "Now I know for sure that you're insane. That sounds like some slimy move a guy in a movie would make. Ugh, Dominic, that's horrible."

"No, it's not. It's clever, it'll loosen you up and I actually think knowing what I do about you, that you'll get a kick out of it."

She hated to admit he was right. Her cheeks were burning. God, she must be mad getting into this. Before she could stop herself, the words were trickling out. "You'd have to bake exactly as I told you and it would have to taste good. In fact, it would have to taste so good..." She was getting into the spirit of the game. "I will take a sample to Oh Crumbs! and force them to taste them."

He raised an eyebrow. "I like your way of thinking. You're on."

"Okay, then."

She had loads of ideas for the afternoon tea. The trouble was the remit for this order was so strange with the sweet pastries having to harmonize completely with the main cake which was a feat in itself. They wanted a theme centered around a summer pudding but using meringues and soft fruits. The pastries would echo this and be tartlets delicately flavored with herbs that would carry through into the savories. As she watched Dominic working on the samples, she frowned. He seemed to negotiate his way around a kitchen well, that was for sure. And he had the kind of ace knife skills a daily would never have. She'd watched him chop a leek and the strips were finer julienned than many chefs could make them. He was enjoying it too. It filled her with a sense of wonder and frustration. Of course, he wouldn't pull it off. No rank amateur could.

"So when do we have this competition?" He beamed at her. "I'm eager to show you what I'm made of?"

"Tomorrow," Carrie Ann said. "That'll give you time to plan things."

"You'll let me borrow the kitchen, that's the only condition."

"I guess so," she said smugly.

Chapter Ten

Carrie Ann tossed and turned before stretching her arms and legs and sitting up. It suddenly dawned on her that today was the day and she'd better get up and face the trial ahead. Before Dominic started, she had loads to do because she needed to get the Oh Crumbs! and The Manor orders ready. For a moment she thought it was a dream, then it came flooding back to her. Downstairs she couldn't hear anything, which was odd. He was generally up and about early. When she walked out into the conservatory, though, he was bent over the table reviewing what she took to be his plans.

"Ready to do battle, then?" He rubbed his hands together.

"You won't pull it off," she replied. "Those savories will have to be up to my exacting standards."

"Aha." He raised a wooden spoon and brandished it. "We'll see. Now be off with you. By the time you've sorted Marcus' new order out and chatted to Nina, I should be finished."

* * * *

It was four o'clock when she eventually mustered up enough courage to come home. As she opened the front door, it seemed remarkably quiet, only the tick of the mantle clock for company. Opening the conservatory door, she saw a pile of pastries on the table and the room was full of an enticing savory smell. Open-mouthed, she stared at them, then after sneaking over and lifting one up smelled it. They were definitely freshly baked and comparable to the prototype she had tried the other day. Yes, there was the aroma of goat's cheese delicately perfumed with oregano and basil. She nibbled a bit, put it down, picked up a mini pizza, then the lamb and mint tartlet. The flavors were amazing, she thought, as she rolled the pastry around her mouth, and that was not all. The finish was brilliant with tiny pastry leaf decorations and little motifs.

"Caught you." He leaned against the door staring at her. "Do you know how sexy you look, tasting things? My mind's in overdrive watching you."

She glared. She was used to this by now.

"I just took a look at the shed. It should only be a day or two until it's finished and…that guy from that catering company called and they're delivering the oven tomorrow."

"I hate you," she said with mock-venom. "What you did is impossible." Brandishing a tart, she licked a crumb from her mouth. She wanted some answers, there was a niggle in the back of her mind and she was determined to get to the bottom of it and she would do it…now.

"Why is it impossible? It was an easy brief. They had to harmonize with the pastries and desserts. It was a clever move on your part."

Before she could move, he grabbed her around the waist from behind and pressed her against his chest, her heart beating in time with his. "I'm determined to prove to you I'm serious."

Any questions were instantly erased as she snuggled back against him. "Serious about what?"

His hands slid around, smoothing her belly through her smock.

"Serious about you. I'll do everything it takes to win you, Miss Jude."

"It'll take more than this. We have to see if these are indistinguishable from my bakes."

"They will be, well, almost."

She didn't want to move away. She felt lighter, as if a huge weight had been removed from her shoulders. It was comfortable here in the circle of his arms, exploring feelings she had read and dreamt about but had never thought she would experience. *Is this for real?* It had to be didn't it? Was love close? She could feel herself loosening, as if the tight rope that had held her in check was at last letting her go. She hardly dared breathe. She didn't want Dominic to loosen his grip, she wanted to revel in his touch, even encourage his fingers to explore, touch her again, touch her harder, even…maybe be rough with her.

"So, tomorrow, we'll take them down to Oh Crumbs!?" he carried on.

"You mean I'll take them down to Oh Crumbs!."

"That's a bit unfair don't you think? Since I cooked them."

"I told you, I don't want people to think we're a couple because we're not."

He turned her round so he could study her face. "No, we're not, Carrie Ann, and you've got to stop being so paranoid about this. First and foremost, we're the best of friends. I think we should behave like two normal human beings, don't you?"

It was as if she was dissolving like a blob of gelatin in water, unable to do anything other than stare back. His gaze moved here and there, everywhere it touched igniting smoldering warmth and starting a corresponding heat between her legs that turned to moistness, desire.

"Why are you holding back so much? Is it sex, are you afraid? Because if it is, I have some amazing techniques to loosen you up." He winked at her. "We could start now. Come on, I've made enough advances and you're impervious. I know you're not really like that."

Why was it he had the uncanny ability to read her mind? "What a funny thing to say."

"It's true. You're bubbling away with passion just beneath the surface, but I can't get to you. I don't believe you don't want to find love again. You're too warm, too vital."

He stroked her arm, running his thumb across her skin.

Her heart bumped so loudly she thought it would burst out of her chest. She couldn't reveal the secret about Rommy. Never. What would Dominic think of her? She realized now her life continued to be one whole long string of secrets and lies. She had only once had an attempt at a boyfriend. That had been the time she had met Tom. He had not been anyone special, only Terry's son at the deli, but he had talked to her, shared her enthusiasm for food and often walked her home when he caught sight of her on her visits to the village. Rommy's unerring nose for detection had found out of course, and he had watched her, played her like a fish on a line for weeks, biding his time until the day Tom had walked her too close to home and had kissed her. When she'd walked through the door, all hell had let loose. Her father had not been angry, no as usual, he had used emotional blackmail to make her feel too guilty to see Tom again.

"Carrie Ann, you have to deal with this. Erase this guy and replace him with me," Dominic stated.

"God!" She crossed her arms. "Talk about an egotistical statement. What makes you think I want to?" She gnawed at her lip. She couldn't look him in the eye after the way he had just touched her, stroking her in the subtly suggestive way he had. What if she had let go and given in to her emotions? It would be easy to and she thought it was only a matter of time before she did. She could barely keep her hands off him. Emotions were liquid, running here and there, creeping into all the crevices, and she couldn't stop them as they swept her away.

Why, why had she ever talked to him at the airport? Life was suddenly becoming very complicated for her. It was like she was possessed, as if every time she watched him, she felt herself drawn closer by a magnetism she couldn't fight against. In her best possible fantasy, Dominic would solve the entire problem by dominating her so he could have his wicked way. That would be good, lift the decision of whether she should sleep with him or not off her shoulders. How sick would that be though? A twenty-year-old or so stud, seducing what must seem to him a mumsy, plump woman. Except she felt none of that inside. Inside she was about twenty and she could give any girl his age a run for her money, she knew she could and — the realization almost knocked her off her feet — she wanted to and she was going to start to. Maybe tomorrow. Yes, that seemed like a good time to start to embrace the new Carrie Ann.

* * * *

Rommy set fire to the sheds. Standing by the window, her feet are cemented to the floor. When she begins to walk she realizes the carpet has become fondant icing and each step she takes is like walking through glue. When she eventually gets out onto the landing, she can see the patterns of the flames licking against the wall. The house has somehow become a large cake — buttercream oozes from the walls, and the brickwork and stairs are soft sponge that with each footfall crumbles away. Until someone grabs her.

"It's all right, Carrie Ann, it's only a bad dream. I'm here. I'll carry you down." It's Dominic and he scoops her up as if she is a piece of thistledown and not a large size fourteen.

She remembers thinking he might drop her, except she knows he won't because for the first time in ages, she feels safe. Really and truly safe.

"Carrie Ann, wake up." He shook her gently, and moaning she tossed this way and that.

Her eyes felt glued together and she realized she'd been crying in her sleep.

"It's okay, babes. Boy, that must have been some dream."

Carrie Ann sat up, feeling hot and indignant. It was then she realized that Dominic was peering down at her and she was only dressed in her flimsy nightgown. She blinked. His face was gilded by the light from a bright moon. She put her hand to her heart, glad to feel it was slowing down. His arm was around her, he was cuddling her. Her cheek rested on his chest and the strange thing was it felt natural for it to be there. As her breathing became a slow trip, he stroked her hair. She didn't want this to end.

"My, you've had quite a night. I heard you right over in the other bedroom and I was worried about you."

She peered at him. He smelled so good, of the unfamiliar mixture of man and cologne and a sexy cologne at that. "I caught you sleepwalking. I mean I realize you like your work and you're stressed out with the thought of this project, but really, Carrie Ann. You won't believe this, but you went all the way out to the shed, unlocked it and you were busy at work on the fondant icing when I caught you."

"I don't believe you, you're making it up."

"No, I'm afraid not. Haven't you done it before? Oh, and you were babbling on about Latham."

"My God." Her hand moved to her mouth in an exclamation of surprise. "How embarrassing."

"Yeah, and you were going on about your husband and muddling him up with your father."

"Why, why didn't you wake me?" Alarmed, she fought to contain her composure.

"You know what they say. You should gently guide the victim back to bed. So, I watched you and when you'd finished fiddling around, I helped you back upstairs. It was amazing, you went to sleep straight away. Then half an hour later you woke me up with your nightmare. You were like a banshee and I couldn't wake you. It was horrendous. You were on about Rommy but muddling him up with your father again."

"I didn't know I sleepwalked."

"I'll have to chain you to the bed if you keep doing this. A guy has to have some sleep." He raised an eyebrow suggestively and a scintillating tingle raced across the surface of her skin.

She hadn't realized she sleepwalked. But there again Rommy wouldn't have told her. How much exactly did she say during these nocturnal perambulations? That would account for why Rommy had seemed to have a sixth sense about everything she did. All those years she had probably been giving her secrets away in her sleep.

"I wouldn't worry about it. I did it when I was a kid and again at university. It's generally down to stress. When the stress goes away, you get better. I had to chuckle though. You were raving on about this icing and getting your feet stuck. Do you always have your dreams filled with sweet secrets, Carrie Ann?"

Thank God it was so dark because he surely couldn't see her shock, her reaction. In actual fact, her thoughts had been venturing down lots of sweetly seductive avenues lately and before she'd gone to bed she had dreamt of how nice it would be to slather Dominic in American frosting and lick every bit off his body, in particular off his cock. How adolescent, giving way pornographic temptation. She wouldn't do that again. What if she had babbled about it?

She yawned. No wonder she had been more exhausted than usual. Sleepwalking made people tired, didn't it?

He kissed her forehead, her lips, and for a moment she forgot she was in her nightdress.

"You smell of icing," he whispered. "I never knew it could be so...so sexy." He carefully teased around the lace collar with his finger and a loosened button popped open.

He turned her face up to his and kissed her sweetly and persuasively, and this time she didn't resist. It was not the hard passion she had been expecting, this was a slow coaxing toward the borderline of lust and she didn't want it to stop. No, it was easy, easy to let go, have him lead her as she relaxed into his embrace.

He teased up her nightdress and stroked her thigh, circling her back as she curled into him. Under the cover of darkness and without turning on the light it seemed somehow easier. And yet she couldn't allow this, could she? Couldn't let him to slide her toward this inevitable seduction, or could she? There was nothing stopping her having sex, so why was she so reticent? She also wasn't that naïve. She might be a virgin, but she had been practical about her needs for ages and had smuggled in a vibrator in one of her more daring moments. Rommy had liked to think he'd kept her in a hermetically sealed box, but it was amazing how incredibly inventive she could become when she had to, and she'd had to. Her passions had been consummated on the occasions when she'd known Rommy had had a tot too much brandy or had been secreted away watching his favorite TV program.

The alarming imminence of Dominic now made her hesitate as his hands danced up and down the keyboard of her spine, circling and pressing. He would notice her caution and he would wonder at it. She'd had no actual practice with a flesh and blood lover, and as for being married? No married woman would be this shy. And yet she wasn't that shy, she noted in surprise. In fact it was coming so incredibly easily. Even now with so little practice all it took was a little creative fashioning. Women since time immemorial had been taught how to fool men hadn't they? She had read enough about that kind of thing in her books.

Her doubts and insecurities washed away under this deluge of ecstasy as she was swept along, reveling in the adventure of sex and the surprising amount of power she seemed to possess over him, a power that made his heart pound as erratically as hers.

"Carrie Ann, I've been longing to do this since the first second I met you. Why did you make me wait so long? You don't know the hell I've been going through every day watching you." He laughed. "Squeezing and coaxing all those icing cocks and breasts."

"Eh." *Oh, my God.* He must have been perving on her in one of her more inventive moments. Lately she had been fiddling with her creations more than normal, just because… Shit, how childish. But no point worrying about it.

What was he saying?

"You have no idea how it turned me on, seeing you fingering those cocks and wondering how your fingers would feel, you know against me, pulling and squeezing."

Part of her wanted to burst out laughing, what he was saying was so cheesy, so ridiculous, or was it? Her thighs trembled. It was not so ridiculous at all, if she was truthful. It made her feel excited and he seemed so serious, so intent.

Pushing her back against the sheets, he looked into her face, stroking her cheek with his knuckles. "Tell me you want me as much as I do you?"

"I do, Dom." She pressed her finger to his lips, and he kissed it and slid it inside his mouth, tonguing it gently, sucking it in. "I do."

"I won't ever take advantage of you, you know that don't you?"

She nodded and he kissed her, holding her so tightly her breasts pressed enticingly against his chest. She could feel the swell of his erection between his legs. How did it feel? His cock felt good, not frightening...kind of hard, elastic and yet there was a vulnerability about it. Her own gasp was foreign to her ears. It was one of need, of fast approaching a borderline she could not retreat from. She wanted this more than anything — she had been a fool to hold back so long from sex when she had craved it so desperately.

He made her raise her arms so he could slide off her nightdress, exposing her skin to the warm night air. She experienced only a flicker of doubt that lasted a split second. As the seduction began, she was consumed by overwhelming need with no time to pull back or rationalize.

He was bare, he only wore sweat bottoms. Now he eased them down his legs, holding her to him again so she could feel each dip and rise of his maleness. She was not in the least apprehensive in the heat of passion. Making love to Dominic was the most natural coming together. It was so frighteningly easy to lose control and love. Her body under the thrall of new impulses, behaved of its own volition — copying and replying as her limbs twisted and tangled with his.

It was not the passion she'd read about in her romantic novels, but neither was there anything scary about it. It was easy, a gently moving surge and fitting together, any discomfort swept away by greed. He explored her with his fingers, gently pressing in all the right places, then at last fondling her breasts and doing what she had wanted since that first second — coaxing her nipples, pinching and bringing her to hardness before using his mouth to wet the hard nubs.

Blowing against them, he raised her to a trembling height before moving on, following her dips and curves, raising delicious anticipation as he moved down.

Her legs flopped open — she didn't possess any strength to resist, this was just a smooth glide to Heaven. His hands slid up her leg, teased through the soft tangle of hair and between her slick, ready folds, finding that place. Ooh yes, that place, which instantly made her stiffen not from fear but pure, delectable ecstasy — burning, needy, throbbing. She raised her arms and gripped bunches of pillow. She wanted to scream and shout as her body writhed, and strange animal sounds came out of her mouth.

"Tell me at any time if you want me to stop, Carrie Ann. Let me wash it all away."

"Ah." Just a sigh, as he positioned the wet tip of his by now rigid cock at her entrance and moved inside. She felt some resistance, no more. It was as if her body had denied this so long, that she was so ready it couldn't wait. She simply felt driven on and it was amazing, amazing how it felt. Different to the vibrator as it teased every inch of her — soft and sliding and harder than she'd imagined, moving with infinite slowness to discover. As if that wasn't good enough, the real journey started as he rotated his hips, cupping her buttocks and pulling himself deeper so she could sense the textures of him. Then he lay there letting her feel him, as she touched up and down his back. It was as if he knew she had doubts and let her play them out before beginning to thrust forward in a measured tempo that matched the bumping of her heart. Sweetly, with lots of coaxing and plenty of caresses, he enticed her toward that first pinnacle and it was an easy climb through a blur of pleasure. It was different to her lusty dreams. It meant something, was intensely deep and satisfying, filling her with a vibrating drumming at the critical moment as digging her nails into his flesh, she arched her body in spasms of pure enjoyment. *Mmm,* all her inhibitions melted away as he pushed against her, his cock entering, thrusting carefully as Dominic indulged in all the lust he had been holding back. Sex was so easy, she thought.

He held her close, his finger in her cleft, moving gently back and forth, circling, rubbing, bringing her to one more orgasm, until she was left swimming in the ultimate finale, a series of never-ending ripples and satisfying conclusions.

God, how much like baking it was, with all the minute additions, mixing and being careful to incorporate. The notion made her want to giggle, any mirth soon washed away, as with a groan they began to make love again and she dissolved further into the heat of the moment. She bucked and slid against him in a frenzy, amazed at her responses as she met him thrust for thrust until at last Dominic came and the warm flood of consummated passion led her to one final orgasm. This time a softer, more lingering one, that left her body vibrating like a plucked harp string.

Her head on his chest, he stroked his hands through her hair. Her mind was doing somersaults. Had she just done that? Was it that simple to fall into bed with a man? She hadn't thought it would be this easy, this good.

"Carrie Ann," he whispered in her ear. "I bet no one ever told you, you're hot stuff."

She smiled as he lightly stroked her arm and the slow rise of passion started again, this time in ripples that expanded outward, gently warming her body.

Chapter Eleven

"What is this, a kind of competition?" Nina peered into the basket.

"Yes, a very important one. It's to do with that order. You know the one about the catering."

"Ah," Nina said. "Sexy, so, you've come around to the idea have you?"

"Not exactly. Dominic and I have agreed to a blind tasting, to see if his cooking measures up to mine. You may as well try the savories as well."

"So, what do I say to Ms Bunting? She's bound to wonder what the hell's going on." Nina arched an eyebrow.

"Well, she knows Dominic's at the house. We'll just say it's something competitive, a bit of a lark."

"Good job, but a bit of a lark? I don't know if you'll get away with that looking at these," Nina replied, eyeing the contents of the basket with longing. "They look well..." Her voice trailed off.

"It's jolly hard being kept in the dark," Ms Bunting said, wandering over to the counter. "I wonder what you're up to, Carrie Ann? Why are you so secretive about what you do? However, you young things these days. You always seem to have your conspiracies."

Carrie Ann smiled. "Just let's say I'm not ready to come out of the closet yet. Look." She rattled the basket. "Are you going to try these or not?"

Nina picked up a miniature pasty. Carrie Ann had done exactly the same bake as Dominic but they had marked their bakes with different patterns. She had to be sure that the order would come out up to her standards and that no one would be able to tell the difference at the event. In that way she would feel better about the whole thing. Baking savories was a real strain for her. It was obvious whose were the best from an appearance point of view. Dominic's pasty was a perfect golden, gilded with tiny leaves and little images of sheep. How daft was that? Daft but clever. The most obvious fault with hers was the crimping. His didn't ooze all over the place and hers did. In fact, hers had caught in the oven and a long dark welt spoiled their appearance. Once she got past the outside, what was on the inside? With her sweet treats she worked almost instinctively adding a pinch of this or that spice or a subtle drop of flavoring. But working those flavors into meat, vegetables or seafood on the other hand, was like learning another language. Perhaps she would have to face facts. Maybe her forte would always be pâtisserie.

Nina licked her lips. "Holy shit. The one good thing about this is we get to taste two." She bit into a salmon mousse vol au vent with soured cream, nibbling slowly around the edges. It was like watching two different species of bird with the two women. The careful sparrow like pecking of Nina as against Ms Bunting, who, after hovering like a bird of prey for several seconds, dove down. Carrie Ann could tell they were both winding her up and taking far too long to make up their minds.

"Come on, you two, you're playing around. You have the slips of paper with the details. You just have to put your marks on them and add it all up. Whoever gets the most positives wins."

"I thought this was important to you so we have to take our time," Nina said through a mouthful of lamb tart. "This is a very clever idea. But let's move on to the desserts."

Carrie Ann had to admit Dominic appeared to be an ace at savories. Personally, she thought he lacked edge and finesse on the sweets, but that could be sorted out with her keeping her beady eye on him and tutoring him in how she added a dash of this and that to create her special trademark taste. It was fun now she came to think of it, and she tingled with excitement at the thought of the outcome of the experiment.

After a great deal of lip smacking and whispering, Nina announced their decision, "Carrie Ann, we can't decide and that's the short answer. We deliberated over it, but we've reached a stalemate."

Carrie Ann thought Ms Bunting seemed rather smug for some reason as she waited for the great reveal and the outcome of the vote, but it was unlikely surely, that the both of them would be that devious to construct some lover's game to force her and Dominic together. That was just too way out.

"Here's how we see it. You have the edge with the sweet pastries. But it seems Dominic has the edge with the savories. You were never good at those though, were you? I mean the ideas are great. It's the execution."

"Eh," Carrie Ann said glumly. That was a bit blunt. "Thanks a lot."

Nina patted her on the shoulder. "Don't worry about it, darling, it isn't your thing. You can't be ace at everything. Think of all the great pâtisserie chefs. They only cook savories on sufferance." She gave Carrie Ann a loaded glance. Knowing more about Sweet Secrets than Ms Bunting, Nina evidently felt well placed to point this out.

"Yes, we all have strengths and weaknesses," Ms Bunting added. "However, I must say these pies are superlative. He has even more talent than I first thought. Actually, if I was you, I'd begin to wonder."

Carrie Ann thought she had a gleam to her eye. "Thanks," she replied tartly, snatching the basket away. It made her feel more wound up. She was getting deeply suspicious of Dominic. When he wasn't looking she had inspected the Julienne and macedoine he'd left in a bowl on the counter and they were so perfect you could have measured them and they would all have been the same. It was creepy. "So, give me the verdict. Who's the winner? Someone must have the edge?"

"That's the thing." Nina smiled. "Like I said, it's stalemate, so we've declared a draw."

Carrie Ann felt a sense of relief. Well at least he hadn't beaten her. Nina pushed a piece of paper across the counter. "Here you are, this is our verdict, in case lover boy doesn't believe you."

"Thanks a bunch." She glared, snatching the paper up and stuffing it in her pocket. Really, Nina pushed the envelope with her suggestive statements sometimes.

"That'll cause a little bit of thunder and lightning." Ms Bunting laughed.

* * * *

"They made a great many observations," Carrie Ann explained.

Dominic kissed her on the lips, touching them with the tip of his tongue. "Did they? Tell me. I want the details."

She snuggled into him, drawing the rug up over her knees. They were sitting on the rattan sofa in the conservatory, contemplating how to tackle the commission. Except easily both their minds had wandered. His finger danced up and down her arm. She glanced at him, punching him mock playfully. "Can you believe it? They actually said your savories were way better than mine."

"Hardly surprising." He yawned teasingly.

She sat up. "How did you get so good? I hate you."

He caught hold of her arm, wrestling it behind her back as he assumed a suggestive expression. Dominic was—she was finding out—very strong and she liked this rough play. It was kinky, turned her on. "I told you, I've had plenty of practice. Like you, I've got natural talent and it doesn't only encompass cooking."

"Practice, yeah, messing about."

"I'm no less practiced at it than you. You don't have formal training, do you?"

For an instant she felt a pique of doubt. He was intriguing and it seemed he had a great many talents, savories being only one of them. Furthermore, he was a fantastic and inventive lover. Take today for instance. When she'd gotten back from the baker's, he'd confronted her with a bottle of buttercream icing and threatened to cover her with it. The possibilities of royal against buttercream and American frosting offered up endless erotic possibilities, especially when he'd caught hold of her and had begun drawing icing patterns over her skin. She shivered at the recollection.

She'd wanted to egg him on, see what daring game he was going to play. And that was another thing, how easily he'd tempted her into bed and during the day when she should have been working. She'd never have believed she would go to bed with a man in the afternoon, but she had and twice. Breathless excitement had managed to sneak up on her. It was as if he had been able to break down her barriers just like that. Even now his hand was traveling on its circuitous course around her collar. "So, are you going to tell me who the out and out winner is? Not that I don't know."

"Would you believe it, they called it a draw." When she glanced at him, he was grinning.

"Wow! A draw. So that means each of us is the winner."

"Mmm." She was barely able to conceal the quiver that rippled through her from the tips of her toes to the roots of her hair.

"So, in all fairness we ought to take it in turns."

"Turns to do what?"

He raised an eyebrow. "Whatever the other person wants."

The new flirtatious Carrie Ann was making an appearance. She sat up. "Why, Dominic, I do declare. You're not suggesting something dirty are you?"

"Actually, yes, yes I am. I intend to erase the ghosts of your past and I think I have the perfect way of doing it. A game, what do you think?"

"I bet it's filthy." She sat pouting with her arms crossed.

"So what, you have a dirty imagination anyway. Who else would make rude figures out of icing and play around with them?"

"That's different."

"How is it different?" He tapped his head. "It's all in here."

"I was going to suggest you do the washing up for a month and be my general skivvy." She vainly attempted to steer the conversation onto safer ground.

"That's two things and besides it's not very exciting is it? Unless skivvy means something outrageous."

"Well." She knew it was going to be dangerous to ask... "What do you have in mind?" That was tempting fate.

He stretched back, giving her a smug look. "I've dreamt up something much more exciting. I want you to strip and let me cover you in different colors and textures of icing. I want to discover the wanton Carrie Ann Jude."

"I bet you do." She leaped to her feet and dashed into the kitchen. It was a silly thing to do, but she couldn't help acting silly around him. She knew he would chase her and he did. Around the chairs, nearly knocking over a mixing bowl then down the path to the shed where they skidded to a halt as she realized he'd snatched the key out of the lock and was now dangling it in front of her before slipping it into his jeans pocket.

"That isn't fair."

"I don't remember saying I was going to be fair."

She took a step back. This was a new, dominant Dominic and he was stirring feelings inside her—hot and uncontrollable feelings. It was as if a wild side to her was waking up. A slumbering creature, uncoiling and totally unfamiliar that made her think and act in ways she hadn't thought she was capable of. "I'm not into that kinky stuff."

He rattled the keys. "I beg to differ."

She lost her senses with Dominic and now, gazing into his face, she was overcome with the warm sliding sensations she'd felt before. It was like being dipped in melting sugar and it turned her body molten. It was so weird. She had never contemplated sex being this easy. When she'd thought about it in the past, been denied it, it had always seemed embarrassing and confusing. Acts veiled in secrecy that the people in her books did but she never dared to contemplate. It was like, well, it was like she was being directed by another force. Wow! Dominic was looking at her body for Christ's sake, evidently wanting to explore her in detail and things felt as natural as getting up in the morning. She tried to stifle a giggle. Carrie Ann was like a sex-starved animal as she explored new patterns of behavior which were multi-layered like the most complex gateau. Yeah, that was a great way of thinking about it. A smooth layer of sweet jam, then the nutty crunch of praline, then something with a bit of a bitter decadent edge—maybe coffee.

"Give me that key." She backed him up against the shed wall, kissing his cheeks and with the one hand eased a finger between the buttons of his shirt, skimming his rigid nipple. Mmm she wanted to mouth it, give it a full-on tasting session. With the other hand she reached into his pocket, pushing her fingers in hard, feeling him stiffen as he became aroused. *Hey!* This was good.

As he moved over her with lips and kisses, she let it happen, dissolving into it, any embarrassment melting away into a pleasant swirling world of sensations that made her concentrate only on the track of finger and thumb and the slide of his body.

At last she found the key and with shaking hands inserted it into the lock, right as his arms came around her waist, propelling her forward so she stumbled into the shed and against the work surface table. Breathless and completely powerless, she felt devoid of strength as she let him lift her dress. He reached up to rip down her panties, fingers wriggling inside her wetness, opening her slick folds and starting that sweet avalanche of sensations. At the same time his other hand expertly popped buttons so he could plunder her breasts and nipples, doing things Carrie Ann had fantasized over Latham doing.

"Dom, slow down, I want to savor it." Her voice came out croaky, hoarse with lust.

The sweet climb to the explosive ending wasn't enough for her, she was capable of that passion, but she preferred the minutiae, such was her eye for detail. Her nervousness gave way to passion, deep and turbulent, as she guided his hands to where she wanted them to be, so she could revel in it and satiate the inner conflicts of desire. A pinch, a nip. His touch was so good, so tender, self-assured, yet at other times, animal hungry.

Dominic obliged. It was generally him who took the lead, well at least in the beginning, until the shreds of embarrassment began to dissolve. Giggling harder, she tried to kick aside the knickers that had gotten tangled around her ankles, but couldn't quite manage it. It was exciting having him move around her clothing, tease it away, slide his fingers under and over it. Strange how he didn't seem to notice her less than perfect body, how he praised the imperfect parts of her. He toppled her backwards, laughing, grabbing her hand as she sat down the floor with a bump. On his hands and knees he approached her, his gaze full of the light of passion.

Grabbing her ankle, he stroked her foot, before holding it as she kicked and twisted. She struggled to pull up the panties while he attempted to tangle them in an act of lace and silk bondage around her ankles.

"You're gorgeous, you don't need them, although they do have their uses."

She couldn't wrestle her legs free, but it didn't matter because it felt exciting, kind of kinky. With his praise, her confidence was growing until she was willing to shrug off any inhibitions and doubts and gradually morph into the kind of woman she'd always fantasized about being. Was it her throat, her mouth that gave those moans and cries and did sinful things? Yes, loads of sinful things, like trying to lick his skin, nip at him. It didn't surprise her. Neither did it surprise her when he went down between her legs, and, parting her lubricious folds, teased her clit with his fingertips, his nail deliciously scraping her sensitive clit and shocking her to new heights of sensation.

Shit, she was actually having sex on a shed floor. Unbelievable! It certainly gave a whole new dimension to the experience. The floor was hard, the ecstasy too much to bear as his tongue circled and retracted, then came on full force to circle her clit. She couldn't help wondering how many girlfriends he'd had. Oh, why did that doubt have to intrude at this second? He was very good at seduction, so where had he learnt it? Her heart plummeted at the technique, the accomplishment of the lovemaking. As much as she loved it, her confidence had been so ruptured by Rommy's constant domination it was hard to rebuild.

She pushed the doubts away. This secret thing could go on a bit longer couldn't it? As they made the headlong gallop toward full-on sex — wild, gutsy and fast.

Too quick, too quick, she shuddered, clenching her fists so hard her nails bit into her palm. He'd stopped his tantalizing seduction and now raised her legs so he could enter her. She wanted to hold back, wanted it to go on forever. She liked this crazy, feral Dominic — the fact he had both a gentle and rugged side. She gulped, unable to hold back as he pushed her to orgasm, stopped and withdrew, then turned his attention back to his oral seduction, plunging back into her with his tongue before entering her again with his cock. He was so masterful as he engaged in this thrust and withdraw, using cock, tongue and fingers to charm, entice and lift her to bursting point, then damp the fires down, before starting all over again, bringing her to the slippery crest of lust once more. Could it get any better? Yes! Now he let her have her turn, as dominant Dominic became submissive. She was being so liberated too, as she straddled him, mussing her hair, eyeing him up as her gaze hungrily consumed him in turn. Now, she could do what she had been dying to do — taste him, lick his nipples and move her hands over his washboard flat stomach before teasing him with her tongue. She had the same craving to tease her mouth through the hairs around his balls and linger with flicking motions of her tongue over his cock, as she did when she tried a sweet treat, except, this was even better. Closing her eyes, she reveled in the sweet and salty tastes of man, as changing role provided even more of a rush.

She would show him how inventive she could be that would give him something to think about.

Sex became a game as the two of them dabbed icing here and there and she painted him with food coloring, following the slippery trails around his muscles. She was a greedy student, any inhibitions dispelled as she sucked his cock. She swirled her tongue around it with the same delicacy and delight with which her tongue and mouth tested the firmness and sweetness of her icing confections. She realized she was trapped in a sticky web she didn't want to escape from, a spun sugar tangle that every pâtissier knew could be so fragile and with the slightest touch could shatter.

"Mmm, Carrie Ann. Know how delicious you are?" He crooned, sucking her sticky fingers as this time he pushed her up against the wall.

Her heated skin melted the icing. She was dewed with perspiration, felt gunky but oh, so sexy. Dominic advanced, teeth bared like a wolf. It ought to have been a bit funny because he had flecks of icing in his hair. Instead it was dead sexy as she pushed her back hard against the wall and raised her knees.

Holding her tight, he showered kisses on her neck, moving her hair aside with his hands so he could mouth her erogenous zones. His cock nudged her slit as she opened her legs wider and wrapped them around his hips. Sitting on the floor now they were glued together by sticky icing blobs like two pâtissiers' models.

Carrie Ann nibbled his ear and bit him rather hard as, without preamble, his cock entered her and the ride began once again. This time sweeter, slower, more controlled, but just as good, as practically locked together, they rocked to and fro, reveling in one another's bodies. The sweet ripples kept on and on and she clung to him, kissing him, murmuring, raising herself up and lowering as Dominic ground his hips in a sexy dance that Carrie Ann would have been happy never to have stopped, but of course, she had to think of some work didn't she?

* * * *

That night, she went back over the menu details, her attention fastened on Dominic's glossy hair, his head bowed as he sat at the table, the way he moved his lips as he read the details out loud.

"So you think you can handle all that?"

"Come on, Carrie Ann, I love a challenge and don't worry, no one will find out about us. I'll go along with your mad pretend plan for now if that's what you want. But I'll expect you to come clean soon."

She couldn't come clean—couldn't have everyone know, they were... Her thoughts trailed off. What were they? Lovers, friends, two people having a diversion? She sucked her lips. It made her feel hysterical to even think about it, which was why she tried to push it to the back of her mind. It wouldn't last anyway. Nothing this good could last. He was too good-looking. He would soon get fed up with her, surely he would, wouldn't he?

"Hey, babes." He glanced up, his face a tangle of worry lines. "Come here."

"What is it?"

He pulled her down onto his lap and she began combing her hands through his hair. He suddenly looked frighteningly serious for Dominic.

"What?" She felt icy cold. He had that look about him, as if he were about to tell her something he knew she wouldn't like. She wet her lips. "You're frightening me, you look so serious. What is it?"

He grinned at her. "You're so crash hot I could eat you."

"Yeah?"

"Yeah."

"But that's not what you want to say is it?" More icy trickles danced down her spine.

"Nope, afraid not. It's tons more serious than that."

Her spirits fell, she actually felt physically sick. This was what letting go did and it was the thing she feared. It made her vulnerable, open to hurt. "It's over isn't it? That's what you're going to tell me. You want to finish with me." She put her finger on his lip, felt his arm tighten around her waist.

"Christ no, Carrie Ann, that couldn't be further from the truth. No, I want to prove something to you. I've been thinking loads about it. It's been driving me crazy, keeping me awake at night. Look, I know we all have our secrets, but I need to come clean, I can't carry this deception around with me."

"What, what deception? You're scaring me, Dom. Is it another girl?" She shook her head sadly. "I kind of knew. Knew I wouldn't be enough for you."

"No, it's not another girl, you idiot."

The room seemed so quiet. That bloody clock on the wall. Its tick was so loud—funny how she hadn't noticed that before. The suspense was killing her as the silence lengthened.

"There's no easy way for me to do this. I kept thinking of ways I could soften it, because I knew all that you'd been through. I know you're going to hate me." He took a deep breath. "Because…because I lied to you, and you're so nice I know you'd never do anything like that. I never wanted to, never intended it, it just happened because, oh, I dunno… Now, it seems so stupid. Because I wanted to impress you, not lumber you with all my crap."

Carrie Ann felt ice cold, she was trembling, freezing. "Okay, lied as in?" Her voice was remarkably level and calm.

"Lied as in my father, the job everything actually. Making myself out to be this brainy hotshot when I'm nothing but. When I'm so thick I had to leave school when I was sixteen. A loser just like Dad and not that nice a person either, I was always getting in fights." He bit his lip, closed his eyes. "Shit, shit." He clapped his hand to his head. "The part about Mum and the maid and the cooking when I was a kid, that was all true. It was just the bits about Dad and me."

"Dom, I..." Any moment now she thought she was going to choke. She felt like she had a large lump of emotion caught in her throat and she was too numb to say anything. He put his finger on her lips.

"I need you to shut up, Carrie Ann, and just let me finish what I have to say, or I might lose my courage. I'm not good at this stuff. Then when I do finish, I want to close the book on it, because I consider what I'm about to tell you a finished chapter in my life. I'm moving forward and it's behind me."

She couldn't look at him, couldn't. Well, she had seen this coming hadn't she?

"Babes, my dad is famous. His name is Winston Everton." He cuddled her on his knee, holding her tightly. "Come on, Carrie Ann, say something."

"You just told me not to."

"I know, yeah. Sorry. You're a cook, you must have heard of him."

She nodded in shock. Who hadn't heard of Winston Everton? He was a giant of a man, very round and loud and with a reputation for causing arguments.

More than that he was exceedingly clever and rich. Her gaze roved over his face. "You're kidding me. The one who was in all the papers, the self-made guy? The one who got in that legal battle when he duffed some other chef up when he criticized his food. The guy who set up Everton's Big Eat?"

"I'm afraid so. The brash, loud-mouthed Mancunian, who dug his way out of the gutter when he found a recipe for mushy peas and added a pinch of this and that and became famous."

So that was why Dominic was so good at pastry. The Evertons had started off as a bakery chain way back in the 1920s. Situated up North, they had set a benchmark for smart eateries that presented class on a budget, while retaining the old-fashioned recipes locals loved.

"But then that would mean you're the son he never talks about. The one he once said he disowned because he wanted you to take over his kitchens, but you wanted to make all those changes, add more modern recipes."

"The very one. It makes quite a story huh? But that's not all. I'm not into beef pies, even if they are best Aberdeen Angus, and neither do I like fancy chips. My father was so clever at overhauling all those hearty favorites and elevating them. He did however, still decide to keep the big portions — lamb scouse and stews and pasties, you name it. It's not me. I hate it. I always wanted to go into haute cuisine and have a little restaurant or even a trendy gastropub business. I love fine dining. I grew up secretly reading l'Escoffier. Dad hates nouvelle cuisine, he says it's sissy."

"Dom, I… That's quite a revelation." She was in shock and not sure she could take it all in. "But why did you decide to tell me now?"

"Because I like you and despite how most of my mates behave with their lies and larking around, I reckon I'm quite a nice bloke and I don't believe in that shit. That messing around with pretty women's heads." He took her hand, smoothed it. "I bet you hate me. A girl like you would."

"I..." She fumbled. "So, is that it? No more dirty secrets?"

Dominic blinked at her balefully. "No, that's the extent of it, I'm afraid. The things I told you about Dad and Mum and the divorce, all of that was true. He's such a shit, my father."

"So that's why you walked out, it wasn't just about the woman?"

"No. I want to make it all on my own even if it means starting out at the bottom of the ladder dicing vegetables and scrubbing pots. I don't want any help from Dad and I told him so. I hate his way of going about things. I'm not going home until I make it. The trouble is wherever I've been they've guessed, so I'm not doing that well getting a job, but I will, I promise you I will. I intend to make my own way, stand on my own two feet and not ride on Dad's back."

"Mmm." Carrie Ann smiled, she felt a sense of relief, such overwhelming relief she could have shouted out loud except something stopped her. "Those are big words, Dom. You can never hate your father, it doesn't work like that. You don't mean it and I should..." She stopped herself just in time. God, what had she been about to say, that she should know...because she had at times thought she'd hated Rommy, but despite the way he had treated her – love was indeed thicker than water. She clammed up, swallowed once again at the lump.

"So, do you forgive me?"

"Yeah, yeah I do, even though I'm in a state of shock."

He cupped her chin, kissed her, moving his lips over hers. But for once, Carrie Ann's lips were firmly sealed. Something awful stirred, something so huge and dark it cast a shadow over her and made her shiver. What was she going to do? Dominic had liked her enough, saw their future as bright enough, to come clean with his secret, and she was incubating this huge lie that seemed to be growing bigger day by day. And that wasn't all. He thought she was nice, he'd never dreamt for a moment she would have a propensity to weave such a web of deceit.

"Fancy going upstairs then, so you can show me you really do forgive me?"

She smiled, a smile of pure deception. Well, she would wouldn't she, she was becoming a queen of secrets, a weaver of such a tangled web of secrets she had no idea how she would extricate herself from them. She took his hand and led him upstairs.

"Yeah, let me begin to show you."

Chapter Twelve

"I need spices, fresh ones."

"There's plenty of spices in the garden," Carrie Ann stated.

"Not the kind I want." He pressed close, his arm nudging her and starting those feelings.

She felt hazy and intoxicated. She was in love and her business was getting better and better. Sue Sleight had raved over the erotic ideas she had put forward including an icing couple in handcuffs encased in a spun sugar cage.

"There's this fantastic shop in town, where they have it fresh daily and I ought to be able to get a great discount. I'm fantastic at getting a good deal."

"Can't you get it online?" She stooped over the table, peering through her glasses at the couple. She was just adding a touch of food coloring to get the details on the prototype exactly right.

"You look dead sexy in those glasses." He slid his arms around her, hugging her close.

She felt her resolve melting and attempted to look normal despite how awful she felt.

"And, no I can't get them online, I like to look at stuff."

"What will you do, take the bus? I don't think I can stretch to a taxi. You're short for time aren't you?" She angled her head so she could look at him.

"No, I have things totally in control."

"Go then, if you must."

He was hanging around by the door.

"What is it, Dominic? I can sense your eyes drilling right through me."

"Yes, that's because they are. Finish what you're doing and put something pretty on, I intend to take you with me."

Her jaw dropped. "But I can't. You know how much I have left to do for the Sleights."

"No more than I do. Don't make excuses. Here's the thing." He came closer. He looked so sexy in a black T-shirt and matching jeans. "I think you've forgotten something very important. It's your birthday on Friday. I realize you don't like being out late, but I booked this lovely restaurant. I want to take you to lunch and I won't take no for an answer."

It would mean going out in public. Why did that trouble her? It shouldn't have done because she was getting better in leaps and bounds with no panic attacks, no crises of confidence. The trouble was, over the last few weeks she had been under stress and that always made her feel just a bit edgy. She would have to dress up nice, look pretty for him and she didn't really have anything suitable to wear. This was a real date wasn't it? Good Lord. Her heart sank. She had no experience with this kind of thing, none at all. Unless... She did have that one nice dress. The one she had taken with her to America and that she had worn at the supper before she'd come home. The gang there had complimented her and said how lovely she looked in it. Made of midnight blue velvet, it caressed her body and had nice flowing sleeves and a square neckline. It was the kind of dress that would take her anywhere. And Casper had said it mirrored her blue eyes.

"Quit making excuses. If you say no, I'll only find some other way of forcing you to come."

"You haven't thought it out very well. I can't walk to the station in my best dress and it's such a drag going any farther on the train. There are at least two changes to get anywhere," she insisted.

"That's an excuse and you know it." He grabbed her arm and pulled her to her feet. "Get your glad rags on, tart yourself up like I'm going to do and I'll see you in an hour."

* * * *

Whatever had made her agree to it? Since Dominic's revelations, she had been torn in two and once or twice had locked herself in the bathroom sobbing as she felt overwhelmed by something so much bigger than herself. Last night she had come to a conclusion, though. She couldn't beat herself up over it anymore. She knew she didn't have the courage to come clean so she might as well face it. She was a coward and now all she could do was just try to hang on to the threads of love for a little bit longer, because despite the arguments in her head, she didn't want this crazy, impossible thing to end.

Now she was sitting in a taxi holding Dominic's hand as they sped along the lane between the summer hedgerows. "You look so delicious I could eat you," he whispered in her ear. "I promise I won't take long. I'm a fast shopper and I have it all planned out."

"Good because I don't fancy a long trek." She caught a glance of herself in the taxi mirror. Under the impulse of love, her skin glowed and she looked more vibrant. In fact, she looked dead sexy. She liked the idea of that.

He was as good as his word. He amazed her with his fast shopping then it was on to the little French restaurant—just the kind of place she would have chosen herself—up a quiet side street.

She watched him through the flickering candlelight. The seating was intimate—little lights set in bowls of blossoms on each table and old French posters on the wall. He had thought of her and that touched her, requesting a quiet corner table out of the way of people, so they were on their own. He told her he had asked for them to have somewhere special, somewhere quiet. The day couldn't get any better and she had done so well keeping herself under emotional control, she congratulated herself. She hadn't even thought of the breathlessness and panic attacks and felt great. They feasted on delicate scallops, followed by poached salmon en papilotte and her one indulgence, panna cotta. She thought Dominic seemed rather edgy as he held her hand across the table.

"Carrie Ann, I want to ask you something."

"Fire away," she said, as she sipped the champagne that had miraculously seemed to appear.

His thumb gently traveled over her fingers in a sensual caress. "Why do you mind so much about what everyone else thinks? Why does it matter so much that we're together? And we are together, aren't we? If you think it'll damage your business, that's mad. I can assure you it won't. It'll make you seem even more mysterious and that can only be a good thing."

He had a point, she knew that, but she shook her head. She had no explanation for why she acted like she did. It was just down to her sense of insecurity. "I don't know, Dominic, I really don't. I think I have to come around to it in my own time."

"And how long will that take you? Will it be today, tomorrow?" he coaxed.

"I don't know. When I feel comfortable."

"Carrie Ann? Is it because you're afraid of committing, or that you're afraid I won't commit? I want you to know that I've thought about this and I want to be with you. Haven't I proved that by coming out of the closet with this thing over Dad and my life, which at the moment seems to be in tatters?"

"Look, Dom, don't take this the wrong way." Her cheeks felt hot and her breath short as a wave of panic washed over her. "I know what you did and I think you're terrific and so honest. But my life's even more complicated than yours."

"Yeah I think I get it, you don't have to carry on about it." He flicked out his napkin. "I know this sounds corny for a guy, but I'm doing everything I can to prove to you I don't want a fling, I never saw this as that. I met you and I felt something click into place. I don't have an answer for it. Only that it was right and good."

She stared at her lap. She had been hoping she would never have to have this conversation and now it was happening, out of the blue. Where had she thought this was going? She realized she had been naïve to let it drift along as her feelings strengthened. Never a day went by when she didn't integrate him into her life, talk to him about her projects, her hopes and fears. Then Dominic had gone and done the unbelievable by metaphorically slicing open his heart and laying it right in front of her on a plate. She realized that the only right thing to do would be to admit her lies. But for some reason now she just couldn't. She had gotten caught up in a moral dilemma and it had happened so subtly she hadn't even noticed how deep the hole of her lies was getting. Now to make matters worse she was trying to pull a lid over that hole and just cover it up, wish as if by magic all the negativity she had created would go away.

"I was kind of hoping that you might have asked me to move in with you?" He glanced up at her balefully and in that instant it reaffirmed to her how young he was and what a total mess she'd made of things.

"Dominic, that's rather childish don't you think. Especially in view of everything?" How could she sound so cool, so calculating?

A flash of anger crossed his face. "In view of what? That man who ruined you for everybody else? This relationship that seems to have destroyed you and made you so confused you don't realize a good thing when it's staring you in the face? I don't believe it. I've seen who you are — you're a strong woman with hopes and dreams. I can't take on-board that anyone would stop you going out and getting what you wanted."

A yawning pit opened up inside her, and she felt queasy, as her thoughts and feelings ran out of control. She should have done what she had thought about in the beginning. Put him up for a while then asked him to move on. What was going on? He hadn't intended to stay had he? She scrunched her napkin in her fist.

"You're spoiling this. I thought this was meant to be my birthday treat?"

"It is and that's why I want to talk to you about where we're going. It's also an anniversary. I've been at your place two months, if you hadn't noticed."

"In all honesty, I had."

"Relationships move on. They don't stay stuck in a rut. Not if two people like one another and we do, don't we? Or I thought we did. Unless I got the signals wrong."

"Of course I like you. It's much more than that and you know it."

"Is it, Carrie Ann? Or maybe you're harder than I thought you were and this is a game. You using me in some way to get over Rommy."

"Now you're being silly."

"Silly." He shook his head. "I'm not getting into this. I don't want to argue."

"No, neither do I."

He still held her hand. "It's just I keep hoping you'll want to take it to the next step and ask me to move in. That's what people who love each other do."

Had he said that? Her heart missed a beat and her head swam.

"I love you."

"How, why?" She pressed her fingers to her temple. "I'm a mess."

"I told you I don't see a mess. I think you're fantastic. I've never met a woman like you. A woman who inspires me, who makes me think there are nice women left. Nice, genuine women."

She wasn't nice. She wasn't genuine. Why did he have to keep on making a point of saying that and making things even worse? There were now so many lies piled one on top of the other she didn't know where to start to explain them. What would he think of her when he knew how much deceit she was capable of, and most of all the fact that she hadn't been married at all? He liked her because he thought she was nice, different. In truth, she was none of those things. And that wasn't the end of the story. All along she had feared Dominic being the shallow one – as she had read lots of men were – of using her, of playing with her, when she was ten times worse. "Please don't do this."

She turned her wine glass slowly. She was amazed the panic had loosened its grip. For the first time she was having a measured argument. Inside her though, something was breaking. She realized she was terrified of losing him. *I must love him then. But how would I know? I have nothing to measure it against. One thing's for certain, it doesn't feel how I thought it would. Yes, it's a giddy whirlwind, but it's so much more. It's comfort, friendship, it's so many things. It's...*

Her thoughts trailed off. *It's like the relationship my father had with Mum.* For some reason that petrified her. She didn't know if she wanted to be like Rommy – so wrapped up in a love that when he'd lost Mary, he'd died inside. But then there was the other side of the coin. That love for as long as it had lasted, had been precious. Not many people could say they had had the kind of relationship where both partners were a harmony of spirits. Now she was even more confused. There was no way out. How could there be?

He wouldn't understand and she was too much of a coward to face facts and let him go. Furthermore, there was a murky and nasty side to her personality. If she were honest with herself she'd had, and continued to have, very bitter sentiments toward Rommy. Gloomy thoughts she had believed long since buried seemed to be percolating to the surface and her head began to throb. On more than one occasion, she had wished something would happen to Rommy. She had told Martha and Casper and they had said it was natural when stressed for her to have those sentiments, that she wouldn't be normal if she didn't, but how could they know what it was like? How could she have done something as cruel as plot and conspire with her projects, against a sick man? A sick man who in the end had died suddenly of a heart attack. It was like she was possessed by another person, a coolly calculating person. She might as well confront her dark past.

After she had planned the escape from Rommy, made the trip to the fair and been successful at it, she had progressed down an even more complex avenue of deceit. The catalyst might have been the fact that after Bennie's visit, her father had become bitter, angry and constantly criticized her. He had wanted to go on a return trip to Australia but since he hadn't been even able to remember where he had put his keys, it had been out of the question.

Maybe she had just snapped. It was obvious she hadn't been thinking clearly because the idea had been to run away and anywhere would do. The thrilling part of it had been that she would let the wind take her where it would, despite her nervousness. With a feeling of obscene delight she'd packed a carry bag, stowed it away and with the diligence of a private eye, had set about planning her escape.

One day, she'd waited for Rommy to take his afternoon nap, then had set off at a brisk pace to the bus stop.

It was only when she had gotten halfway there that the realization of what she was about to do had hit her and she had had to sit down breathlessly at the side of the road. She was a horrible person, moreover she was not as brave as she had thought she was. She hadn't been able to go through with it, hadn't been able to leave a sick man. Feeling stupid, she'd gone home, then had pretended nothing had happened. Rommy had somehow guessed though and had treated her differently for a few days, had actually been quite nice.

Her mouth tightened as she snapped out of the reverie.

Dominic leaned across the table, tightening his grip on her fingers. "I won't let you go without a fight. As trite as it sounds, don't you think we're meant to be together? Why else would we have bumped into each other and kept on bumping into each other like that? I know he hurt you, but, Carrie Ann, surely you can move on. Unless of course, I got it wrong and you don't love me. There is that point to consider."

"Don't be silly." She tried to draw her hand away.

"Well say it then."

"I, I can't. Don't be mean, Dominic."

"I'm not being mean. If you loved me you'd say it."

"This is getting childish."

"Shit. Do you know something, the worst thing is, why I keep putting up with this. Why I keep giving you all the benefits of the doubt, Carrie Ann. It's like you're something addictive, do you know that?"

And before she could move out of the way, he came around the table and, grabbing her by the arm, pulled her up out of her seat and kissed her full on the lips.

* * * *

By some miracle, he didn't mention it again, but she knew he was waiting and like a pressure cooker placed on the back burner, the awful secret bubbled away in the background getting ready to explode. She would take each moment as it came, each swift kiss and caress and long nights spent making love.

On the actual day of her birthday, he'd presented her with a pretty friendship ring made of green jade. There had been a question written in the lines and grooves of his face as he'd playfully slipped it on her finger and she knew he expected an answer she couldn't give.

She was doing the finishing touches on a wedding cake and Dominic had gone into town again to fetch a few last minute supplies. It was a blistering day and she'd just gotten the cake in the fridge to harden up when there was a knock at the door. She frowned. Callers were rare at the cottage. She inspected herself in the mirror. She looked a mess, her hair was awry and as usual she had specks of icing over her face. Still it didn't matter.

She opened the door to see a girl staring at her. She was very pretty that was the first thing that struck her. A disheveled head of hair was the perfect frame for a heart-shaped face and bright blue eyes.

"Hi." She tried to peer past Carrie Ann into the hallway. "I know he's here so can you let me in?"

"Who?" Carrie Ann asked as her stomach lurched like she was on a rollercoaster ride.

"Dominic. I know he's here. The old biddy at the sweet shop said you had a Dominic staying with you. She gave me directions to the cottage."

"And you are?" Carrie Ann asked pleasantly. She was amazed at how in control she felt. Her voice was cool, her smile genuine.

The girl frowned. "What's it to you?" she said with venom as, hands on hips, she looked Carrie Ann up and down. "I see. You've got your eye on him do you? Good old Dom. I knew he had unorthodox tastes, but this is amazing."

Carrie Ann couldn't believe her ears. This couldn't be happening.

"I'm his girlfriend, for your information." She began chewing on a piece of gum. "Bet he didn't tell you he had a girlfriend. That figures. He likes to run away from things."

Carrie Ann's mouth went dry. This was her worst dream come true. She ought to have known there was a girl lurking somewhere in the background. She was the type she could imagine him with, although she would have thought he'd have gone for a girl with a nicer personality.

"Well, uh." There was no use denying it. She leaned against the door.

The girl seemed to be reconsidering. "Look, I'm sorry, okay." She had studs through her ears and bright, sparkly blue nail varnish. "I didn't mean to let off at you like that. But he kind of walked out on me without an explanation."

"He's not here."

"Can I come in and wait then?"

"I don't think so. He's gone on an errand into town. I don't know how long he'll be."

"I don't mind waiting. Come on, babes, let me through."

Carrie Ann could tell the girl didn't believe her. "I can't. You caught me in the middle of something important."

The girl's eyes were doubtful. "He didn't mention me to you, did he? That's typical." She carried on obliviously as if she hadn't heard, but there was now a tone of doubt in her voice. "Well, okay. Look, I'm staying overnight at The Angel." She took a piece of paper out of her bag and after scribbling something on it, handed it to Carrie Ann. "Could you make sure he gets this please? I need to talk to him." She waved it under Carrie Ann's nose. "Come on, babe. You don't look the kind who wouldn't give it to him."

"No, eh, I suppose." She took the paper. "And who uh...who should I say's looking for him?"

She was half way down the overgrown garden path and her hand was on the front gate. "Just tell him Alice, Ally called."

Carrie Ann wandered back into the kitchen. Now the truth was sinking in, she felt sick. She sat down at the scrubbed kitchen table with her head in her hands, before thoughtfully smoothing the keypad of her mobile. She could call him but what would she achieve if she did? He would probably only say he wanted to talk about it when he got in. She didn't know why it bothered her so much. It wasn't as if it was totally unexpected.

The trouble was, the very thing she'd dreaded had happened. She hadn't been able to resist and now she'd gone and fallen in love with Dominic. It was a bit like her crush on Latham, but ten times worse, no a thousand times worse, because Dominic was real. *Oh, Carrie Ann, how could you be so stupid?* A tear squeezed between her eyelids and plopped onto her hand. It was the emotional turmoil of the last few weeks that was the trouble and his girlfriend was yet another obstacle in an increasingly complex puzzle. There was no denying her life was going through so many changes and getting her business off the ground was pressure enough. She didn't need this to add to it.

Love, it seemed, had turned her life upside down. If this was a story she would be superhuman and find some solution. In books the hero and heroine had arguments all the time and overcame them. This wasn't a story though. She pushed her mobile phone away. Life was a million times more complicated than a book.

The worst part was, Dominic had exposed the deepest part of her and made her feel vulnerable. Her wanton behavior in the bedroom that revealed a deep and greedy side to her personality, and the fact she was making up for lost time.

She glanced at the kitchen clock. He was really late, but if he had been back any earlier he would have bumped into Alice when she'd left, or seen her upset. Carrie Ann got to her feet and splashed her face with cold water. She looked awful when she'd been crying. She'd try to take her mind off it. She'd take the newest batch of cakes into Oh Crumbs! ready for Marcus to pick up. Her heart sank. That was another thing. It was getting harder and harder to manage without some form of transport. The more orders she got, the more she realized that the old bike parked in the shed that she had used to put the bread orders in wasn't anywhere near suitable enough to transport the delicate cakes. Now, if she had a sizable load she used an old pull along cart Rommy had used for the gardening. She had painted it pretty colors and it was large enough for her to stack the cake baskets in. But what she needed was something with a cooler. Her flesh crawled at the thought of driving lessons. Dominic had already joked about it when she'd shown him the pristine old Sunbeam in the garage. "Hey, that's vintage, Carrie Ann, you'd look so cool in it. I could teach you to drive in that."

She'd shoved him playfully. "Don't be so silly, I don't have a driving license."

"Easily solved. Come on, you can't have a business and not have transport."

That was true. She sighed woefully. It was stupid, she must look like a terrible novice not being able to drive. The Manor was perched on the hill and the driveway up to it was about a mile long.

She forced the thoughts of Ally out of her head. She still felt shaky all over.

Yes, that's what she would do, she'd take her mind off things and pack the stuff up for Oh Crumbs!. At least she had been lucky with the bakery. They had been great about her burgeoning orders with Marcus, well they would be. Marcus' patronage had put them on the map and no end of tourists were stopping off at the tea rooms to sample the cakes. *I mustn't think about what just happened.* She tied her hair back, then after changing into a summer dress, she packed the cakes and set off down the lane, tugging along the trailer that squeaked and whined behind her. It was a hazardous journey that Nina had once likened to taking her life in both hands. This time of year the tall hedges were obscured by flowers, meaning visibility was nil. Dominic had gone crazy when she'd told him she sometimes negotiated the twisty lanes twice a day. "Are you crazy, it's only wide enough for a car and have you seen the speed people come down there from the crossroads?"

"I've been walking along that lane since I was a kid. I know how to do it. I walk on the verge," she'd argued.

"Carrie Ann, the verge isn't safe. What if something came the other way and a car swerved."

"It won't. You can hear stuff coming a mile away anyway. I'm tuned into it."

He'd cupped her chin. "You know something, I'm beginning to notice a stubborn side to you."

She wandered along the side of the road. She wasn't thinking clearly and tears were threatening. She was proud of her latest triumph. Marcus had gone wild over it. This time chocolate cups were scented with the gardens special basil and black mint infusion.

The wheels of the trolley jammed and she tugged it as it got progressively harder to pull. She really ought to have a look at it, something was sticking, meaning she had to use all her energy to drag it along. She couldn't help thinking about Dominic and going over things time and time again in her mind. She didn't know what she'd say to him when he got back. He hadn't mentioned a girlfriend. Perhaps he had been steering her away from his love life all along. She ought to have listened to her hunches in the first place. She was so deep in thought, she wandered out into the lane which meant she didn't hear the car approaching at speed, only heard the honking horn as it swerved around the corner, startling her as it rode up on the bank. There was nothing she could do. Hauling the handle, she tried to drag the trolley out of the way and lost her footing. The next thing she knew she had tumbled down the bank and into the ditch.

Amazingly the car roared off without checking if she was hurt.

She blinked and opened her eyes, gingerly moving her arms and legs. She appeared to be lying on her back in the ditch in a patch of nettles and they had stung her bare arms and legs. She had also acquired multiple scratches during the steep tumble. She sat up, gingerly palpating her limbs and moving them this way and that. Things seemed okay, well at least she hadn't broken any bones, although her ankle was really throbbing. Bending forward she massaged it carefully. It was blue and already swelling. She must have twisted it as she'd fallen.

She tried to stumble to her feet but had to lean forward, biting her lips against the pain. It hurt and she couldn't seem to put her weight on it. Her heart began to beat an uncertain tattoo. The ditches along the lane were deep and steep. It would be hard enough to climb out of if she was okay, but with her injured ankle it would be impossible.

"Hey, anybody out there, help me. I'm down in the ditch," she called out once or twice but soon realized how mad that was. No one ever came down the lane. She sat down with a bump, her heart increasing in tempo as a wave of panic descended. How would she get out? She could try to walk farther along. She remembered there was a farm gate somewhere and there was a pile of rubble at the end of the ditch. Perhaps she could climb out there. As she tried to put her weight on her foot, though, the impossibility of that struck her. There was no way she was going to get very far. She glanced up. It was sizzling and the sun was beating down fiercely. The weather forecast had said it was going to be exceptionally warm today, and she reckoned the temperature must already be in the seventies.

"Help," she called again vainly, as she hobbled around, falling over again, palms down in the nettles. If she moved back she thought she could just see the edge of the trolley. Well that was something, at least it hadn't overturned. The cakes, however, would be ruined in this heat.

Sitting down, she burst into tears. Damn. If Rommy was up there looking down on her, she bet he was having a laugh. Maybe it served her right. She was crying so hard she barely heard the motor.

"*Mon Dieu*, I am hoping you did not ruin the chocolate order?"

She peered up into the bright sun, startled by the voice. There was no mistaking the accent and the trademark broken English. A shadow was leaning over her. Her heart sank at the embarrassment. It was Marcus and she didn't want anyone to see her like this.

"Do not move, Carrie Ann, for I will be attempting to help you."

That was all she needed. She was glad someone had come to her rescue, but she felt so silly she wished she could curl up into a ball and die. She had no makeup on, there were leaves and sticks in her hair and she was covered in nettle stings that smarted. It made her want to cry even harder.

"I have a rope in the car. I will throw it down and then I want you to tie it around your waist. Do you think you could manage that?"

"Yes, yes, I think so."

A rope landed with a thud beside her. It must have been out of the boot of Marcus' old Land Rover because it smelled of oil. When she glanced back up, she still couldn't see him because the light was shining in her eyes. Her fingers fumbled as she tied a knot.

"Are you ready, *petite chou*?"

"Yes, but be careful. I think I twisted my ankle."

She planted her good foot on the side of the ditch as she managed to find some purchase. Eventually he hauled her up and she flopped down with a gasp on the grass verge. It was such a relief to be out.

Anything was better than the ditch. For a small man, Marcus could be amazingly strong.

"*Sacré bleu*, are you all right?" He sank down on his haunches. She didn't have time to object as his hands manipulated her leg and ankle.

"Ouch, ouch."

"I think it is only a sprain. We have a doctor up at The Manor. He will look at it for you and bandage it up."

"So, you're the expert are you?"

Marcus paused, a queer expression flitting over his face. "How you know? Not all chefs are born from great chef's family."

Scowling she stared at the blossoming bruise. "No, no thank you. Can you run me home?"

"I do not think so, *ma petite*." Marcus began to assert the personality he was legendary for. "You will allow Marcus to escort you to The Manor. Luckily it seems my precious cakes are not damaged and I have time to get them in the cooler. It will be quicker to get your leg looked at up at the house than to call the doctor anyway. And you must bandage it up, get ice for it. Here let me." He helped her to her feet and over to the Land Rover that was pulled over onto the side of the road.

"Is that all you can think about, your cakes? I could have been killed."

Marcus shook his head. "I am thinking that Carrie Ann is a silly girl because she knows how dangerous this road is."

She sat in the front seat burning with embarrassment, while Marcus took the boxes out of the trolley and put them in the back. It was even worse when she glanced in his rear-view mirror. She looked hideous.

Marcus climbed in beside her. It was then she was struck by something. With his thick black hair askew he looked handsome. A bit on the short side, but she could see why women found him charming.

"Good thing that monsieur was traveling in your direction, I think."

"Mmm. Thanks, Marcus, and sorry for sounding so mean back there. I feel totally stupid, but thanks."

"Why you feel stupid? It was an accident, no? This lane far too hazardous for walking. You need to see about a van, a cool van to transport the cakes in."

She stared out of the window. "You're not the first person to say that."

Marcus gunned the ignition and they pulled off the verge. It was then Carrie Ann remembered the trolley. "What about my trolley?"

"Trolley no problem." He leaned over the steering wheel. "I will get Richard, the commis chef to walk down and fetch it."

She couldn't help it, it had been such a day she burst into tears again. "I'm so stupid."

He grinned at her. "I do not think so. I think that Carrie Ann Jude is woman full of emotion, which is a good thing. Emotion very important for art of bakery. Every cook need passion. Look in glove compartment, there is a box of tissues."

She took one out and blew her nose. Marcus kept shooting glances at her.

"There is nothing prettier than damsel in distress. Makes a man come over, how do you say...? Even after all these years in England I still find it hard to find the correct words. Ah, I have it." He put his hand on her knee then quickly removed it. "It make man very romantic and...protective...that is word...make man feel like knight in armor."

She was amused by him. She hadn't known that Marcus had such a sense of humor. She twisted the tissue in her hands. It was too late to do anything so she might as well go along with what he said. They soon turned off the lane and through the gates that led up to The Manor. It was quite a while since she'd actually been up here. Either side of the road, well-kept fields stretched away, full of the sheep that Marcus' restaurant was famous for.

"Why is it I invite Carrie Ann many times to come to The Manor to see where she sends her cakes and yet each time she say, 'No thank you, Marcus'. Why is that, *petite*?"

She shrugged. "It's just a few cakes, Marcus."

He turned to look at her. "What is that you are saying? You get me out of some sticky situations with your delightful recipes and you do not take it seriously. Michelin star chef take your cakes, Carrie Ann. He put cakes on menu and that is all you can say. Do you not know that a top chef would be delighted to be on menu of The Manor?"

"Of course, I know that."

A smile quirked his lips as they drove toward the square imposing manor house. "I fool with you. I understand about Carrie Ann. You do not think so, but many years I help with people, you know that."

She nodded. This was true. For the past three years Marcus had been taking part in a program that gave underprivileged and inspiring young men and women the chance of training with him. Many of them had problems. He was a bit like Arlem but a miniature venture. "I know about it and I think it's great."

"Marcus is well aware of Carrie Ann." He winked at her.

What did that mean? She was unsettled but so overcome with the approach to the house that any other emotion was simply swept away. It was much larger and grander than she had first thought. The imposing tall rectangular windows festooned in swags. At the front a large semi-circular gravel forecourt had wide steps leading up to a stone terrace. She leaned forward, taking it in.

"This is my humble abode. Although, not as imposing as the chateau of my father." Marcus stopped the car and came around to her door to help her down. "Rest on me, yes, that is right."

She leaned on his arm as they went up the steps. Inside and to the left there was a beautiful lounge full of antique furniture for the residents to relax in. On the right was a bar room and at the back was the restaurant. Upstairs were the guest rooms. The Manor catered to staying guests as well as having the Michelin starred restaurant. At this hour, day service had ended and the hotel was peaceful and quiet. It was an atmosphere of hushed opulence that was at the same time comforting.

Marcus led her through the kitchen where preparation was already underway for evening service. Out the back, a man was leaning against the wall with his earphones in, listening to some music. He took his earbuds out when he saw Marcus.

"Alain, this is Carrie Ann, she met with an accident. I wonder if you could look at her foot for her and clean it up."

"Sure. What did you run into, a truck?"

He meant it good-naturedly, but it only made her feel worse.

Marcus sat her down in the conservatory out the back. "How about a cup of tea. What is it an English lady would like? Earl Grey or coffee?"

"Marcus, none of this is necessary."

"Of course, it is. You have had a nasty shock. Look, Alain will take care of you. Before he had a life-change he was going to be a doctor. It's jolly handy having him around. I will unload those cakes and then I'll come back, see how you're doing and you can have a spot of lunch before you head back."

"No, Marcus." She wailed as she attempted to lever herself up. "I have tons to do, I have to get home."

"Even the maestro of cakes has to eat. You will see how much better you will feel afterwards. Then I will run you back. I'll get Amelia to book you into a room and you can clean up."

She was horrified. "No, you definitely can't do that. I won't hear of it."

"We can't have you walking around looking like you do. *Mon Dieu*, Carrie Ann, you are a hard woman."

He was only trying to be helpful and it was nice, nice to be looked after and to enjoy the peace and quiet. Plus, it would give her more time to decide what to say to Dominic.

"Good, that is settled."

Alain brought a glass of water and while she sipped it, washed her foot with some antiseptic out of the kitchen, manipulated it and decided it was a sprain. After applying an icepack, he bandaged it up. As he did so, she relaxed, her mind floating as she listened to the tweeting birds through the open doors. It was a fantastic place. When he finished and pronounced her fit to get up, Amelia the receptionist poked her head around the door. "There you are. Marcus has given me an instructions to look after you. Goodness, what happened?"

"I practically got knocked down, some idiot, hit and run. He didn't stop to see how I was."

She now felt a sense of rage at that. Anything could have happened. She could have hit her head.

"They're maniacs on that road. Once or twice, Marcus nearly got a prang turning out of The Manor. Can you walk?"

"Yeah." She tested her weight on her foot. "It's much better now that it's bandaged." She followed Amelia through the lounge, surprised to see a small, rather unique looking lift, with extravagant iron grills and ornamentation.

"I can guess what you're thinking, it's kind of weird having a lift in a manor house, isn't it?" Amelia explained. "The guy who privately owned it back in the '20s was eccentric, though, and ahead of his time, rather like Marcus. He liked his gadgets."

Carrie Ann was amazed that for once she didn't feel panicky in the lift, since her panic attacks had often come to the fore in enclosed places. Instead she enjoyed the short ride. When she stepped outside she was in a carpeted corridor. Amelia slid a card into a door and opened it. "Make yourself at home. This is the guest suite that Marcus reserves for special VIPs. There are towels in the en suite so you can have a wash. Here let me look at you. Turn around." Amelia looked at her appraisingly. "Your dress is okay, but you have a tear. Put a dressing gown on and I'll get housekeeping to fix it."

"No." She felt a sense of despair. "Don't go to all that trouble."

"It's no trouble. It'll take half an hour. They'll press it and you'll look as good as new. Just enjoy it. Have a nice bath."

"I'm not meant to be here, I'm meant to be back working."

Amelia laughed. "We haven't kidnapped you, you're five minutes down the road and this is the story. You can't walk far and Marcus insists you are his guest and he'll run you back. If you want you can look at it another way. You provide those amazing cakes so in a manner of speaking you work for him, don't you? I'm fascinated, we all are. You're so talented, Carrie Ann. Now stop whinging." She went into the bathroom. "I've started to run you a bath. Slip that dress off and then you can have a soak. Come on, a couple of hours off won't hurt you. I'll pop your dress straight up when they've finished."

When she left, Carrie Ann wandered around. She couldn't believe it. She felt like a film star, although The Manor's accommodation was what would be termed modest. The furniture was in keeping with the period with mod cons cleverly fitted in so they were concealed and there was a gorgeous bed that she bounced on once or twice. No wonder the house was used so much as a honeymoon venue.

She emptied a bottle of sweet-smelling bubble bath into the tub and had a brief soak. Then after washing her hair and blow-drying it with the hairdryer provided, she sat down in a chair by the window. Only twenty minutes or so had gone by, but it felt like a whole day and now to top things off she had a headache where she had banged her head.

There was a light tap on the door. God, how stupid – she had forgotten to lock it.

"Carrie Ann, it's Marcus." He brazenly wandered in. He had changed into a denim shirt and jeans and looked completely different.

She opened her mouth and closed it. This Marcus looked as Nina would say 'hot'. He had Byronesque looks and a quirky manner about him. She blushed. "Oh!"

"Don't look so worried, I have seen women in bathrobes before." He sat down in a chair opposite her. "You look miles better. How's the foot?"

"Great, thanks."

He nodded. "Housekeeping is getting your dress fixed, then I have a light lunch laid on with a number of things I think you will like. I am afraid I have an ulterior motive in keeping you here. I want to ask your opinion on our new trifle."

"Marcus, I hardly think I'm qualified to judge a Michelin starred chef."

"Carrie Ann, I am not expert in all things. I am not a pâtissier. Now come along, you are too shy. You realize you have skills." He leaned forward. "I happen to know about the craft competition. While Latham is not a friend, we often, how do you say...? Rub shoulders, and I know you won a craft competition at the fair."

"It was nothing," she mumbled.

"What, nothing to be judged by the world's best cake maker?"

"He is not the best."

"You don't want to let Latham hear you say that." He grinned at her.

"I don't like people to know." She gripped the chair arms tightly.

"Okay, that's fine. So, we won't tell anyone. But in my view someone with your talent is qualified to give me an opinion and I am sure you will like my dessert." He made a kissing motion on his fingers. "I make what I think is delicious trifle, but it could do with how do you say…"

"Tweaking?" Carrie Ann ventured.

"Yes, *parfait*, tweaking."

At that moment, Amelia came in with the dress. It had been patched up so well she couldn't see the rip and it had also been pressed.

Marcus stood up. "Fine, as tempted as I am to stop and see a gorgeous woman dress. I will leave you. When you are ready come downstairs, I will be waiting for you in the conservatory. You know where that is now, don't you?"

"Yes, yes I do."

He paused at the door. "That is what is so wonderful about The Manor. It has the aura of one of the biggest and best hotels and restaurants. Yet, it is still comfortable and intimate."

She was in a frenzy of mixed emotions. She dressed quickly then found Marcus out in the conservatory where the food had already been laid out. An exquisite light Mediterranean lunch of grilled salmon, salad, focaccia and sparkling local wine.

"That's miles better, how do you feel?"

"Terrific except I have a mighty headache."

Marcus pulled out her chair, then sitting down spread a napkin. She liked this different Marcus.

"I thought you'd appreciate something light. That must have been quite a shock for you. But that road is a death-trap. You shouldn't have been walking up it, are you *folle*?"

"*Folle*?" She raised an eyebrow.

"In French is mad," Marcus clarified.

"No, not mad. Eh, I realize how busy it is, but there's no other way of getting cakes to Oh Crumbs!."

"No, that is a problem." He stared at her intently.

She tucked into the meal. It was outstanding.

"I realize it will seem selfish. But I am so glad we have this conversation. I have wanted to speak with you for a long time, but you make good job of avoiding me. You know I was serious about the apprenticeship in my kitchen, don't you?"

She nodded. "Yes, Marcus, but can you keep a secret...? I want to go my own way." *Wow!* This was a step forward for her. She wouldn't have stood up for herself or divulged Sweet Secrets to anyone else like this before. "I've always had a dream of my own cake making company. But that was all it was, a dream until Rommy died. Even then I didn't know if I would be brave enough to carry my plans through."

"And let me guess. You sold your cakes to me and got an order and the rest is history."

"Yes, I suppose so."

He sighed. "It is my loss. But if you had say six months off and gave it a go, maybe you would change your mind about the direction to travel in. Training in a first class restaurant cannot be bought. If you are as good as I think you are, my restaurant and hotel would be your ticket to do whatever you wanted to do. Perhaps to travel the world."

"I don't think I'm that good." She nibbled a rocket leaf.

"I think you are and believe me I have seen enough aspiring chefs. I am happy to put you on the program." He laughed. "I am delighted to imprison Carrie Ann Jude."

Was there a hint of flirtatiousness in his voice? She couldn't tell with Marcus. It was part of his Gallic charm.

She shook her head. "No, my mind's made up. Besides things are almost off the ground now."

"And I don't suppose you'll talk about these things?"

"No, no, I won't. Not until I'm ready to make the launch."

"Make the launch. You know something, you've changed over the last few weeks, it's like a new and very exciting Carrie Ann. I'm so pleased. Your father was like a jailer."

She bristled at the memories. "It wasn't his fault. He wasn't well."

"We can all make excuses." He slapped the table. "Well I have lost and no Frenchman likes losing. Maybe." He winked at her. "I'll have to try again. Attractiveness and brains, I wonder why I didn't see it before."

"You're being silly."

He lounged back in his chair. "We'll see."

She glanced outside. A couple were playing tennis on one of the courts and a flight of ducks had just taken off from the lake. It would be a great place to work and he was right, the perks were tremendous. She must be crazy. However, Carrie Ann had a dream and before Rommy had been ill he would have said it was important to hold true to your dreams.

"I think you're pretty amazing. Now, shall we taste my trifle?"

She caught his eye. "I won't be kind. If I don't like it, I'll say so."

"You would be blunt with the maestro, you would make me angry. Make me into a crazy animal." He joked, jumping to his feet and dancing around her. Before she could stop him he grabbed her, planting a kiss on her mouth. "There I have done it. I have been aching to do that many weeks. I think I begin to thaw the ice maiden."

"Marcus. Don't be silly, don't play around."

"I am not. Did you not know? Everyone else seems to. I have liked you from the first second."

"Oh." Her spirits that had been riding so high on his praise suddenly fell flat as her old worries came creeping back—self-doubt, lack of confidence—was that the only reason he had taken her cakes and pastries? Because he fancied her? It was an infantile and silly thing to think. Marcus was a businessman after all. But she couldn't help it.

"Now I upset you. You think is that the only reason I take Carrie Ann's cakes?" He lightly pinched her cheek. "It is nonsense. Many women, and even men, want to get in the bed of Marcus de La Tour. I could have my pick. But I am not interested. You interest me because you are like refreshing wind that blows down the valley in the village where I come from in the Alps. It is a bracing wind, at other times warm and bringing the promise of summer. Yes, you have much promise. You are different to other women and more than that. It is as the great Latham said to me. That girl, what her name? Carrie Ann Jude, she have talent. I remember her name Jude, because he is saint of desperate causes."

"Thanks," Carrie Ann said not understanding either the broken English or the sense of the argument.

"I think she would be great addition to kitchen and life of Marcus de La Tour. I will wait, I will be patient. I will not give up and one day Carrie Ann Jude will be…how you say? Lady of The Manor."

She laughed as he turned his back to go to fetch the dessert from the cooler.

The trifle was a wonderful confection of layer upon layer of fresh fruit and sponge interlaced with a fine English custard. She let the flavors roll over her tongue. However, there was in her opinion a subtle nuance missing and she said so, "Perhaps a shot of elderberry cordial, or a layer of almond sponge?"

Marcus was amazed. He said her idea was exceedingly daring. In the end they ended up in the kitchen where they tried to make the trifle again. By now it was getting very late. Time had sped by and she had spent much longer at The Manor than she'd intended to. But the thought of having to return home and face Dominic filled her with trepidation.

Marcus ran her back in the car and dropped her outside her cottage. Dominic was in because the lights were on. So, she would have to front up. There was nothing for it.

"Hey," he shouted out to her from the kitchen. "I was worried to death about you so when I got back from town I popped into the bakery. Nina said she'd seen you heading up to the house with Marcus."

She nodded, coming to stand in the doorway.

"What the hell's the matter, Carrie Ann, you look dreadful?" He caught her around the waist, holding her tightly. "Oh shit, you're foots bandaged, what did you do? Are you all right?"

"Let me go, Dominic I'll explain later, I'm not in the mood."

"Why, why aren't you in the mood? You generally are." He shouldered his way through the door. "I got the stuff you wanted and picked up a few extra bargains. I think you'll be proud of my negotiating skills. Where do you want them?"

He stopped in his tracks when he saw her expression and clenched fists.

"Why didn't you tell me, Dom? Why didn't you tell me you had a girlfriend?"

"What's happened?" He opened his arms for her to walk into them. "What are you on about?"

"Alice, Ally whatever you call her. She turned up here on the doorstep. How the hell did she know where I lived?"

His face fell. "Oh, Christ, Ally." He looked genuinely nonplussed. "Come on, you can't possibly think there's anything in it."

"Is that all you've got to say. Oh! What I'd like to know is how she found out where you were. Don't play games with me, I'm not that dumb." She sank down at the kitchen table. "I ought to have guessed. I wondered why you were bothering with me. What was I, an interesting diversion?"

"Carrie Ann, don't be like this." He edged forward, coming to stand behind her so he could tease his fingers through her hair. "Honestly, you don't have anything to worry about."

"Don't I? How come she turns up here then? She must be very keen if she wants to see you that badly."

"So, you think there's something in it? Are you mad? My goodness, you are low in confidence aren't you? It's ages since I saw Ally. She's mad, she's always been mad. She could always find out where I was. She followed me everywhere—it was a bit like having a stalker. You know. I met her at this gig and I tried to shake her off, but I couldn't. I thought she'd given up, evidently she hasn't. Come on even you're not that daft. You must have realized what she's like."

"To be honest, I don't. She was very together, very pretty and she seemed keen on you."

"She can be like that. That's Ally. She's a good actress."

"And you expect me to believe that, do you? Isn't that what most men say?"

He spread his hands in a gesture of supplication. "It seems like you've made your mind up and whatever I say, it won't make any difference."

"I don't know what to think. Only that I've been foolish. I knew it was a bad idea falling for you in the first place." She frantically combed her fingers through her hair in frustration. "I should have stopped myself but it was so easy to give in to something I wanted and had never had." She glanced up at him tearfully. "Contrary to what you think of me though I'm not such a mess and I won't let anything destroy what I've worked for."

He sat down at the table. "Destroy what? I don't get it."

She pushed the piece of paper across the table. "Here you are. She's staying at The Angel and she wants to see you. You'd better go. She strikes me as a girl who won't take no for an answer."

"I don't want to go. But I suppose I'll have to. Then at least I can tell her again, in no uncertain words, that I've met someone else."

"Then you can pack your stuff," she carried on boldly, steamrollering over his words.

For a second his expression didn't change then he blinked at her. "You're not serious?"

"Yes, I am. Very serious. If I can't trust you, I don't see that we have a future together." She didn't know how she was finding the courage to say what she should have said ages ago, but if she acted quickly enough who knew, perhaps she could come out of this with some of her emotions intact. Yes, it was much better to end it now because the thought of how intense she might feel later on and what a wrench it would be then, didn't bear thinking about.

He put his hand over hers and she drew it back.

"It's not just about Ally is it? You're just grasping at anything to find an excuse to ruin this. It's because you're afraid of confronting your past and what went on with your husband. I felt this, felt it coming. You and I were like the proverbial house of cards. One day we would come toppling down."

"You'll stop at nothing to get what you want, will you?"

"No, I won't and I'll prove it to you," Dominic insisted.

She got to her feet and stood with her hands on her hips. "Mmm."

"You've got to let this go. When you liberate yourself, you'll free your creative muse. It'll make you free to create more wonderful things. Even bigger and better things."

"You know I wonder about you."

"Yes, and I wonder about you, Carrie Ann." He stroked the loose strands of hair out of her face. "I wonder how a beautiful woman like you can be so shell-shocked she's afraid to love again. I've been very patient, but I want to know what happened in that awful marriage so I can put it right."

Alarm bells began ringing, she shivered. "No one can put it right. It went too deep. That's why I can't talk about it and don't try to pull a veil over you and this Ally, whoever she is."

"Ally's irrelevant, why won't you listen? She means nothing to me, she never did. She's just a remnant from the past, we all have them."

For once she seemed to have gotten to him and Dominic was getting angry. "You know the problem here, Carrie Ann. You've never believed in us. From the start you were out to scupper this with every excuse you could find. Shall I tell you how it looks to me? It looks as if you're scared, scared to let loose and love, so you try to find every reason you can not to trust me despite my honesty — to stick the same label on me that this guy, this Rommy had. He treated you bad, crushed your confidence and you want to be able to say I'm the same. Well, I'm not and I won't give up, I'll just keep proving it to you. I won't let you cast this dark shadow over us all the time."

Her heart pounded, she was sure it had become one continual echo in her chest now, the beats were so close together. He was right, she was trying to scare him away, but the sense of relief she'd thought she would experience at the prospect of being free and on her own, now filled her with a horror so great, she didn't know what to say.

"I think I need time that's all. Time to work things through."

"No, Carrie Ann. That's not a good game to play. I'm not sure I just want to hang around until you decide love is right for you. For once I'm being selfish when I say, I want you now."

She glanced up sharply. He wasn't joking. She had never seen Dominic so serious.

"And one more thing, you took my ring off. Why did you do that? Are you ashamed of me? Well, you must be. Either that or you never took me seriously?"

"I..." She blushed. She had taken it off but only because she didn't want anyone to question her. The ring was after all, on her wedding finger.

"I have a feeling it will never be the right time for you, will it?" His expression had changed to one of abject defeat. "I want you to let the cat out of the bag and tell everybody around here about our...our relationship. It's not a dirty secret."

She blinked at him. She should have known Dominic would come around to this old argument again. He had constantly gone on about it. She knew she ought to be pleased. If he was fooling about and using her as a distraction, he would hardly want Puddleford to see them as an item, would he? She cursed her lack of confidence. She was probably being far too juvenile, but she couldn't help it. It was down to Rommy, it was all his fault and yet...yet. She had read the self-help book Nina had bought her time and time again and it had said about apportioning blame. That she couldn't do that, couldn't shift the blame onto someone else, because when it came down to it, the real reason she was acting in the way she was, was because the issue rested with her not being able to face up to her own inner demons. She must seem weak to him. "I'm not a superwoman. I don't have all those strengths women in books have, Dominic."

"I don't want you to be a superwoman. I simply want you to let go and decide to move on. I have."

"It doesn't matter. It shouldn't have gone this far."

"You're being impossible."

"No, no I'm not." She peered at him. "Please don't make this any harder."

He stood up and wandered to the door before turning. "I get it. I saw you with Marcus, so that's how it is, is it? You've set your sights a bit higher, have you?"

"And what's that supposed to mean? Now you're being childish."

"I'm childish, am I? When Marcus has got his eye on your French Fancies or whatever."

Had it of been at any other time, Carrie Ann would have burst out laughing it was so ridiculous. What had happened was so huge though, she couldn't properly take it in. She didn't have the energy to argue as she struggled to her feet. Her leg was throbbing. It wasn't worth telling him what had happened. He would only lecture her about the dangers of the lane.

"Okay, I realize when I'm beat." He bounded upstairs.

Five minutes later, she heard him slam the front door.

Evidently he was going to see Ally. She made herself a cup of tea. She had no appetite for the supper he had laid out. Then she took a couple of aspirin and decided to have an early night. She was tired and numb as she pulled the duvet up to her neck. She'd had to do it hadn't she? There was no other way.

Much later the front door clicked and through her open door she could see the light on beneath his. A while later he came in and sat on the edge of the bed. "Here, I warmed you up a glass of milk." He stroked her hair out of her face. "I realize you didn't mean any of those things you said earlier, it was just anger."

Did he have to be so nice all the time, so understanding? It just reaffirmed to her how impossible things were. Basically he was far too nice a guy for her, a girl with a dark stain on her life, one she couldn't seem to wash away. She took the cup and sat up as he switched on the bedside lamp. His expression was stony.

"Listen, Carrie Ann, I'm sorry. We seem to be at a kind of stalemate, but it shouldn't pull us apart."

"It has though, hasn't it?"

He was silent a moment. "Like you said before, this isn't a book, this is real life. In real life you find solutions that are practical and not simply romantic dross."

She wished he wouldn't do that, study her lips as if he was considering kissing her. She knew she wouldn't be able to resist. Even as he bent over her and reached beneath the sheet to cradle her breast, she gave in, and after pushing the plate aside she arched her body up toward him, seeking, needing solace. They came together so easily. For now she would concentrate on his hands, moving and guiding her toward the familiar dipping and soaring as the crescents of ecstasy ebbed and flowed. Love made it easy to forget, which was why she supposed they said love was a drug. He pushed her back and she dissolved into the rhythmic dance of sex. Neither of them said a word it was enough to just let their emotions find vent through a meeting of flesh on flesh.

* * *

When she woke up in the morning, he had already left to finish the baking at Oh Crumbs!. She stretched and made herself a cup of coffee, the thought of what had happened yesterday hanging over her like a black cloud. They'd had fantastic sex, but it felt like she had the weight of the world on her shoulders.

She knew the event was going to be a stunning success as she stared at a plate of the savories that were laid out on the table. It seemed that she and Dominic had even more in common, notably their attention to detail. She felt a sense of pride that things had turned out exactly as the client wanted, the themes carrying through both pastries and savories, all the ingredient choices overlapping so there was a common theme of herbal infusion in both the sweets and savories. Perhaps it was best if she didn't try to think too much about what she was doing with the task at hand. It was a simple menu, but all chefs knew the simplest things were the hardest to pull off successfully because they had to be flawless. The fruit cups had a perfect swirl of limoncello and mascarpone running through them and the rum infused homemade sponge fingers echoed the delightful cake arrangement, the crowning glory that was the centrepiece – the Genoese and Victoria sandwich cake. It was a stroke of genius.

She added the final few flourishes, carefully applying melted sugar to anchor the sugar basket onto the main cake. She loved the magic of working in spun sugar and seeing what textures and shapes she could pull off. The main cage was mirrored in small cakes with tiny baskets, each one containing a little miniature figure for the bondage theme the Sleights wanted. She sat down with a sigh. Everything was done. Now all she had to do was package the cakes ready for Nina to arrive to pick up the precious cargo. She was lending Carrie Ann the use of the van from Oh Crumbs!. She didn't know what she would do without her friend.

"It looks like you're going to have to come out of the closet completely with Sweet Secrets," Nina pointed out when she came to pick Carrie Ann up a bit later on. "We have a genius working for us, so it's bound to get out."

"If you've told anyone, I'll kill you," she groaned.

"What, *moi*? Come on it's not that hard to figure out."

For once Carrie Ann didn't argue about it. What was the point? Anyway it hardly mattered. People kept coming into the shop and asking her for pricelists. It was amazing how these things spread with word of mouth. That wasn't her biggest worry. It was Dominic now who dominated her thoughts.

"Can I look?" Nina asked as Carrie Ann loaded the boxes into the van. "Just a peep."

She lifted a lid.

"Ooh." Her eyes were round. "Goodness, it amazes me. You truly are a genius. You know what Marcus is saying?"

"No, what is Marcus saying?"

"That you have the makings of a Michelin starred chef."

"Pull the other one." Carrie Ann laughed.

"No, I'm telling you the truth. He says it's easy to make a brilliant looking cake, but not one with the taste as well." She looked skyward as she attempted to mimic the chef. "Now what little gem did he come out with, ah, I remember. He said, 'a fabulous looking pastry that fails to deliver on taste, is like ze woman with fur coat and no knickers'."

"I don't want to be a Michelin starred chef, thanks." Carrie Ann groaned. "I'll just be happy if I can have fun and make a living with Sweet Secrets."

"Well, it certainly looks like that's going to happen. Your client's bound to be impressed." Nina jangled her keys. "Where exactly are we going? Other side of town isn't it?"

"Yes, through the new estate to that select new development. They're having the reception at home."

"Goodie." Nina leaped into the driver's seat. "It makes a change from serving rolls," she said through the open car window. "Where's the boy wonder?"

Carrie Ann frowned. "I suppose you mean Dominic?" That was a point. They had seemed to reach a truce last night, but he had been lost in thought all morning and when Carrie Ann had tried to find him earlier he'd seemed to have vanished. "I don't know."

"He packed things up at Oh Crumbs! and left the kitchen like a new pin. Cleaned the counters down and everything. It was spotless."

"That's Dominic, he's very particular."

Nina watched Carrie Ann as she slid onto the seat. "So, he's not joining us on our escapade? I rather fancied feasting my attention on him."

"No, it doesn't look like it, does it?" Tight-lipped, Carrie Ann stared out of the window. She couldn't focus on anything much when she had an order. Besides it was too worrying contemplating her feelings about Dominic. She'd think about it tomorrow.

"Did you hear about Samantha and Raphe?" Nina stated, deftly changing the subject.

"Samantha?" For a second it didn't dawn on Carrie Ann who Nina was on about. Then the penny dropped. She'd indirectly met Samantha last year when the ex-model had been on a whirlwind visit to England from the States where she had been living at the time. She had been inviting tenders for her birthday cake from local suppliers. Raphe, her fiancé and one time top goal scorer for one of the major teams was keen to support local business and was fanatical about preserving their pretty little enclave. He had already fought a vehement protest about the new bypass and won that, and was now in the process of setting up a new training center for young football talent.

Carrie Ann had not been able to resist putting in a tender and she had gotten a formal typed note back with a few lines scribbled on the bottom. It had been rude in her opinion and made out she was too much of a novice to even be considered. It seemed Samantha's reputation, which was not good, preceded her and she was 'a right cow', as Nina put it. A self-confessed WAG, she now lived permanently up at The Pines, Raphe's footballers retreat the other side of Puddleford. Because it was behind tall gates no one saw the occupants who lived in a state of secrecy.

The fact Raphe had chosen to live near Puddleford was another one of its claims to fame, and Ms Bunting and Nina often joked about it in the bakery. He had apparently bought it as a retirement pad because he was thinking of giving up the football and going into farming. No one knew much about Samantha other than that she'd once been a page three model and roamed the world and had a terrible temper to boot. Quite what bad boy Raphe saw in her no one could guess. Inflated boobs, Carrie Ann speculated uncharitably. That was what most men went for wasn't it? Botoxed lips, blonde hair.

"Earth to Carrie Ann." Nina nudged her before putting her foot down. "They buy your bread. You ought to be interested in them. Their Thai housekeeper is always in Oh Crumbs!. I bet the paparazzi don't know she has a partiality for your buns."

"Are you trying to be funny?" Carrie Ann asked, crossing her arms defensively.

"No. Well yes. Someone needs to try and cheer you up. You old misery guts."

"What, what is it with them. More scandal?"

"That's not fair."

"No, well I don't like people like that, they give the village a bad name."

"No, they don't, what's got into you?" Nina grumbled.

Carrie Ann shrugged.

"They're getting married."

Carrie Ann glared at her. "As if I should be interested in that? Good luck to them."

"I would have thought you'd be all over it, since that other French cheese..." Nina grinned at her and her own sense of wordy cleverness. "Monsieur Jacque Forrest, whoever he is, is doing their cakes. If you'd played your cards right and angled for it, you might have got an invite up the The Pines."

"You're talking nonsense as usual." Carrie Ann wriggled her feet. "Why would they invite me to their bash?"

"Why?" Nina chortled. "Because you're up and coming local business talent and Raphe would be ecstatic to have that kind of coup."

They were approaching the outskirts of town and Carrie Ann's heart picked up its tempo. Whenever she came out of her comfort zone of Puddleford, she was still panicky, although she knew she was beating her phobia. Especially since... A sharp dagger of pain sliced at her heart. Dominic. *Get a grip, Carrie Ann. You're imagining this feeling of panic. Do you realize that could be half your trouble, imagining things?* That made her think of the argument. Maybe, she'd been a bit rash and there was nothing between him and Ally after all. No, she must be more stoic and stand her ground on this. She would be better off out of it anyway. There was no point going over old ground. She was heading for the inevitable fall.

"I don't think it's only the Thai maid who's partial. Quite a few of those chocolate and mint things with the frozen raspberries seem to go back to The Pines." Nina nudged Carrie Ann again. "Think if you had got an invite you would have got to meet Forrest. Or do you still only have eyes for naughty Latham?"

"I'm over that," she said. "It was a childish infatuation."

"Which means someone sensible has taken his place." Nina winked at her. "That wouldn't be Dominic, would it?"

Carrie Ann bit her lip.

"I thought as much. The last few days both of you have been going round with long faces. So, what's the story?"

She stared hard at her. "Aren't you going to lecture me over dating a guy half my age?"

"No." Nina was concentrating as they drew up to a set of traffic lights. "Why should I say that? We don't live in the Middle Ages. It's just obvious you like him. You changed when he turned up. Everyone has guessed you fancy him like crazy, so if you were thinking of keeping it a secret...?"

"Great. That's all I need."

"Lucky you, you mean."

They turned left at the supermarket and began down the long road into the estate. Carrie Ann yawned.

"So, what, does he get a cut of the profits or perks?"

"I hate your filthy sense of humor," she snapped. "Shut up will you, or I'll clock you one."

"Feisty," Nina quipped.

"No I'm not. I just don't want you to go on about it. It's practically over, finished. We had a major row."

"What's new? Most couples have rows."

"Not like this. I lied to him, like big time." She gripped her seat and thoughtfully considered the sat nav, as they pulled into Howarth Close. It was one of those estates where none of the house numbers made sense.

Carrie Ann looked straight ahead. She didn't know why she had picked this moment to come clean.

Nina rested on the steering wheel. "Right, what's the problem? We all tell white lies."

"No, it was larger than that. And that's not all." She sat back, pressing her palms to her temples. "I can't talk about it. It's way too complicated."

"I think that's the very thing you should do, talk about it." Nina squeezed Carrie Ann's hand. "Look, I'll help you with this and then you can maybe tell me on the way back. Okay?"

"Okay," she said glumly. But Carrie Ann felt nowhere near ready enough to tell her friend everything, at least not just yet.

Chapter Thirteen

He was gone. She couldn't believe it, but he was. As soon as she walked through the door, the cottage had the feeling that all vacated properties had. She could sense it. Nonetheless she shouted, "Dominic. Dominic are you there, I'm back." When she got upstairs it was to find his wardrobe empty and his rucksack gone. He had left his toothbrush in the bathroom, though, a niggle, a small reminder of possibilities.

She felt a bit numb, even though she was riding high on the success of the afternoon. The catering had gone down a storm, her client in tears of excitement as Jayne Sleight tore about, shouting how wow, simply wow it was. And for her mother and bridesmaid to come and take a look.

Carrie Ann had as a result, gotten a massive tip and the promise of more work. She sank down on the couch in the conservatory, tucking her legs beneath her. She was worn out as the tears trickled down her cheeks. Well, Dominic up and leaving like this was hardly a surprise since, as she had kept telling herself, she had known it wasn't going to last. She had set her sights way too high. She was simple, plain Carrie Ann Jude and the only reliable thing about her life was her work and fantasies. She would get over it. She was much better off without a man. She would be married to her work, that was much safer. Yes, that was the answer. Work was something she had a grip on, something she knew, understood and could control. Before long, exhausted, she drifted into a deep sleep, slipping over the borderline into her fantasies of Latham. At least he was safe. She could manipulate Latham in her dreams. He was at her mercy. She smiled to herself. That thought actually gave her a thrill as she snuggled down and prepared to enter her private world.

* * * *

She is busily piping icing onto cakes in Latham's kitchen.

"Carrie Ann, I told you, you must finish those cakes or you won't be allowed home." Latham stands with his back pressed against the door. There is an evil glitter to his eyes and a twitch to his kissable lips.

She quivers and the tip of her piping bag slips so the icing slithers out like a long snake all over the table. Latham pounces. He snatches the piping bag out of her hand and presses her against the table, his cock sandwiched between her legs. Does he know she has nothing on beneath her dress and catering apron? She never wears knickers in Latham's kitchen now, not since he asked her not to, because it gives him an erotic kick. Her body becomes liquid.

"You know where I want to pipe that?" His lips close to her ear, she quivers as he lifts her apron and skirt and caresses her buttocks.

She thrusts forward and feels the nozzle of the piping bag guided by his other hand pressed into sensitive places, the warmly oozing icing heightening her libido. Latham is strong and muscular and he lifts her in one easy movement onto the table. Her legs dangle off the edge, as he tugs at his buttons. Underneath his chef's whites he has on a T-shirt he proceeds to rip off.

"I like a bit of danger don't you?" he murmurs in her ear and his breath makes her body erupt in goosebumps.

"What if..." she stammers. "What if?"

"What if what? Someone walks in, the world explodes...which in a second, I think it will."

It would not be the first time Latham was caught fucking. She hardly ever thinks that word let alone says it. But now it fills her with filthy possibilities.

"F...f...f...fuck me," she stutters. The words are deliciously naughty.

Latham laughs. "I intend to."

Dirty monster, *she thinks as he inserts the piping bag farther and maneuvers it as far inside her as he can. It is plump and squidgy and she is so wet and ready it slides in easily, much too easily, which makes her wonder what kind of woman she really is. She clamps her thighs together to hold it in place. It is kind of culinary bondage, a game she has played with him many times. Once, Latham forced her into the cooler and they had a kinky sex session that was all the more thrilling as the temperature dropped. There had been something super sexy about the ice cold droplets mingled with the contrast of their red hot tingling skin and fluids.*

When finally, her leg muscles protest and she can't bear it any longer, he edges the bag in even farther and the sweet sticky confection as it slips everywhere, surpasses her wildest erotic dream. He moves the bag around so the nozzle rubs her clit and she is ready to explode already. She wriggles her bottom on the service table. Service that about says it all.

"I...I..." Why won't any of her words come out?

She can see the bulge under his chef's trousers. He tugs at the ties and his pants slither down his hips and pool around his feet, leaving him naked. She only has a moment to savor his penis at full mast as she wonders how it will feel sliding into her icing-lubricated tunnel. He squeezes the piping bag. Soft and warm, it collapses inward, expelling its cargo of vanilla scented sweetness.

"I'll get my revenge," she croaks. "I'll plaster you in chili paste. The hot one you put in that new chocolate."

"You will, will you? I don't think you ought to have said that, Carrie Ann. Never let the enemy know your intentions." Just to make his point he gives the by now limp bag a final squeeze before rotating it. She is oozing, but she doesn't care as Latham gets down on his knees and licks her thighs and her swollen flesh while she stares at the top of his head. The bobbing motion makes her more turned-on, especially as she feels his tongue sliding in and moving around her labia. She wants to flop back on the table but there isn't much room. In desperation she has to, and her back slides against the floured surface as a bowl clangs to the floor. Latham laughs. Standing up, he holds his cock in one hand while he teases the tip with more icing, to lube it up. This dream is so filthy she hopes it doesn't stop right at the vital second like it normally does.

"You're going too fast." She tries to look coquettish, as she twirls her fingers through her hair. Her body, though, is vibrating and crying out for passion. As her body warms, the icing becomes more liquid, more sexy. She wonders if later on he might insert a hard plug of sugar paste like he did the other day. Then he could spend ages using his lips and tongue to pull it out.

"Ooh...ahh..." she groans as he grabs her and moves her legs so he can slide in. Then he begins to do the Latham dance as he grips her, her body jouncing back and forth. Latham, she has discovered, has immense creativity and staying power. He can keep pumping with metronomic insistency for well over ten minutes, lulling her into a soporific state with his smooth seduction before he begins pounding away. His thrusting makes the table shake and as he moves in deeper he grabs her breasts and squeezes and massages them, pinching the delicate nubs with his fingers.

Her tentative ripples of pleasure become tidal waves of euphoria. It's amazing how the sensations pile up one on top of the other and her control melts away to be replaced by animal fever. Sex with Latham is like a terrific cake recipe. He adds the ingredients one by one – sugar to sweeten, a good beating to amalgamate, then some folding in, of something especially fruity to finish things off. After she has shrieked and cried out, stirred by his orgiastic feast to an incredible orgasm that seems to go on and on, he stays inside, pushing against her until her last spasms resolve. Eyes closed, she floats on a wave of bliss, wondering how she will be able to clean up so much icing before someone comes in. This is not the first time they have consummated their passion amongst the kitchen paraphernalia. On more than one occasion she has ended up on the floor, subjected to the mercies of egg whisks and wooden spoons. Her eyelids slowly open. Why does this dream seem different to the rest? Something is wrong. Dominic has come into the room and is watching their kinky sex. He flicks a pinch of icing out of a bowl onto her nose and kisses it away even as Latham begins seducing her again.

* * * *

She woke with a start, feeling on the one hand remarkably turned-on and on the other bereft. Something was different. It was then she realized Dominic was gone, or was he? She ought to have been thankful for Latham waking her though. She turned her head and jumped up. Yes, she had heard a sound, a person creeping up the stairs. She pushed open the bedroom door to see Dominic opening his bedside drawer.

"Dominic, you scared me."

"I forgot a couple of things," he said coldly. "Plus I just wanted to know. Did everything go okay? Did she like it?"

"Better than okay, it was brilliant and she loved it. I couldn't have done it without you."

He turned to look at her. "You know, things wouldn't have seemed half so bad if you hadn't wanted to keep me a secret. I thought about it on the way back with Ally and I realize you couldn't have taken us seriously if you wanted to hide me away."

"You took Ally back? Back where?" Her fists clenched at her sides, her mind still fogged by the erotic dream. "Everyone seems to have guessed anyway, so it doesn't matter, does it?"

"Yeah, maybe they have. But that's not the same as saying it out loud. It was like I was your dirty secret."

"You aren't, don't be silly. You're my sweet secret."

"Very clever, Carrie Ann. But I know you're a genius."

He went to push past her, but she put out her hand to stop him. "Don't go, Dominic, I've been doing some thinking too and I realize it's time I came clean on a thing or two."

"You've been saying that for a long time. It's always been a case of, I'll tell you tomorrow or next week and it never happens. This thing that's between us, is killing us. Don't you see, it's all adding up to create a recipe for disaster."

She swallowed. It was now or never. Her mouth seemed to be acting independently of her mind. Only this morning she had been congratulating herself she was doing the right thing, now for some reason the thought of him leaving filled her with panic.

"This time...this time, I promise."

"No, Carrie Ann, I don't think so."

His mouth was tight and she couldn't force him to look at her as he went to push his way past, pausing to place his hand on her cheek. There were tears in his eyes.

Well, at least he was not totally unaffected.

"Can't we?" she stuttered. "Can't we?"

"I think you'll agree, this has got into too much of a mess."

She stood at the top of the stairs wringing her hands as he walked down. "But, you can't go, Dom. You said you loved me."

"I do love you, Carrie Ann. Look." He turned around. "I think we ought to at least take a break from one another."

"And what does that mean?" It was like her insides were melting. She had read about relationship breaks and it was as good as the end. It meant the other person was uncertain and needed to spread their wings, in her opinion often into other relationships. So he couldn't make his mind up now between her and Ally, could he? It made her want to pound him to a pulp with her fists.

"If you loved me, you'd have wanted to tell the world about me long before now, wouldn't you?"

Chapter Fourteen

She had lots of plans, Carrie Ann thought one morning when she was half way through the shortbread batch at Oh Crumbs!. In cake making it was important to think ahead to Christmas and even further afield to Valentine's day and Easter. She had fought hard to keep Dominic out of her head but each day was a fresh challenge. Sometimes she woke up in the middle of the night expecting to feel him curled up against her with his arm around her, but despite the warm summer nights, the bed was surprisingly cold and empty.

There was only one thing to do and that was immerse herself in her work and there was plenty to do now that the sheds were completed. The new ovens and coolers meant she could produce lots more food and she had decided to take out an expensive advertisement in *Cake Maker's World*, not that she needed it. She was getting loads of commissions. It was just that now she thought she ought to follow through on what Casper had told her, about pushing herself. One thing was for sure after the success of the catering event, she began to wonder if she had overlooked an important opportunity. She was no good at savories and Dominic was. Maybe—although it was a bit soon to consider it—she should think of diversifying at some point and taking on that much needed assistant. There was no shortage of the good local produce that she, like Marcus, favored and which she could add to her repertoire. There were loads of herbs in the garden and a supplier of good local cheeses just down the road that The Manor used.

"Hey." Nina poked her head around the door, there was a wry twist to her lips. "There's someone to see you in the shop. You'd better gird your loins."

Carrie Ann continued manipulating the pastry. Ms Bunting had roped her in to help with an order for a huge tray of shortbread with salted caramel topping and two more dozen seeded loaves for the stall at the local market that she ran on Saturday. She hesitated for a moment. What was it Dominic had said about her hands—that they were soft and sensual? Caught out again, she couldn't stop thinking about him and it was agonizing. It was almost as if he were right there stroking her skin, his seductive voice whispering to her. Heart racing, she blushed and her spirits sank. She wished she could stop thinking about him—he obviously didn't want anything to do with her because if he had he would have come back. She had eaten her pride several times and texted him. But he had ignored her. That hurt worse than anything.

"Who is it? Can't you ask them to come back later, when I'm not so..." She viciously pummeled then leaned her weight against the rolling pin. "Tied up."

"I don't think so, he's so insistent. Look, get that flour off your hands and come out will you."

She sighed. For Nina to call her like this it had to be important.

When she walked out into the shop she stopped in her tracks, her hand flying to cover her mouth. "My God." It was none other than Raphe and he was here standing in Oh Crumbs! not that they hadn't had other famous people in the bakery of course.

He pushed his hands in the pockets of his jeans and grinned at her. "Thank goodness. I need you."

Carrie Ann's gaze wavered back and forth. She didn't know why coming from him that sounded so sexy, or maybe she did. Raphe had had a daring reputation in his prime.

"Yes, here's the very person," Nina said. "The county's finest and best kept secret." She shot her a glance as she brushed by. "If you need to talk business, you can use the café."

Carrie Ann's jaw dropped. Raphe was even more handsome in the flesh than she'd imagined. He came forward and leaned against the counter. "I'm sorry to shock you and I guess it must be a shock, but I'm here to ask for your help."

"But I…"

He gestured through the doorway. "Look can we go in and sit down and then you can hear me out, see what I have to say, before you say no?"

"Sure." She wiped her hands on her apron and Raphe burst out laughing. "Go in for a new line in cosmetics do you?" Bending forward he brushed a smudge of flour off her nose. "There, that's much better."

Despite his flirty manner and what she'd heard about him, she liked Raphe instantly. He was open and friendly and not like his interviews made him out to be.

"I'm here on a mission on behalf of Samantha, my soon to be other half. You must have heard about her and our plans?"

"Yes," Carrie Ann mumbled. "A bit." Since Nina had mentioned Samantha she had found out more about her and it was an interesting story. Raphe had chased Samantha half way across the world to win her affections. An American socialite, her family had been against the liaison, but Raphe had been determined to trap her. He had won her with his romantic gestures, and she had defied her parents once again, like she had over her modeling, to leave the States and come and live with him. It was like a romance novel in the best tradition.

"We're due to get married next week. I expect you know that as well. A smallish do at our place. It's what she wanted."

She raised her eyebrow.

"Yep, I realize what you're thinking. Folks judge Sam, but it's an act. If you knew her you would know that her bark is worse than her bite. Anyway, as I say, it's going to be a small wedding by celebrity standards, but she wanted things just so. We're having it themed. 1890s Paris. It's a secret, by the way. She'd go nuts if anyone found out. The paparazzi have been hounding us ever since they knew we were getting hitched."

Carrie Ann nodded mutely as she wondered where this was going.

"Samantha saw that wonderful cake you made for Miranda, you know the peach one done in those amazing colors. She said it was fab, reminded her of a tequila sunrise."

"Mmm." She mumbled, resisting the temptation to blurt out, 'That's not what she said last year'.

However, Raphe was nervously fiddling with his cufflinks as he marched on, "She dithered over asking you in the first place and then she decided that because she wanted the desserts to match the cakes, it would be too big a project for a small baker so she went for that dork, Forrest. I guess he piled it on." Raphe sighed. "Samantha's a sucker for the latest society hotshot and he doesn't pass up an opportunity to have another hot catering notch on his bedpost."

"Pardon."

"He likes to store up celebrity victories for his portfolio. He's so jealous he can't bear any of his competitors snatching one away from under his nose."

Carrie Ann bent forward. "I don't mean to be rude, but I don't have too much time. I have to get the bakes in the oven."

"Of course, I realize you still work here part-time. I'm sorry. I'll cut to the chase. Samantha has lost him, it's a bit of a disaster and it's too short notice to go too far afield. We wondered if...we wondered if you would consider doing it, Carrie Ann. I know it's last minute and it would be a terrific amount of work, but if you could see how cut up Samantha is over all this."

"I..." She was dumbfounded. "I mean, this has come rather out of the blue."

"Sure I realize that. That's why I think it's best if you talk to Samantha. I'm sort of the advance guard because she felt bad about turning you down like that, last year. Actually, she didn't know I was coming here, although if you call her she will." He seemed thoughtful and there was a gleam in his eye. "She can be a wildcat, but I have a hunch she wanted me to come and sound you out." He scribbled something on a napkin. "Here's her mobile phone number. If you could give her a call, we'll take it from there."

He stood up, holding out his hand. "Pleased to meet you, and don't write things off. I think if you knew Samantha you'd see..." He was stammering along uncertainly. "I'm making a hash of this. But I know you've not had it easy, have you, and neither has Sam? You have quite a bit in common, you might even like one another." He leaned across the table. "Don't worry about the catering. I've got the catering covered. It's the cake Samantha's wound up about. That was the centerpiece for the whole theme. Everything was constructed around it."

She wasn't stupid and Carrie Ann knew what this could mean. The publicity from the event would be huge. From the point of media attention it surpassed her wildest dreams. She clasped his proffered hand. It was like being in a mental fog. She followed him out of the shop.

Raphe turned at the door. "Eh, I almost forgot. You're making your name aren't you? People say you have this great talent. Well, I realize the importance of publicity and this could be a great move for you. We have this media thing surrounding the wedding and they want to showcase the theme. It would give you a massive push in your career." He gave her a wink. "Anyway I'll leave it with you."

Just as she thought. She stared as he walked out to his car. She still couldn't believe it. When Nina patted her on the shoulder she jumped.

"Well aren't you the hotshot. Hobnobbing with the WAG fraternity."

"Get off." She shrugged off Nina's hand. She felt so anxious she didn't mean to snap but couldn't help it.

"It's true. How many more people are you going to enchant. First it's Marcus and now it's gorgeous Raphe. Mr Sex on Legs."

"I hate you," Carrie Ann croaked, flapping her hand, then sat down hard on a chair. "I think I need a strong coffee." It was surreal, Raphe approaching her like that. She bet she knew the real reason. Samantha wanted the cake done in superfast time and no professional bakery would take that on. She must think she would be a mug to agree to it.

"I'll get you one, then you can let me have the details."

"Can you share?" Nina asked, when she came back with the coffees. "Or is it all secret service stuff?"

"They had a disaster and their cake maker can't fulfill. Raphe seems to think Samantha wants me to do it."

"Wow don't that beat everything." Nina sat fiddling with a teaspoon and twirling it in her fingers. Then she said slowly, "That's bloody unbelievable. You realize in a month or two you could make your name with that kind of thing. Soon you're going to be too grand for Oh Crumbs!." She pulled her lips down in a mock expression of disgust. "Soon we will be on our hands and knees begging you for your cakes and buns."

"Don't be so soft." Carrie Ann slapped her lightly with a napkin. "I'll be working for Oh Crumbs! when I'm ninety."

"That's what all the mighty social climbers have said and then, tis a sad thing…but they are overwhelmed by the bright lights and off they go. You'll be decorating cakes for the rich and famous in Beverley Hills."

"Rubbish."

"Don't let Marcus hear you say that. He's determined you will." Nina stirred her coffee. "So, honeybun, what are you going to do? You're not going to toss the idea are you? Not even before you hear what she has to say. I'd love to see her groveling, she's apparently such a bitch."

"I don't know if I want to confront her. Can you imagine what she'd be like to work with? A nightmare."

"And what if she's not. I mean you haven't met her have you, and neither have I, come to that?"

"No, she's too up herself to shop personally in Oh Crumbs! isn't she?" Carrie Ann was flushed and becoming hotter with excitement by the second.

"My, my, has the boyfriend got you in a spin."

She glared then she pushed her cup away. "Dominic wasn't my boyfriend. He just left. We both knew he would sooner or later."

Nina's mouth fell open. "Oh dear, so he has gone. I did wonder, but I couldn't believe it. He was so into you. What happened?"

"Nothing, we, well, you know. Nina do we have to talk about it please, it really hurts?"

"But you seemed to get on so well together. He seemed mad on you."

Carrie Ann realized she was through with lying, as much as she kept putting it off. She was being cowardly and it had caused so many problems. Today would be a landmark, she would tell Nina the truth. "He wanted me to be more open about our relationship for one thing."

"But you were, weren't you?"

"No, that's the point. He wanted me to tell everybody and I wouldn't."

"Eh, eh, I see." Nina blinked at her. "Yes, men can be touchy creatures but surely he understood. I mean you've told him about your insecurity issues haven't you?"

"No." She screwed her eyes tightly shut and ground out the words. "Oh, God, it's all so awful it hurts to say it. I lied, which was why I didn't want anyone talking to him. I sort of backed myself into a corner."

"But why the hell did you do that?"

She paused. "Because it was easy and I just did." She shook her head angrily. "It simply happened. It's so easy for you isn't it? You've had boyfriends. Well, when I met him I thought it was a bit of a laugh, a bit of a flirtation. I didn't think for a second he'd want to see me when we got back. So, I lied. It seemed pathetic to tell him about Rommy. No one would believe how a father could dominate you like that. I didn't want to look an idiot or have him feel sorry for me."

"But why do it. What came over you?"

"It was the end of a holiday and a bit of a joke. I wasn't thinking straight and then it was too late. I thought." She hesitated. "I thought, when I got to know him, that then I would tell him. But picking the right time was harder than I reckoned and it never came along."

The room was silent. Nina glared at her. "You ninny. You meet this great guy who evidently thinks the world of you and can actually cook, and you throw him away."

"I did not throw him away. There's more if you must know but it's too long a story for now."

"God, is it? I'd like to hear this story," Nina said with interest.

Carrie Ann searched in her pocket. She'd forgotten about the ring and now her fingers closed around it. She took it out and put it on the table. "He bought me this and I took it off. I realize it was the wrong thing to do. At the time I thought it was a joke and he was just winding me up, but..." She chewed her lip. "It wasn't." She slid it back on her finger. It was right being there.

"I should think so. Are you nuts, Carrie Ann Jude? No, don't answer that, you are nuts."

"Then she turned up. This girl called Ally and he wouldn't tell me anything about her. It was obvious they knew one another."

"Carrie Ann," Nina wailed. "It could have meant anything. Surely you talked about it?"

"No. We had this awful row. It's all right for you. It's not as if I have boyfriends crawling out of the woodwork is it? How would you have liked it, if an old girlfriend of Robert's turned up on your doorstep?"

"That wouldn't happen," Nina said, shocked at her friend's outburst.

"No, but if it did, you wouldn't be so magnanimous."

Nina turned her cup around slowly, she always did that when she was thinking. "I still think there's more in it. I think he'll come back."

Chapter Fifteen

It took her a day to muster up the courage to call Samantha. Any person getting a new business off the ground would have to be crazy to turn down a publicity venture like this. Carrie Ann chewed on a nail. It was at times like this that her nerves came back to haunt her. How would she cope with a personality like the infamous Samantha? Well, it would take all her courage, but she would have to bite her lip and see what the ex-model had to say. Her hand hovered over the buttons on her keypad. In the end she took a deep breath. There was one thing she would not be and that was beaten. She punched in the numbers, hoping Samantha wouldn't answer and almost dropped it when she picked up.

"Oh hi, hi, this is Carrie Ann Jude."

"Thank God, my fingers were itching," Samantha replied. "Raphe, bless him, told me what he'd done…but I thought no way, he wouldn't have snuck off and talked to you, that's just, well…" There was a vulnerable edge to her voice. "Look could you come to The Pines to talk things over? I would come over there, but I'm up to my neck in the prep for the wedding and I have the dress maker arriving, I think that's her at the door right now…to alter one of the costumes."

"Sure." Carrie Ann was wondering how she'd walk all the way to The Pines. It was half way up the hill and right on the other side of Puddleford, practically in the town of Weston. Not driving had its disadvantages. She could take the bike out of the garage, but she was a bit nervous since the accident.

"Um."

"I'll send you a cab," Samantha leaped in. "I wouldn't dream of you being out of pocket and The Pines is so hellish to find. The local cab company know where we are. They should be with you in about…let me see…half an hour."

"Well, I… Half an hour's…"

"Good settled."

"Well…I…"

It seemed Samantha seemed to intuit exactly what she was about to say.

"I suppose."

"Good, I can't wait to see you, Carrie Ann." Before she could say anything else the call ended, the line went dead and Carrie Ann was left staring at her handset. She hadn't given Samantha her address so would she know where she lived? She supposed Samantha knew everything.

Carrie Ann dashed upstairs and pulled some clothes out of the wardrobe. What did she wear to a meeting with a woman that had been on the cover of nearly every glossy magazine in the world? She nibbled her lip. She didn't have much choice. She took out the velvet dress. It was the only decent thing she possessed so she slipped into it. Then she pulled a comb through her riotous curls and put a slash of nude lipstick over her lips. That would have to do. She was about finished when the cab pulled up outside and she had to snatch up her handbag and notebook. She sat like a statue on the ride, her knees pressed together and her heart pounding. This was such a big deal and Samantha and Raphe were so famous.

The Pines was even more imposing than she'd imagined. Tudor black and white beamed, it looked the archetypal country house and was in a glorious position within the edge of the pinewoods that looked down the hill toward the river. She knew what the interior looked like since it had been featured only a few months ago in *Interiors*. Apparently, it was incredible. All white and cream and very high-tech. Thankfully the door opened as she came up the steps.

Her eyes widened. So this was Samantha. Well, at least she didn't look as immaculate as she'd thought she would. Her long blonde hair was pulled back in an elastic band, she had no makeup on and was wearing a loose, rather grubby blue tracksuit. She did, Carrie Ann thought, also look pale.

"Thank you for coming. I thought you wouldn't."

She seemed uncertain of herself Carrie Ann was pleased to say.

"Forgive the outfit, it's what I use to pig out in, in front of the TV." She swept through the house leaving a trail of expensive perfume behind her.

Carrie Ann's throat was dry. A lot hinged on this. Samantha was known to be volatile. Up one minute and down the next.

"Anyway great to meet you again."

"My what a lovely room," she said, awestruck as Samantha led her into what had to be the back lounge.

"Thanks." Samantha gestured to a chair. "I'll cut straight to the chase because every second counts. Raphe approached you and he shouldn't have. The trouble is, I'm a bit of a coward."

Carrie Ann began to warm to her. When she was up against it, Samantha didn't have quite so much side. "Yeah."

"Stunning isn't he? I feel so lucky every day I wake up next to him. Same as you feel with your boyfriend I would imagine? Look, maybe we ought to go into the kitchen, it's less formal and I feel like I'm giving an interview to a maid in here."

The house yielded up more of its secrets. It seemed to have endless rooms as Carrie Ann followed her through. Every one was painted in cream and finished off with matching accessories in the same color—from the sumptuously upholstered furniture to the carpet. There was also a conservatory lavishly filled with tropical plants. She was so nervous of marking the carpet she slipped off her shoes and padded about in her stockinged-feet. Samantha, she noticed, was barefoot anyway.

The kitchen was Carrie Ann's dream, her gaze sweeping around to appraise the four ovens. Who would need four ovens? And the state-of-the-art sink that was situated in a work station in the center of the room that sported a bunch of flowers that Samantha must have been in the process of arranging.

"Neat, isn't it?" Samantha's American accent was charming. It wasn't a drawl just a nice accent. "I realize what you're thinking. You expected the brash American." She took some stems out of the sink and finished arranging them in a vase. "The thing is, that's the other Samantha." She gestured to a stool at the workstation. "Park yourself, I'll only be a beat."

"Who did you mean when you just said, same as me with my boyfriend?" Carrie Ann asked naively, as she picked up the trailing length of conversation from a moment ago.

"I mean your boyfriend, Dominic."

Samantha must have heard her sharp intake of breath.

"Dominic isn't my boyfriend." God, that hurt — it felt like a knife twisting in her heart.

"Well, sure he is. I saw you two together one day walking down the lane. You can tell when two people are in love. He's so dishy isn't he? I remember I went to this function some years back and I saw him there with his dad. I guess I was kind of privileged to see them together, Dominic doesn't like the limelight does he? Probably why he's managed to remain a bit incognito in Puddleford."

Carrie Ann was about to ask when that was, but thought it was better not to. The most terrifying thing was that Samantha knew anything at all about it.

"Yes. I suppose he is."

"If I wasn't engaged to such a delicious specimen as Raphe I might have tried my luck, if you know what I mean. Come on let's get a coffee, there's no need to sit on ceremony. Plus, you could have left your shoes on. Raphe likes a change around every six months or so with all the soft furnishings and carpets."

Wow! Imagine changing your furnishings that often. It must cost a bomb. The French doors that led out of the kitchen were open onto a crescent shaped patio or terrace. She would never have believed she would step inside a WAG's house but here she was and surprisingly she wasn't as out of depth as she thought she'd be. She warmed to Samantha the more she talked to her. She stifled a yawn. It was so relaxing here.

She shot her a glance. Samantha seemed serious as she glanced up with a grin. "But as I say, I'm getting married to Raphe." She turned the huge diamond engagement ring on her finger.

Carrie Ann had heard rumors about the colossal value and size of the ring but never imagined she would see it close up.

"Although, there's always time for one last fling." She brushed past Carrie Ann whispering in her ear. "Only kidding. Would you like something stronger? I need a glass of champagne if I'm honest."

"Coffee would be lovely. I don't drink."

"Wise thing. Neither do I usually, well only champagne. I'm scared to death of alcohol after seeing the ravening beast it made of Mom." Samantha was exceedingly direct. "The demon drink they call it, and it's very true."

"Unless it's used in cake." Carrie Ann made a witty quip. She hadn't done anything like that before. For a second she wondered if she had offended Samantha.

Samantha blinked at her. "That's true. I have such a decadent weakness for champagne truffles as well, but you would know about the sweet treats side of things."

That afternoon, she and Samantha talked. Carrie Ann didn't want to look as if she was leaping at the job and anyway she couldn't, because it was such a lot to take on, but Samantha seemed to enjoy detailing the food. She was nothing like the woman she presented on camera, which showed that Nina had been right in what she'd said only yesterday. You couldn't judge a book by the cover. In fact, in her own home she was so laid back, it was untrue. Samantha spent some time on the telephone discussing the wedding preparations while Carrie Ann sat in the lounge cradling yet another cup of coffee and totted up her sums. After finishing her calculations, she strolled through into the kitchen and put her notebook on the table. Samantha had flicked on the coffee machine again and was in the process of opening the oven, taking something out and emptying it onto plates. It smelled out of this world.

"I thought I'd rustle us up a snack, so sit down." She burst out laughing. "Well, that's a lie. I get my stuff in from town, all made up from this great restaurant and then I pop it in the oven, I'm afraid." She picked up knives and forks wrapped in a napkin. "I do lie and say it's my own work. In fact I've got in rather hot water over that." She pushed across a plate of salad and pasta before settling onto a stool opposite Carrie Ann. "So, how long have you known Dominic, then? I can ask you since you're having your lunch and not technically at work now are you?"

"A fair while. Look do we have to talk about him? It's like ripping off a painful plaster."

"Ouch. Like that is it? So he was your lover?"

"I didn't say that."

"You didn't have to. I told you before, it's written on your face, besides which, he doesn't stop talking about you for a second. So what happened? Why did it end? It seems to me like he's the perfect match for you."

Carrie Ann felt an unexpected warm glow tempered with anguish and despair. So he had been gossiping to Samantha about her, had he? How well exactly did they know one another? The thought of that made her mad. It might have been all water under the bridge but she still felt like she was ready to explode. She dug her fork into the salad. "It's very complicated. My life is very complicated."

"I know about your life. Half the village does." Samantha was tucking into the meal, seemingly oblivious to what she'd said.

The knife in Carrie Ann's heart dug and twisted even deeper. She was horrified. "They do. Who does? And I know you met Dominic, Samantha, but you seem to know him awfully well, if you don't mind me saying so."

"Everyone knows about your life. It's common knowledge what an ogre your father was keeping you tied to the house like that. I should know. My father was a dreadful bully too. Why do you think I escaped and got into modeling? I wasn't allowed to do anything. It was the only way out. And as for how I know Dominic." She blinked at Carrie Ann. "These things just happen in my set and I suppose"—she peered at her fingernails—"I harmlessly flirted with him and he liked me and we just got chatting. Don't make such a big thing of it, because it's not. These things happen."

Carrie Ann tried to rein in her emotions as she pushed her food around her plate and Samantha continued.

"Keep that one about my father close to your chest. I have a feeling I can trust you, Carrie Ann, but not that many people know that. I like to keep personal parts of my life, secret. You see it took me ages to get over it." She leaned across the table and squeezed her hand. "As for you and Dominic, it's okay, darling, it's old news. I wouldn't worry about it. You can't keep anything secret in these villages."

"No, no, I guess not." Now the shock was wearing off, surprisingly Carrie Ann didn't feel as bad as she thought she would. "Look, can we change the subject, if you don't mind?"

"I do mind," Samantha mumbled through a mouthful of zucchini spaghetti. "But if you must."

"I need to talk about your cake. The decorations are notoriously difficult and I don't know yet what you want."

"Raphe told you."

"Raphe didn't tell me much, only that it was themed."

"Yeah and boy it's terrific. You ought to see my dress and the costumes for the bridesmaids. It's going to be the talk of the town. Let me tell you about it, I love talking about it. It's Moulin Rouge. I adore Paris, it's where Raphe proposed to me and I so love everything about it. And I adore that film I must have watched it a hundred times. Instead of having a simple bride and groom model, here's what I thought and it's my only *must have*. I want me and Raphe on top of the cake in Moulin Rouge outfits."

"Okay." This seemed quite a challenge but not beyond her capabilities. "I can manage that, but I'll want to add my own little twist here and there. Are you all right with that?"

"Babes, I'm fine with that so long as we're on top." Samantha winked at her.

Carrie Ann took a deep breath. If she intended to do it, she would have to set to work right now. As with Miranda's and the Sleights' cakes, she didn't have long and the most tiresome part of the procedure was the planning and approval by the client. Why did this keep happening? Oh, she knew of course. She couldn't afford to pick and choose her jobs yet. She wanted to make an impression and so she was forced to take everyone's leftovers, so she could show her tenacity of spirit.

"What happened with Forrest?" she asked.

"You wouldn't believe it if I told you." Samantha stared at her over the rim of her glass. "The premises burned down but they thought it might be a bit you know..." She raised her eyebrow.

"What, suspect?"

"Yes." Samantha lowered her voice as if someone might hear. "Afterwards I found out some juicy gossip, as you do. Forrest wasn't going through such a hot time. He threw a tantrum and it got him booted off his cookery network contract. After the fire, it wasn't as if he didn't try and put things right. He said this other guy would do the cake but you know, I don't trust that. I didn't know this" — she made quote marks in the air with her fingers — "other guy, and I have to feel this kind of empathy with people who do things for me. I was always like that with photographers." She blinked at Carrie Ann. "I realize what you think, babes, you think what a shit I was to you before, and I was. I was very rude. Although it isn't an excuse I was going through a lot of crap at the time, and you know that's half my trouble, I open my mouth and the words come pouring out. Do you think you could forgive me, I feel enough of an ass as it is?"

Carrie Ann opened her mouth then closed it again when she saw the tears that had collected in Samantha's eyes. Sam fiddled in her pocket for a tissue. "You don't know how I feel. I mean everyone thinks I have it so together when in fact I don't. Underneath the surface I'm a jibbering wreck. The whole wedding could be a shambles now and I so wanted it to be memorable. A couple of other cake companies said they could do it, but they needed more time. I won't lie to you, Carrie Ann, I realize what this must look like. That I'm treating you as a last resort. But it isn't like that. I forgot about you and then Raphe pointed out how cool it would be and that you were local. I really, really want you to do this. Please." She grabbed Carrie Ann's hand. "Please say yes, you wouldn't ruin my big day, would you?"

"Why didn't you come into Oh Crumbs! and ask me yourself?"

Samantha twisted her ring nervously. "Sure. I can see how this looks. You reckon I think I'm too above myself to come in there. Shit, what a mess." She bit her lip. "God, I need to tell you something but I'm scared to. Oh, what the hell here goes. The reason why I didn't visit your little bakery is because people steal things out of my mouth and write it down wrong. They're continually wanting a story out of me, just because I lose it and I have such a temper in public. The fact is I'm scared shitless walking into places. People recognize me everywhere I go. You don't know what it's like not being able to go down the road for a loaf of bread without being pounced on. I thought about it, naturally I did and then I thought what if some paparazzi follows me. You'd better get used to that because when you get famous, which I am sure you will, they'll rip you to pieces and misinterpret everything you say. I'm not at all like the picture they paint of me, well most of me's not, I promise you."

"Paparazzi in Puddleford, I don't think so."

"You'd be amazed. They're everywhere." She burst out laughing. "Now I sound a nut don't I?"

"No," Carrie Ann said. "I think I can guess how you might feel. It doesn't look like you leave me any option, does it. But your wedding's only ten days away, isn't it?"

Samantha nodded enthusiastically, leaping to her feet. "Yes." She was beaming, her tears forgotten. "I knew you'd turn up trumps." Before Carrie Ann could move out of the way she hugged her.

"There's miles to go, I haven't said yes." Carrie Ann felt as if the air was being squeezed out of her, as Samantha continued to hug her.

"Please, please."

"Okay, okay." How could she turn her down? "I'll give it my best shot. I don't know if I can pull it off though."

"Yes you can. I could pay you what I was going to pay Forrest, honey. It's a lot of money."

"It's not about the money, Samantha. I'm not a genius. I don't have much time and I have to sketch out the ideas first."

Samantha grinned at her. "I think you are a genius, Carrie Ann. The genius of Sweet Secrets. Anyway to pick up the story about Forrest. I know I shouldn't say anything, but the fire looked so suss. He's a prodigal spender and he's not that flush, so I don't think it would have been beyond him to dream up some insurance scam. The way I see it, I bet I had a lucky escape. I don't know why I went with him in the first place. He's a right pig—have you ever met him?" She puffed her cheeks out and put her hands on her hips making a swaying movement. "He's blustery and very camp and so, so rude. Actually"—she winked at Carrie Ann—"I think I might be quite glad his place burned down. Can you believe the nerve of it? When I showed him the dresses because I wanted to harmonize them with the cake, I overheard him talking to one of his flunkies and he said I would look like mutton dressed up as lamb, I mean I know I'm thirty-eight, but that was a bit harsh."

"So you reckon the fire could have been a set up job?"

Samantha shrugged. "Who knows. It wouldn't be the first time would it?"

"For God's sake, do something," Raphe said.

Carrie Ann thought she'd glimpsed him silently watching from the door and he now strolled into the kitchen. "I'll never hear the last of it if this wedding's spoiled. Samantha has her heart set on a Moulin Rouge theme and the cake was going to be the centerpiece with the burlesque dancers. She has the pictures, she helped design it."

"Raphe," Samantha wailed. "I didn't want to go into that."

"Go and get your portfolio of ideas, sweetheart."

Samantha gave her fiancé a withering look then slithered off the stool and left the room.

"Sorry to butt in. I couldn't believe my ears when she told me you were coming. I half expected you to turn it down."

Yes, Carrie Ann had decided she truly liked Raphe. For a footballer and TV personality, he was down to earth.

"We're pinning our hopes on you. I told her she should have gone with you in the first place but you know Samantha. She had to have some hotshot, just because she read about him."

"Look, Mr Jenning."

"Raphe."

"Look, Raphe. I'm a small scale operation at the moment and even if I could do the cake, I don't know if I could do the rest of the catering. I'm not a catering company. I know you said you have that in hand and you were having the catering took care of by someone else." She took a deep breath. "The point is, I operate in a certain way, it's kind of my trademark. I like to harmonize things myself. I don't like working with other people."

"Yes, but it's the cake that's the important thing, right? I'm sure we can work our way around that problem just this once, can't we?"

Carrie Ann was deflated. Raphe was forthright and direct. She doubted she could get the better of him. It was a gargantuan job. She kept thinking of excuses not to do it but Raphe was so nice and looked so earnest. The time factor was a nightmare, though, and she wasn't feeling on top form. She knew she shouldn't let her emotions get a grip on her like this, but she couldn't help it.

"I'm going to take this away with me." She snapped her notebook shut. "I have lots of ideas, but Samantha might not like them."

"Not like them?" Samantha came into the room carrying a thick book. She gripped her fiancé's shoulder and he hugged her. "I think I'm bound to like them."

It gave Carrie Ann a warm feeling just watching them. She could tell they were very much in love. How could she say no? She sighed and sat back down. It was going to be a long afternoon.

Chapter Sixteen

Latham offers her a spoonful of chocolate mousse and she runs it over her tongue. For some reason she doesn't feel as excited as she normally does when she's pressed this close to her lover.

"What is it, Carrie Ann?" Eyes glittering, he flicks his tongue across his lip as he nudges her legs apart. "If I didn't know better I would say your mind isn't on us this afternoon?"

"Don't be silly, Latham. How can my mind not be on you?" Carrie Ann is pushed up against the work surface in Latham's high-tech kitchen and a blob of chocolate is trickling slowly down her cleavage.

Latham's finger follows it as he pops the buttons on her smock and her dress pools down around her ankles. She loves the feel of his tight, muscular body against hers, the way he dominates her and makes her feel submissive.

Edging his finger under her black lace bra, he pushes it up, trapping her nipples and pinching one, coaxing it between his thumb and finger. Carrie Ann lets out a low moan and clutches the work surface behind her. Her body kicks into overdrive with Latham and she can normally feel the crackle of lust in the air, today though that crackle is not there.

I don't love him anymore, *she thinks.* He isn't real. *Now where did that thought come from? Then as she stares at Latham, she begins to edge away, because something, something awful is happening. Latham looks kind of odd. It is then she realizes her lover is actually nothing more than an icing figure and all his features are blurring around the edges as the organic food coloring softens and melts dripping down his skin and his hard muscles become doughy and gloopy. No sound will come out as she tries to say something, digs her fingers into his arm and finds he is nothing more than very soft royal icing and he smells far too sickly sweet, so sweet it makes her feel nauseated. Carrie Ann is about to scream until...until...*

It's just a dream, *she tells herself.* Pull yourself together. *But even if it is a dream, or more accurately a nightmare, the sight of her fantasy man is so horrible she has to screw her eyes tightly shut. When she opens them she finds herself in exactly the same position, except now where Latham stood, there is Dominic. She feels like weeping with relief but she doesn't, because now it is Dominic's fingers beneath her bra.* This is a dream *her inner voice insists again, but so what. This feels real, this feels right.*

"Oh, Dom, I missed..."

She can't say anymore because Dominic is down on his knees. Hands on her hips, he presses his lips to her cunt and sucks it in while his hands travel around her to cup her buttocks and jerk down her pretty lace panties.

"I don't think we have the need of any of these props do you?" He gazes up at her. "I know this sounds super corny, but you don't need the embellishments of any chocolate, sugar or icing, Carrie Ann. You're great as you are."

It's just a dream, *she chants as he bites. Yes gently bites her flesh and nuzzles her belly. She fizzes all over.* "Ooh." *Her hands sink into his hair urging him on, this feels so good. His mouth is inside her, tonguing her cleft and sliding back and forth, circling her hole then tickling her clit. She can't resist this climb toward orgasmic bliss.*

There's so much to say, but it doesn't matter, nothing matters because this feeling melts everything away, just like it melted Latham into the little sugar puddle on the kitchen floor.

"I, ahh…"

He pulls her down onto the tiles and they tumble around, Carrie Ann kicking and twisting her legs around him. He wrestles her bra from her shoulders and wraps her hands in it so she is left squirming and at his mercy. Then he stands over her dripping the rest of the chocolate mousse, plop, plop onto her belly and between her legs.

"I thought you said…no props."

"I lied."

God, she can't bear it as his hot tongue travels over her. He pins her down and no way can she push him away, not that she'd want to. But there's something she has to say, something very important, she thinks, mind clouded – all of her secrets melting away under the force of this – this lust…love. How could she ever have imagined that she craved Latham more than Dominic? Dominic is…

Nudging aside her legs, he unzips his jeans and snuggling down between her knees caresses her with lazy sweeps of his tongue. He tastes her like he would a fine dessert. He does not rush things, he nibbles and licks and digs, just a little bit deeper with each movement. His mouth is pressed against and nuzzling her mound as he pushes his tongue higher and higher still to stroke her velvet walls. She begins to work her hips in tune with his thrusts, pushing him deeper, wanting more, knowing how this will feel, can feel. It can feel even better with time as they get to know one another's bodies. A dark thought intrudes and she cannot identify why it is there. Wrapped within this sugar bliss, is a sweet secret she can't quite extract. It is like one of

Rommy's mysterious flavors that she can't pinpoint. But what does it matter? A smile paints her lips as her whole body becomes liquid and pools out. Dominic's sex-scented tongue is now in her mouth, she wants to hold him but is at his mercy as he pushes her legs wider apart with his, and positioning his cock rotates it, coming into her right up to the hilt with considerable finesse. Something unlocks inside her belly. It is like a tidal wave of lust and all of her emotions pent up for so long, release in a crazy swirling vortex of pleasure. Raising her legs higher still she welcomes him inside, hears his purr of pleasure as he sinks his hands into her curls.

"Oh, Carrie Ann, you sweet secret."

Then it is the mad ride again, the slow seduction giving way to pumping, hot needy lust, a flowing of juices, just like he is stirring her, beating her up to just the right consistency to make her burst with flavor and texture. As she reaches that orgasmic moment and Dominic fills her, hot, pumping – his thumb buried in her cleft, helping her reach the pinnacle of the mad whirling sensation – her cry sounds as if it comes from a long way away.

She comes down a fraction from the ecstasy only to feel it start again on and on. Will it never end?

* * * *

It was hard, so hard to push away all her conflicting emotions and the dreams that kept coming back at her as if they were trying to remind her or force her to face up to something. She had to get a grip, had to concentrate, but it was difficult.

She had to admit the new job at least focused her and gave her a multitude of opportunities to show off her talent. First of all, Carrie Ann made her sketches on paper. These showed the cake at its various stages of assembly including the models. Then she put a crayoned color chart up the side. When she was ready she would take samples of the cake and the various icings over to Samantha who could make her mind up. She was at least grateful her client had decided to go with a Genoese sponge because they were one of her strengths. She had her own idea on fillings though and they were at variance with Forrest's.

* * * *

Her stomach was full of butterflies on the day she was due to go back to The Pines. Samantha had kept on ringing her and the two of them had struck up an unlikely friendship.

"So let's have a look." Samantha could hardly keep still with excitement, as she turned the notebook around so she could look at the new sketches. "My God, these are brilliant. They're miles better than Forrest's. Carrie Ann, you're amazing. Do people know how good you are?"

"I'm not that good. I've had no formal training."

Samantha blinked at her. "So what. Do you want me to let you into another secret?"

Carrie Ann nodded.

"The most qualified chef that I know — and I know a lot, I can tell you — is Marcus. Most of them are self-taught and in my opinion the self-taught ones are generally the best. They're ready to learn and they're innovative. Why do you think Marcus has taken a shine to you?"

"Pardon me." Carrie Ann laughed. "Everyone keeps matching me up with Marcus. As if. Look at me."

"I'm looking at you," Samantha said. "And you're gorgeous and talented. Why wouldn't he like you?"

"I'm not gorgeous. You're the definition of gorgeous."

"Gorgeous can be bought, darling." Samantha propped her chin on her fist and stared at her. "It's amazing what they can pull out of the bag with a good hairdresser and some makeup."

"That's a joke." Carrie Ann bit into one of the cookies she had brought with her. "You look fantastic, even with no makeup."

"Know something?" Samantha who had been revered all her life for her rigorous diets, picked up a cookie and nibbled it. "I'd give my looks up to be respected and have an ounce of talent. Do you know they turned me down at the WI even though I was willing to help with their fund-raising?"

"That's Puddleford for you." Carrie Ann giggled.

"Rumors are rife about you and Marcus. Raphe and I dined up at The Manor the other night and he's apparently gaga over you." She didn't look at Carrie Ann although a smile quirked her lips.

"Marcus is from Paris. I bet he's deluged with sophisticated Parisian women when he goes home."

"So what?" Samantha blinked at her. "He's into you. All he could talk about was the zing and pop of your jam fillings." She winked and it was a very dirty wink.

"Thanks a bunch."

Samantha took an age to turn the pages of her notebook before looking up, and Carrie Ann was compelled to cross her legs and rub her ankles together nervously as she did so.

"You're a magician."

"Do you mean it?"

"Sure, I mean it. Will the figures look precisely like that? I mean she looks like me and he looks exactly like Raphe in the pictures."

"Well." Carrie Ann dragged over her holdall. "Just so you could see, I brought this along." She reached inside and pulled out a container before placing it on the table. "Here's some sample models so you can see the dimensions and color ways. This way you can decide if things are fine before I start. It's an awful lot of work." No wonder she had had that dream, she mused, her entire attention had been concentrated on the figures.

"Think you can do it on time?"

"Sweet Secrets prides itself on never failing."

Samantha reached in the box, taking out the icing figures. "Shit." She clapped her hand to her mouth. "Excuse my French. These are brilliant, ten times more detailed than Forrest's. They look real. She even has pink cheeks." She turned the Burlesque dancer in her fingers.

"You said you wanted burlesque in the manner of Moulin Rouge. So I'm going to put you and Raphe right on top in burlesque dress and then around the edges of the cake I'm going to do the cast from the movie. Instead of flowers I'm going to put small fans on the edge of the cake and maybe a few playing cards. It's given me artistic scope. I like to take people's requirements down and then ask for some artistic license to work on expanding my ideas."

For a second she thought Samantha was going to pose an objection. Then she nodded. "Yeah, yeah. I can't see any problem with that. Just don't go too mad. That's fantastic. If I didn't know better, I would have said you'd been trained by Latham. I remember going wild over his figures. He's hot stuff, we've rubbed shoulders more than once."

"Mmm." Carrie Ann's hands shook. The thought of Latham still sent her into a juvenile spin but not such a heady one. The trouble was Samantha had noticed.

"Well hey, you like him." She grinned. "You have a crush on him."

"Only a little one," she replied.

Samantha exploded into gales of laughter. "That's not what he'd have you believe. He's always going on about how gargantuan it is. I, though" — she tapped the side of her nose — "happen to know different."

"Big as in?" Shit, she realized. How could she sound so naïve? She was getting hotter and hotter. Samantha could be very suggestive.

"Don't be embarrassed, I know how filthy I am. I don't need to spell it out do I? The thing is I was on a photo shoot and they were doing a few takes of him while I was there. He's such an ass." She lowered her voice and leaned across the table. "What's stuffed temptingly down his jeans isn't what you think. I caught a glimpse." She held her stomach as she burst out laughing again. It was ages before she could compose herself enough to go on. "He sticks something down there to impress the women."

Carrie Ann's eyes widened. She couldn't help her surprise.

"Want to know what?"

She shook her head. It seemed like Samantha was going to tell her anyway.

"This plastic parsnip called Eric." Samantha said high-spiritedly.

"A...a..." Carrie Ann stuttered. "No way."

"Yeah. Sick isn't it?"

"So, who's going to do the catering? It would be good if I could have a word with them about the desserts." She wanted to swiftly change the subject.

The smile vanished off Samantha's face. "Mmm, I want to talk to you about that."

"But I thought you and Raphe had it sorted."

"Yes." There was a slight flush to Samantha's cheek. "We kind of do."

"You can't kind of. You either do or you don't. Oh, Samantha, come on. Don't throw a spanner in the works at this late date."

"You see the thing is, I couldn't stop thinking about that spread you did."

"What, the one for the Sleights?"

"Yes."

"But that was a one off. I told you. It was way out of my comfort zone. I wouldn't do it again. I'm a cake company." Carrie Ann sat back in her chair. "That was Dominic being clever. He stuck me in it with that one. He never gave me any choice about the catering lark."

"But it was such a success maybe you ought to think about having a sideline. I mean it went down a storm, everybody was talking about it."

Carrie Ann didn't like the direction this conversation was taking.

Samantha seemed nervous. "Actually, I don't think you're going to like what I have to say very much."

Carrie Ann pulled her notebook back across the table and replaced the figures in the container, experiencing as she did so a weird feeling in the pit of her stomach. "Okay, what is it. You'd better let me know?"

You could have heard a pin drop in the kitchen, it was so silent.

"The thing is, after I saw that spread it got me thinking that I wanted Dominic."

Carrie Ann's jaw dropped. "Are you mad, Samantha?" She put her head in her hands. "How could you spring that one on me?"

"It's tried and tested. I liked what I saw and heard. Better still the two of you together, well you seemed to harmonize. It was perfect. Every one said so."

"No way and besides he's gone. I told you we've split up." That hurt, truly hurt to say it.

Samantha's mouth formed a thin line. She swallowed. "I hope I haven't been silly and prejudiced my chances because…"

"What?" she said slowly. "What have you done, Samantha?"

"It was like fate, when he approached me and said he could handle the catering. It wasn't as if I pressed him or anything. He offered."

"What? How?"

"He didn't have any problem with it. When I said about my ideas for the cake and pointed out I could somehow liaise without the two of you actually having to, you know…?"

"He what?" She leaped to her feet. "I don't believe it, he had no right. I don't think you realize, Samantha. I haven't seen him for days. I don't know what he means." She held her hands to her head. It was like a nightmare as her world came tumbling down around her. "Besides, Samantha, oh, it's impossible. You're nuts to even think it would work."

"Babes, I think it would work, the two of you are on the same wavelength."

"That's not the point." Carrie Ann felt like screaming.

"Honey, I don't think he went as far as you thought. Look, I don't want this to appear like I'm sticking my nose in, but he's staying at The Angel, I honestly think you ought to see him and talk about this."

She couldn't believe it. She was filled with a mixture of anger and elation. Anger for a variety of reasons mainly because Ally had been staying there, and she hated to admit it, but she was as jealous as hell. Elated because he was still here, almost close enough to touch. But why hadn't she seen him around? Frowning, she paced the floor. She must have looked mad.

"How could you do this to me?"

Samantha peered at her fingernails. "Look I don't want to tread on your toes especially since you're doing my cake and we don't have much time left. But he's an ace choice for the job and you have to admit we're up against it." She paused. "How much do you know about your boyfriend?"

"I told you he isn't my boyfriend."

"Far be it for me to say anything, but in view of who his father is, it seems Dominic is well placed to do the catering."

She felt as if she was going to choke. Her throat closed up and the room began to slowly spin. She clutched the table. "I know all that... I know who his bloody father is, Winston bloody Everton, super chef." What was happening? She hardly ever swore and now...now Samantha's voice seemed far away and she felt incredibly light-headed.

* * * *

She'd fainted. She'd never passed out in her life. Carrie Ann woke up thinking she was in a surreal dream. She was lying on a wonderful pink swagged four poster bed and Samantha was leaning over her patting her forehead with a sweet smelling cloth. "There you are, babes. I'm so sorry. I went and put my big foot in it as usual."

It seemed easier for Carrie Ann to close her eyes and pretend nothing had happened. "Ooh." She massaged her temples. "What happened?"

"You're exhausted. Been burning, as you say...the candle at both ends. I think that's part of the problem. I should know, I had it when I was modeling." Samantha helped her sit up. "Sorry I broke the news like that. I really blunder into things and you must think I'm a right busybody."

"Well, to be truthful, Samantha, that is how you come across sometimes."

"Yeah, I know. But I get so bored up here sometimes and I'm so good at listening in on gossip. And to be frank, I've been so interested in following your story..."

"Mmm, I suppose I can forgive you then." Carrie Ann burst into tears, she couldn't help it. "I'm an idiot. I've been an idiot ever since I met him. God, I'm stupid." Her pent up emotions flowed out in one rush and to Samantha of all people. She couldn't hold it in any longer. "You don't want to hear this."

"Of course, I do. You need to talk about it. Don't tell me you've been bottling it up because that leads to all sorts of problems? I could tell you a thing or two about that. I've been going to shrinks my entire life."

Carrie Ann subsided into silence. She didn't want to think about what Samantha had told her, it was too complicated. She plucked at the bedcover. "When he took off, I thought he'd gone for good. How could I not have known he was staying at The Angel?"

"I don't know. All I can say is it's easy to overlook the obvious. He evidently didn't want to leave did he?

Perhaps he needs to think things through. I mean..."
Samantha curled up beside her on the bed. "There's
lots of ways of looking at this. He must still want to
see you or he'd have taken off home. Maybe you
should go and see him."

"I don't think so. You don't know what went on
between us."

"What, what don't I know? I know about falling in
love with the wrong person."

"Yeah, but I bet you didn't lie to Raphe."

Samantha punched a pillow then rolled over to stare
at her. "Boy, what have you done?" She smiled.

"Something idiotic." Carrie Ann traced the pattern
on the bedspread as her mind tumbled. It was good to
get it out in the open to someone else other than Nina,
like a kind of catharsis. "My relationship with
Dominic has been a string of lies from start to finish."

Samantha shrugged. "So what. Just go and tell him
the truth."

"Are you kidding? I wouldn't know where to start."
Carrie Ann peered at the ceiling and more tears rolled
down her cheeks. "When I met him it was terrific, I'd
never had anyone half that attractive show an interest
in me. And the trip to Arlem had been so brilliant,
made me feel new and shiny and like I could do
anything. That's how they make you feel there. Then I
came home and it was like a last thrill. He sat next to
me when I was waiting for my flight and before I
knew it I had to make myself sound more interesting
and I lied."

Samantha frowned. "Why?"

"What do you mean, why? Look at me. Dull, plump,
uninteresting Carrie Ann." She knew she was being
cynical.

"But you're so clever, why would you want to lie and especially about a tyrant like your father? If anything I would have thought he would admire you for what you did. I certainly do."

"Don't come that one, Samantha. I realize what you're trying to do. You're attempting to make me feel better. Well, it won't work."

"I am not, honey. One thing you should know is that I tell it like it is.

When Samantha talked about it, it seemed so simple, so trivial.

"It was so easy and the more I told him the easier it got. Then it became harder to undo it all, until I'd kind of barricaded myself in."

"He strikes me as a great guy. I'm sure he'd understand."

"There's much more to it than that. I mean as if saying he loved me wasn't enough, it took guts to come clean about his father when he felt so sensitive about it. It's so sort of one-sided and it made me feel heaps worse. It's a shipwreck."

"Loves you, eh, lucky you," Samantha interjected.

"Look, will you be serious." She shook her head. "It doesn't matter how perfect we seem for one another, despite him coming clean about all the stuff going on in his life, it just wouldn't work. Besides, to add insult to injury, I tried to hide our relationship. It looks like I was ashamed of him. So, you see. See how impossible it is?"

Samantha seemed to be considering something. She helped Carrie Ann sit up. "Come on, babes, you have to pull yourself together. Let's go out into the conservatory, I've got a nice bottle of champagne. Let's christen new beginnings."

The sun blanketing her shoulders in a golden glow, her anxiety ebbed away and she began to feel warm and happy. The champagne fizzed on her tongue and the bubbles went up her nose. The both of them sat on the garden seat on the terrace enjoying the evening and munching away on the selection of cakes Carrie Ann had brought with her. She felt an inner sense of triumph that Samantha, aficionado and patron of the green salad brigade, was feasting on her food again.

Samantha licked a smidgen of cream off her fingers. "You see I'm far from perfect. There's another one of my secrets for you." She paused. "By the way, I was wondering if you'd like a regular catering event at one of my afternoon tea events. You're on your way and I want to bag you now before you get famous."

"What, me?"

"Yes, you."

"God, Samantha, I'd love that." Carrie Ann, having gotten over the initial shock of Samantha's revelations, was now reveling in the warmth of a new found best mate and frighteningly candid friendship with this most unlikely woman.

There was nothing like a shared confidence to make her feel better. It turned out Samantha had done a fair amount of lying herself because Carrie Ann was now party to one or two exclusive secrets that could make her a fortune if she sold them to the press. "What if I go and blab about what you've told me today?"

Samantha laughed. "What, you, Carrie Ann? You're terrific and far too nice for that, that's why I told you."

"Yeah, yeah. I wish people wouldn't keep saying that about me when actually I'm a dreadful person."

"A few white lies and a few nasty thoughts geared at a father who treated you like the mud on his shoe doesn't make you a bad person. I think you've learnt your lesson haven't you? You won't lie again."

"Not on your life." *No, I most certainly won't, because I'll never fall in love again. I don't think I could bear to.*

* * * *

One good thing came out of her despondency, she immersed herself in work so she didn't think of Dominic and created a cake that far surpassed even her highest expectations. She was aware of a dark cloud on the horizon, though, that made her feel sick every time she thought of it and that was him. Samantha had created an invisible tie as fragile as spun sugar between them that she couldn't yet break completely. Hard knowing he was close, working with her even though she had chosen not to collaborate face to face with him. Every day when she was in Oh Crumbs! she wondered if he might come in and make the first move, which would probably be a good thing since Nina was getting fed up with her crying out the back.

"Look I know we're called Puddleford, but we don't want a second ford."

She knew Nina was trying to cheer her up but for some reason the comment simply annoyed her.

"That's not funny."

Nina winked, before coming over all stern. "You could be the one to make the first move, perhaps that's what he's waiting for."

"No, I won't. Then he'll think when we have a bust up, I'll be the one to give in and I'm not doing that."

"You're impossible. One of you has to make the first move. If not, these stalemates have a habit of blowing up in someone's face."

She shrugged. Dominic had had a pretty large secret of his own, but her lie was a lot more serious in her book, because it seemed there was no reason for it, she shouldn't have done it in the first place. She was being so self-righteous with herself though and she had to be realistic. People didn't always think of the right thing to do, they acted on impulse and especially when they bumped into a one in a million guy. She shook her head to try to loosen the cobwebs. It was better not to think about it because then she started going around in circles.

* * * *

Carrie Ann glanced up from a tray of seeded baps and he was standing in the doorway with his hands in his pockets. She couldn't control her reaction and she dropped the serving tongs with a clatter.

"Hey." He smiled at her sadly. "As pretty and obstinate as ever."

She couldn't speak, it was as if the words had become lodged in her throat like a traffic jam.

"I just came to tell you I finished the catering for Samantha and Raphe, totally to their satisfaction I might add, so I won't let you down. I paid that nice guy who owns The Angel to let me use the back room there." He slapped some typed sheets down in front of her. "Here's all the details. Samantha filled me in on every explicit detail, so I think everything will tie in to your satisfaction."

"Don't be like that," she said softly, trying to quell the stirring, the wanting to reach out and touch him. At the same time her emotions were reaching boiling point. She felt her anger flare but just as quickly die down. She thought she could guess the reason why her new friend had been so quiet lately and had carefully steered any conversation away from Dominic. She had wanted to protect Carrie Ann from more pain. Once Samantha's tarnish had been rubbed away that was what was revealed underneath, a bright, caring person.

"Like what? How do you want me to be?"

"Not like this, that's for sure."

Before she knew it, he had come around the bench and had hold of her wrist. "Why?" He was angry. "You knew I was staying at The Angel. So why didn't you come and say something?"

She stared up into his face. "The same reason you didn't come and find me here and do the same thing." She prized his fingers free. "One of us had to make the first move. Don't touch me, Dominic. You came to say what you had to, now I think it's best for both of us if you leave." *There, he had not expected that.*

He actually looked shocked.

She thought the feeling of power would buoy her up, instead it upset her. The truth of the matter was, she wanted to make it up to him, but she couldn't back down.

He seemed to deflate, shoulders sagging as he spread his hands. "All right, I don't want to argue about it. It's your big day tomorrow and I don't want to spoil it for you. You deserve your big moment, Carrie Ann."

"By the way," she shouted as he reached the door. "It makes me wonder why you bothered with me in the first place, Dominic Everton. I bet you could have any woman you wanted."

He spun to face her and he looked very, very angry. "Just as shit low on self-esteem as you ever were, aren't you, Carrie Ann? Some things never change and it's crap. Why the hell did you think I bothered? Because I loved you. Why do you persist in writing yourself down when you're so lovely, so trustworthy, so sexy?"

Well, that's it, isn't it? Loved you, past tense. So she had really blown it.

Chapter Seventeen

When she woke up, Carrie Ann rushed to the window. It was another sunny day, perfect for the wedding and she had to make an early start. Nina would arrive in an hour to take her up to the house to make the final preparations, although she had done as much as she could yesterday. Samantha was having a huge marquee. Because in her own words, "You can't rely on the English weather not to spring a few surprises."

Now all Carrie Ann had to do was take the refrigerated stuff in the Oh Crumbs! van up to The Pines.

She showered then changed into the neat, light woolen two-piece she had chosen for the day and pulled a comb through her tight curls. After Nina had moaned at her, she had seen the sense in looking good. God, she didn't know if she could go through with it. What would it be like meeting those celebrities? Samantha had assured her they were only normal people and she would introduce her so she felt at home, but it was hard to believe that when Raphe and Samantha rubbed shoulders with so many sports and TV stars. Still, she had to be brave and do it. The first time at anything was most often the worst. Instantly, that made her think of sex with Dominic. On that particular occasion the first time had surpassed her wildest dreams. She felt grim as she headed out to the van. She would have done anything to make this day perfect and it would have been if Dominic had been there.

Nina went to say something, but Carrie Ann stopped her. "If you say anything I'll kill you."

"How do you know I was going to say anything?"

"I can tell. You get a look on your face."

Her friend shrugged. "You're spiky, but I'll let you off because you've got nerves."

Carrie Ann tugged down her skirt.

"You look nice. I hardly recognized you."

"Thanks."

They pulled out of the drive and headed out of town. Carrie Ann wound down the window. Even this early it was baking.

"So where is he? He's bound to be around isn't he?"

"By *he* I take it you mean Dominic. No. He saw me yesterday."

"Wow." Nina bounced excitedly on her seat. "So you made it up. I knew you'd see sense."

"No, we didn't make it up. He came to see me to explain about the catering and to make sure I knew he definitely would be gone by today." She struggled with her composure as she bit her lip and stared out of the window at the fields.

"Oh, you didn't let him slip through your fingers? How could you? He's so yummy."

Carrie Ann said nothing. The fact she ought to have said something and fought for him had been playing on her mind ever since. It had not been worth this pain. If it had meant her backing down, maybe she should have. "I don't want to talk about it anymore, thanks. It's over. I need to focus."

"No." Nina patted her knee, giving her a queer look. "Of course, darling."

They turned up the hill toward the house and made the short journey between the towering pine trees. Carrie Ann got out of the van to ring the buzzer on the electronic gates. There was only the beautician's van and a couple of BMWs in the drive, the guests wouldn't start arriving until lunchtime. Samantha's maid answered the door because apparently the bride to be was having her nails done. That was Samantha, she smiled. She didn't mind because it gave her plenty of time to check everything was in order.

Nina kissed her cheek. "Well, I'd best be off. While you're hobnobbing with the snobs, us mortals have to get back to the mill."

"For goodness' sakes, I know you love Oh Crumbs!."

"I'll pick you up later then?"

Carrie Ann hugged her. "I don't know what I would have done without you, Nina, you've been such a cool friend."

"Pah." She made a dismissive gesture with her hand. "If you can't help your best mate, who can you help?"

* * * *

Samantha seemed distracted and so she should be, Carrie Ann mused as her friend did a slow pirouette. The outfit took her breath away. She had opted for a corset dress in clinging pink silk finished off with feathers and ribbons. On any one else it would have looked ridiculous but the provocative flourishes suited her since she had such an extravagant personality and could carry it off.

"Wish me luck," she said.

"I will but you won't need it with Raphe." Carrie Ann kissed her cheek and was enveloped in Samantha's trademark scent.

The happy couple were off for the short wedding ceremony at the church in Weston and things had to be ready when they got back. Carrie Ann was glad of the peace and quiet and the assistance of the rented catering staff who were fantastic and had the buffet organized instantly. Out at the front of the house was parked a large camper van that belonged to one of the satellite stations which had exclusive rights to film the private ceremony. She was intrigued as she watched the cameramen setting up equipment in the conservatory for Samantha and Raphe's interview. Then she caught sight in the distance of the American anchorman, Tony Smythe. His height and steel gray hair were unmistakable.

She checked the plates, knives and forks then adjusted the cake slightly. It was then it struck her, a mixture of crippling emotions that were so intense she had to sit down. What had she done, when she could have had what Samantha had? Sure, it wouldn't have been this glitz and glamour, but she had found love and that was rare. A crawling sensation spread through her belly. She didn't know why she was torturing herself like this because it was far too late to save the day.

* * * *

"There you are," Samantha said, brandishing a glass of champagne. "I want you to meet some of my friends." She was back from the church and swept up in the celebrations as the hired band began to fill the summer afternoon with music.

Carrie Ann noticed Fred Ames, the local politician, a couple of WAGs and even a famous pop star who had won one of the popular talent shows and who she had seen on TV only the other week. She had to maintain her cool, this was what it was all about. For once in her life she'd been dealt a lucky card. But it was hard, hard holding it together without Dominic. She hadn't realized how much he had helped her and what an added sparkle he had provided in her life. Like a memorable recipe, it took a special pinch of one essential ingredient to make it perfect. God, she had felt like another person around him. He had been so good for her in so many ways. It had not only been a case of the physical attraction, but so many other things. He had been supportive and she hadn't had one panic attack since he'd been with her. In fact, she felt great and like an entirely new Carrie Ann. She smoothed her suit, wondering what he would make of her today. Would he like her new look? Would he be proud of her?

"I was about to have a word with Tony the anchorman for the satellite cookery networks, but he beat me to it. Now"—she put her hand on Carrie Ann's arm—"don't freak out but he would like to do an interview with you today. They have it set up." Samantha said.

"Me?" Carrie Ann spluttered. "Come on, Samantha, I can't. I..." Her voice trailed off as Samantha gave her one of her looks.

"Now, don't start that again. Of course you can, you have to. You owe it to Sweet Secrets. This is the best possible occasion for a launch. You have to climb out of that dark little closet you inhabit and embrace it. I would if I had a finger full of your talent. You might not get another opportunity for some free publicity like this and people are saying such good things about you."

"They are?"

"Yes, they are."

It was no good she was too overwhelmed by the occasion and every time she thought of Dominic she wanted to burst into tears. "I know I'd make a hash of it, don't force me." Her voice quavered, a reappearance of the old Carrie Ann.

Samantha shook her head. "I can't help but think you're making a huge mistake. But no one can make you do it, if you don't want to. I have a hunch when you've mingled though, and heard what everyone thinks of your cakes, you'll change your mind."

As if... Gazing about, she caught a glimpse of Raphe moving through the crowds looking incredible in his outfit.

"I'll chat to you later but right now I have to give my undivided attention to my new husband."

She smiled as Samantha drifted off. Who could blame her? He looked fantastic, very sexy.

Everywhere she walked the guests were talking about the cake, pointing her out and coming over to congratulate her. She soon lost count of how many times she was stopped and asked about her inspiration. That took her mind off her troubles. The one thing that was sure to loosen her up and get her talking was her work, because then everything seemed to slip away and it was as if she had put on a different coat—the new more confident Carrie Ann who was an ace at icing.

The afternoon was a sizzler. She found a tree to sit under. She had no appetite. She had to face facts she had made a big mistake. She obviously wasn't as together as she thought she was. No, it wasn't just that. She realized she loved Dominic. Yes, she loved him. She had probably loved him from the beginning if she was honest with herself. Now, she had gone and blown it, it was inevitable to be frank. Her confidence still wasn't brilliant, she doubted that it ever would be and it was her confidence that had let her down in the end. Maybe she expected too much from herself. After all, the world around her was full of more together and brilliant women than her, women who had everything—looks, careers and the toy boy.

She turned away, Samantha was coming toward her again. She sat down next to her. "Raphe's been whisked off for more pictures, I've had enough and I'm going to sit this one out."

Carrie Ann burst into tears. "I…I'm sorry, I think it's the stress. It was so difficult getting it together at the last second like that."

"Yes, yes, I know, you were brilliant, though, and I can't thank you enough. You know I've been racking my brains to try and find a personal way of saying thank you and I came up with this." She pushed an envelope into Carrie Ann's hands. "It's not much just a spa day, I thought we could go together."

"Argh…" Carrie Ann shook her head. "Sam, it's not necessary, this is so embarrassing, you're paying me a packet as it is."

"Contrary to popular belief, I'm not that hard-assed bitch they think I am, you know that. I've told you most of my secrets."

"I know. I think you're fantastic."

"Thanks. I think you're fantastic, too, and that's why I want you to enjoy a little treat, you need it, you look bushed. Lord, listen to us, we're like a mutual admiration society." She put her hand on Carrie Ann's arm, the large diamond solitaire flashing. "You're going places. Funny isn't it. When I got into modeling I thought I'd be doing it all my life and then along came Raphe. He's not like people think either."

"I know that. I love Raphe. He's so funny." Carrie Ann sniffed.

"Yeah, he is. I'm very lucky, but what seems like a miracle relationship hasn't always been like this. We've had our rough patches and we've had to make some tough decisions. Take for instance, the fact I've decided to give up work at least for a while and kind of retire off the scene. That sounds daft because I love my career and it's sort of in my blood but I need a break."

"What you?"

"Yes me, sounds mad doesn't it. I might go back later, there's plenty of work now for older models." She hesitated. "There was another decision too, it might seem wacky to some people. I know I seem a bit old, but more and more women are having children late in life and me and Raphe want a kid."

"Hey, that's brilliant, I'm so pleased for you." Carrie Ann couldn't conceal her exuberance.

Samantha nudged her. "Looks like a christening cake coming up some time soon." She fell silent. "Getting back to what I was saying about thanking you. I think I know what happened."

Carrie Ann stared at her.

"You fell hard and fast for Dominic against your best instincts, didn't you? Just like I fell for Raphe. I'll let you into another little secret no one knows about. I had vowed never to get married and I held out pretty well until he came along. He wore away at me, wore away that hard bitch until he revealed the *me* underneath. Sure, that old girl is still there, but I like the new Samantha immensely and it's the same for you."

Carrie Ann could sense this conversation was building up to something and half of her wanted to run away.

"You split up with him for loads of reasons and not just those staring you in the face. I bet you were scared. Yes." She wagged her finger. "I've been there, through those doubts, and I understand how you feel. You wonder what the hell he sees in you? Well, I've had that same inner voice nagging away at my self-confidence. I realize I scrub up okay but underneath this, well you've seen it, you've caught me often enough on a bad day."

"Pardon me, Sam, we're hardly the same." Carrie Ann laughed, her tears forgotten. "I told you before, even without your makeup you're stunning."

"You're very kind but we all know what a bit of slap can do. Come here." She hugged her warmly. "Boy, I like you, I'm so glad we met and got to know one another. Anyway like I say, I know how you feel and because you were scared you began looking for excuses. Excuses to ruin your relationship before you got more hurt. Rommy made you like that didn't he?"

"What do you know about Rommy?"

"I told you before. Everybody knows about you and Rommy, sweetheart. When I came to live at The Pines the village was rife with talk about how his daughter was his virtual slave and had no life of her own. Naturally, I was curious. I watched for you, saw you on several occasions and was amazed at this pretty girl who had no confidence."

"You did?"

Samantha nodded. "People make you think things. They drain your confidence away until you think you can't cope on your own. It was the same for me. My mother made me out to be this bimbo, whose only purpose in life was to hang onto the arm of a man. It took me years to find my inner self and Raphe helped me over the final hurdles. Needless to say, now people accuse me of letting Raphe have too much control over me. Like for instance in this decision about giving up my job. The difference this time is I made the choice and I made it look like Raphe's idea. In actual fact, I've been playing him because for once in my life it was what I wanted to do—to make him feel good and to hell with what anyone else thinks."

"So…the point being?" Carrie Ann asked.

"You spent enough time nursing your father, so don't be a martyr. You don't know if you'll ever find love again, so are you going let it pass you by?"

Carrie Ann took a deep breath. "It already has," she blurted out. "I don't think he'll ever forgive me. I guess the demons of the past took me over."

"I know, honey, and now I'll tell you one more thing. One of my largest failings is I can't keep my nose out of other people's business."

"And what does that mean? How does that relate to my situation?"

Samantha held her hand tightly. "You remember when I said about wishing there was something I could do for you? Well, here it is. I want to offer you…" She made a gesture with her fingers. "A little smidgen of advice. Carrie Ann, life really is too short and that perfect guy might only come along once. You need to be brave and get this all out in the open. Tell him the truth. Sure, it'll hurt some, might even be the biggest thing you've done in your life, but it'll be worth it."

Carrie Ann sprang to her feet, almost knocking over her chair. "My God. I feel sick. I can't believe you're even suggesting it, Sam, you know how I feel about the whole thing."

"I've got broad shoulders, I can take it if you hate me. Just go for it, Carrie Ann. I hazard a guess he's worked out the situation more or less, probably guessed there was more to the story." She pulled Carrie Ann back down beside her. "You have to tell him the truth. I can't let this fiasco with two of my most favorite people go on forever."

Surprisingly Carrie Ann didn't feel as angry as she'd thought she would. What Samantha had done was water under the bridge now wasn't it? It was a huge relief to have her new friend point out some of the big issues she'd been agonizing over, but the biggest remaining problem was that even if, and it was a big even if...she could find the courage to confront Dominic, it would be the nail in the coffin of their relationship. He would never forgive her lie. "I shouldn't have lied in the first place, it's my own fault," she murmured.

"I think he's a big enough guy to understand why you did what you did."

"But I bet he wants nothing more to do with me. I bet he's as mad as hell."

"Babes, I don't know." Samantha fluffed out her gown and clambered to her feet. "I think what hurt him most was you didn't want to face up to your relationship."

"Mmm, yeah, I realize I was wrong over that, now that I think about it."

"One thing I will say." Samantha gave her a sly look. "It says something that he slaved away for you here today."

"What do you mean?"

"On the catering."

"He didn't have to." Carrie Ann was quick to point out.

"No, but don't you get it? It still had to harmonize with your theme didn't it and he put you first, didn't want to see you fail. What kind of a man's that? I would say a million dollar guy like Raphe."

Carrie Ann folded her arms as she glared at Samantha petulantly. That was true. How could she have missed that important point? Her frustration rose up in a tidal wave. She thought she saw a weird expression cross Samantha's face. Was she up to something else? "Samantha, I can't help but think you're up to something."

Her new friend made a gesture with her hands. "What, *moi*? You're being paranoid. The only thing I did was have a word with Tony about how utterly brilliant you are. Honey, you need good sex to get that frustration out of your system. Come to think of it, lover boy number two is over there, ogling you."

Carrie Ann looked up and caught a glimpse of Marcus over by the marquee. He waved and smiled at her. She turned back to Samantha who now looked awkward.

"So why did you pick Dom for this job, you must have known what agro it would cause? I don't truly believe what you told me before."

Samantha put her champagne glass down on an empty table. "Believe me, despite you and Dominic being two of my two favorite people, I hold true to my view. He was the best man for the job, especially with his father's credentials."

"That's it." Carrie Ann clapped her hands to her head. "I've had enough." She felt funny as if her thoughts were whirling faster and faster out of control. "No, Sam, I don't take that on-board, with your money you could have had any caterer you wanted."

"I wanted Dom. I thought I was the shallow one. It's not all about technique, it's about other things. Look I don't want to go into deep and meaningfuls here. Besides he's going places and Raphe is dead keen on helping young people realize their dreams. You should know about that better than anyone."

Carrie Ann became angrier and angrier. "What else do you know? What's he said to you?" She grabbed Samantha's arm hard. "Tell me, Samantha."

Samantha's lips seemed sewn together and no words came out. She quietly prized off Carrie Ann's fingers. "Calm down, Carrie Ann, everyone's looking. For once things are very simple."

"You contrived this. You thought if you hired Dom and put me in this awkward position, by some miracle we would be forced together and we might make it up. And I thought I was the idiot." The nerve of it. She felt like she would explode.

"You're wrong, but I'm not arguing. Anyway here comes lover boy," Samantha said smoothly, grinning at Marcus.

Carrie Ann glared at her retreating back. She didn't know whether to shout or burst into tears.

"*Eh bien*, there you are, *enfin*. They're doing a waltz. I wanted to ask you to dance with me." Marcus sat down beside her.

"No thanks."

"The fact you make yourself unobtainable, makes you more...how can we say...tasty?"

"Marcus, for God's sake."

"It is true, *chérie*. Do you not realize that a woman who does not show interest only makes a man madder?"

She did like him, she couldn't help it. But she didn't fancy Marcus, who was now gazing at the sky. There was only one person in the whole world Carrie Ann would ever truly fancy and she knew that now.

"You know something, *petit chou*, it is case that love grow and especially love with two people who have an immense amount in common. I think my father who has chateau in Loire would be fascinated with you."

Carrie Ann peered into the distance. Was she going mad? Her imagination must be playing tricks on her because she was sure she'd caught a glimpse of Dominic's blond hair. Her heart missed a beat.

"One dance?"

"One dance then."

Marcus flicked a glance at a tall man with a glass in his hand who was bearing down on them. Then taking her by the arm, he whisked her away before she had chance of finding out who he was.

"Who was that?" She frowned as Marcus steered her toward the tent where the band was now playing a medley. "You're being very rude, I think he wanted a word with you."

"Not me, you." Arm around her waist he moved her onto the dance floor, where couples were now shuffling about. "You see how everyone looks at you and forgive the metaphor — how everyone wants a slice of Carrie Ann." He breathed in her ear. "And why is that? Let me tell you. Because she is going places."

Not far away, Samantha was dancing and she looked breathtaking, like a spread from *Vogue* and so did Raphe. Carrie Ann was pleased for them.

After the dance she stood holding her glass and applauding, but she hardly heard what Samantha was saying in her speech. Every so often she would be distracted by someone else coming up to her and asking for one of her business cards. Then the tall slick man who'd tried to catch her attention before took hold of her arm.

"Carrie Ann Jude, my name is Laurence Teebon. I'm responsible for Cake Artists Forum."

Marcus glared at him. "What is this? This is very rude."

"I'm sorry to butt in, but I have to leave. I kept waiting, hoping to catch you alone, then I talked to Samantha," the man carried on obliviously.

The name seemed familiar—she trawled her mind for information. Samantha and Raphe were just heading out again onto the dance floor, surrounded by dancing girls. She would certainly sit this one out.

"Teebon, you must have heard of me?" He smiled at her. "I have a proposition that might be of interest to you."

Marcus stamped his foot. "Well, you know where I am."

"Don't be like that," Carrie Ann squeaked, surprised at the outburst as Marcus stomped off indignantly showing his Gallic pride.

Laurence smiled. "Always the impetuous Frenchman. Honestly, though, I have to talk to you." He maneuvered her out of the crowd to a quieter area. "I know this sounds funny but I want to get in before anyone else does. I want to offer you a blog on the forum." He grinned as he saw her look of surprise. "Yeah, I know what you're thinking, that you're not a blogger. But you could be and I know folks would think you were great."

"Oh shit. Teebon, yes of course. What must you think of me? Of course I know about you. But...I don't think I heard you. The forum's largely American based isn't it?" Was this a dream? It must be. In a second she would wake up tangled in her bed sheets.

"Well yes," Laurence said. "Naturally, and it would mean you having to be there. The forum is largely participant based as you already know. Our members are interactive through their blogs but don't just remain a name behind the keyboard. We have meet ups, cookery competitions and TV appearances, so we all get together, as well as doing the blogging. That's the part that reaches out worldwide." He winked at her. "You didn't think you'd only stay this side of the Atlantic did you, not with your talent. All of you come across the pond at some point. If you want to be huge that is."

"Do we? Yes, I suppose we do." Of course, she'd thought of this with America still being such a golden land of opportunity, but not so soon and not right now. She wasn't prepared, although having said that she never seemed prepared for anything.

He pressed a card into her hand. "Here's my number. Believe you me I want to get my pitch in early because you're going to be big, very big. My forum will give you a massive chance of spreading your wings. Soon, the sky will be the limit. There's not many places you couldn't go. Anyway, think about it."

"Yeah, yeah I will." She felt like she wanted to scream and dance a jig. This exceeded her wildest expectations. It was then she experienced the return of the sharp knife stabbing her heart. It had taken Laurence Teebon to point something incredible out to her. She wanted to share her happiness with Dominic and he wasn't there and she didn't know if she could stand that. Life was nothing without him and over the last few weeks it had lost its sparkle.

I know what I would like to do. I want to be with him, I want for us to have this adventure together. As a one man show she knew that Sweet Secrets could be a terrific success but there was more to it than that. The added force of the two of them together could be even better, and Dominic's know-how would provide an added ingredient making Sweet Secrets more of a success than she had dreamt possible.

Her heart thumped. It wasn't only about love and amazing success, it was about a partnership. Of course, she still realized she had a long way to go to heal, but he had added something. And it wasn't about having a muse either. No, it was much more than that. She wanted to hear his voice every day, have him hold her. No, she did not know what the future might bring, but she had to take the risk. And that was what her life was all about now, wasn't it? In that instant she knew the next step she had to take, despite its mind-blowing magnitude. Even at the risk of him turning his back on her, saying he despised her for her lies, she had to take her courage in both hands and tell him the truth about Rommy.

"Excuse me, Mr Teebon. Yes, yes, I will think about it, I promise. But right now." She hesitated. "Right now, I have to do something very important."

Pushing her way through the crowds, she headed toward the edge of the dance floor where Samantha was standing, her lovely blonde hair blowing in the breeze. Breathlessly she grabbed her arm. "Samantha, I will do it. If it's not too late. It isn't is it? For just a moment I got cold feet, but you're right. This kind of opportunity won't come up again. I want to do the interview."

She saw her friend hesitate and wondered if she had blown her chances. Then Samantha laughed. "No, it's not too late. I'm thrilled. I'll go and get Tony." She patted her shoulder. "I'm so delighted for you. I was so hoping you'd change your mind. Come on." She began steering her through the crowds. "Let me get you back over to the makeup van. They have a place next to Tony's where they do all that stuff."

"Makeup van. Shit. My God, I don't know if I can." The bright lights, the sight of the mirrors, pots and hairbrushes made her feel shaky and nauseated.

Samantha mock glared at her. "Stop being a ninny." She clambered up the steps and pushed Carrie Ann down in a chair in front of a mirror. "This woman's called Steph and she does the glam bit. Let her get you ready."

Carrie Ann stared at the young girl who was sitting in a corner eating a sandwich. Then taking her courage in both hands, and electrified by her sudden decision, she leaped to her feet. Something had happened, something momentous. She realized this opportunity might not come again. It was an opportunity to at least put things right and she couldn't and mustn't blow it. Her plan might not work, but she had to give it a try. Tears filled her eyes and one trailed down her cheek.

Samantha darted outside and returned with a full glass in her hand. "Here's some champers for my favorite girl and you're to drink it all this at once. It might just give you the courage you need." She pecked Carrie Ann on the cheek. "Now go for it, girl, it'll be..." She chuckled. "A piece of cake for you."

Carrie Ann went to object but Samantha was already heading out of the door.

She sat back in the chair staring around her at the array of makeup and brushes.

"Hi, don't look so petrified. You look like a rabbit in the headlights," Steph said.

Carrie Ann picked up the champagne glass and took a sip. "Just Dutch courage," she said to Steph as she came toward her wielding a makeup brush.

"You'll be fine, everyone feels nervous their first time being interviewed. You'd be amazed. Once you get on there you forget about it though and Tony's one of the best interviewers. He really makes you feel at ease."

Carrie Ann's hands were shaking but surprisingly not this time with nervousness, but with excitement.

"And," she carried on. "You'll have to get used to it won't you, because you're a genius. Tony will be delighted he bagged you. I'm not kidding, they're all saying it, everywhere you go everyone's on about you. They think you're amazing and it's so clever, so very clever, the ideas you have with icing. It's fresh, original. You have to be a genius to think of something like that."

"I don't think so."

Steph shook her head as she placed curling tongs into Carrie Ann's hair and began arranging her curls over her shoulders. "Modest too. I think you're wonderful and I've met some arseholes I can tell you.

Take that ninny Latham Crosswick. He makes me mad."

Once Carrie Ann would have jumped to Latham's defense. Not today. Instead she sat stock still. She had to think exactly what she was going to say, or did she? Maybe it would be best to go with the flow and be her normal self. One thing was for sure. There was no going back.

"Ninny?"

"Yes, ninny. He's so up himself you'd need a flash light to see where he's gone."

Carrie Ann burst out laughing, for the first time she could see the funny side in the situation and it helped to lighten the mood. How would she be able to do it? Could she manage to go through with this huge step?

Her breath caught in her throat as the girl led her to the interview van and she saw the technicians standing to attention, the blazing lights and of course, Tony Smythe, mumbling away like he always did. He was famous for rehearsing his lines out loud.

Something odd was happening as she felt a weird impulse seize her. Carrie Ann stood in the doorway of the van, then turned around to blink at the assembled partygoers. As she did so she saw a figure move to the back of the crowd. A suave figure — Dominic. His hair curling across his shoulders, eyes sparkling but still that look of doubt on his face. Her heart leaped. A feeling of pure joy and relief. Something released inside her, it was like her heart and soul were opening up to fly and in that second she felt lighthearted, practically euphoric. Nothing else mattered. She had to make her own choices now. She was free.

Tony settled her into a chair and winked at her. "It'll be fine. I think you're going to be a natural. People love you. Be yourself, be easy, I won't ask you anything you can't handle. Remember, though, this is going out live as part of the wedding diary."

She tugged down her skirt and took a deep breath. "I know and I'll be okay."

"So. Carrie Ann, introduce yourself to everyone and let us into the secrets behind the owner of 'Sweet Secrets'."

"Yeah, eh, sure. My name is Carrie Ann Jude and I'm the owner of erotic cake design company Sweet Secrets." As she spoke the words came to her naturally and she realized she had the uncanny facility to easily express how she felt about cakes and her hopes and dreams.

Tony kept nodding at her, it was all the encouragement she needed. Every so often he held up his fingers telling her how much time she had left. Ten fingers for ten minutes, then seven. It went incredibly fast and she didn't falter once. Time was sliding away and she had to get in what she must say.

"And what about romance, Carrie Ann? A pretty, talented and, dare I say it, hot woman like you, must have her eye on someone special?"

She took a deep breath and nodded. "Mmm, actually this leads me on to one more thing I want everybody to know. I met this amazing guy, yes I know how that sounds. You kind of expect someone of my age to be settled down with kids already. The fact is I never thought I would meet a man I felt so intensely about because I've led a pretty hard and sheltered life, well you'll get to know more about that as you find out about Carrie Ann Jude.

"I thought life had passed me by and then out of the blue I met Dominic. It was scary at first and I tried to run away, but he wasn't having any of that. but the trouble is I bungled it up and my inner fears became so bad, I made sure I pushed him away." She paused.

Tony nodded encouragingly at her. "Come on, Carrie Ann, this is the human element of a story that I am sure your audience will absolutely love. Tell us more, so everyone can associate with and get to know you better." He made a gesture for her to continue.

"I honestly thought I wouldn't get this wedding cake done on time, especially since Dominic and I had split up. Yeah, we split up over something silly. Lies and misunderstandings. The trouble was, I was living in the past. I also thought I was able to go it alone. Since he left I've had to face some hard facts though and something struck me. I was afraid of letting love into my life. I was afraid of the love of a man I realized I wanted to know so intimately he could melt me." She smiled. "Yeah, stupid isn't it? Love is just like a great recipe and to make the perfect cake you have to sometimes add a bit of a sour note to the sweetness. Recipes sometimes don't seem perfect until they come together at the end, all the elements blending to create a final product that will blow your socks off." This was ridiculous, she ought to be thinking of winding it up. The trouble was when she got started she didn't seem able to stop.

"Hey, Carrie Ann, you have a real way with words, but I think your listeners want to know where you're going with this." Tony grinned.

Carrie Ann stopped. "Oh, sorry. I was running off then, letting my thoughts get the better of me. I can't help myself. Everything I think of is in terms of food and especially cakes. I think of life in terms of cooking. What I'm trying to say is I like to see my relationship as stronger through him. Like a pastry crust with holes in, he just patched them up. Now I have to get risky with flavorings and textures and see what happens."

"Perhaps you ought to save all those wonderful metaphors for your cookbook."

Carrie Ann looked up sharply, she was about to say something else then realized it was probably better not to. He had to be kidding didn't he? A cookbook? Tony indicated to her she only had a couple of minutes left and he looked deadly serious.

"Anyway, Dominic is such a sexy guy, but he is also the loveliest man on this planet. He might be younger than me, but he is warm and kind and I realize that he loves me. I hope, Dom, if you're out there you hear this because I know I was wrong, wrong in lots of ways, but I'm not afraid anymore." She glanced again at Tony, who waved his hands as if to say, *What do I need to do, Carrie Ann has it all together.*

She'd done it and rather than feel exhausted she was exhilarated. As she left the van, people clapped her on the back, tried to catch her attention and get her to sign the odd autograph. Carrie Ann, though, was intent on scanning the crowds. She was sure it had been Dominic, but where was he? She'd been certain that following her revelations he'd come after her and forgive her. But he'd gone. No happy ending for her then.

Chapter Eighteen

Samantha and Raphe had left on her honeymoon and Carrie Ann was desolate as Nina helped her pack up the plates. They were practically licked clean as Nina liked to point out, which had to be a good sign. There was nothing left of the buffet and she had a notebook bulging with orders. Next week the backbreaking work would begin, since today she'd truly given birth to Sweet Secrets, hadn't she?

Nina patted her back. Carrie Ann sagged against the table and burst into tears. Nina hugged her.

"Oh, Carrie Ann, I'm so sorry. But you know it isn't that easy to fix something. You can't just say a few words."

"I did it for him, Nina. It was very difficult."

"No, you didn't. You did it for yourself because you knew it was the right thing to do. I'm so proud of you and it was sweet and lovely and even had me going."

"Thanks," Carrie Ann said tearfully, blowing her nose.

* * * *

She was so tired she'd left all the stuff in the shed to sort out the next day, before making a cup of chocolate and sitting down in the conservatory. It was dark now but the night was warm. Outside the garden was fragrant with the smell of elderberry. Already her mind was spinning through new ideas. It was then the knock came.

She was so tired that for a second the truth didn't dawn on her. Carrie Ann went to the door and opened it, to find Dominic standing there, hands in his pockets, with a carrier bag of Chinese food at his feet.

"Well, are you going to let me in?"

"I hate you." She ran at him, pummeling him with her fists. "How could you run out on me? I was in pieces. I thought all sorts of things." She stopped, staring up into his face. "I thought you had gone forever. Why, why?"

He grabbed her hands, kissed her fingers and led her inside, forcing her to sit down at the kitchen table.

"I had to do it. There wasn't any other way. It wasn't what you thought. I knew that if I left you alone, you'd think things through because you're one tough cookie, Carrie Ann. It was a gamble on my part because I'm so crazy about you and I risked losing you. You needed to reach that place inside though, where you felt ready for *us* and ready to let go and embrace the future and I know how hard that can be."

"I still hate you." Face screwed up she began to sob. "I thought you'd gone back to her. Eh, I dunno I thought all sorts of things."

He shook his head before taking a deep breath. "At the very least I had to leave knowing that you were sure of the facts about Ally, that it was nothing like you thought." He hugged her and for a moment she struggled.

Then she became submissive in his arms. This was where she wanted to be, this was where she belonged. He stroked her hair, circled her nape with his fingertips. "I took Ally home. It was rough, but I pointed out to her it was really and truly over and she oughtn't to delude herself anymore and I think she understands. Then I did something silly."

He held her away from him, smoothing her tears, a wry twist to his lips. "I came back to drop in on Samantha's wedding, just to see how it went, to see you were okay, and that was when I heard the interview and saw you. I knew in that second you'd healed, that you were ready. Ready to truly talk."

"I took too long to heal." She sobbed into his shoulder.

"No, no you didn't. We heal in our own time."

"I'm sorry, Dom, so sorry. It wasn't as if I was ashamed of you, of us, of anything like that, I was scared of shadows that weren't ever there. Now, I don't care. Don't care so long as you're going to be around."

"I'm going to be here for a hell of a long time." He pushed her away from him and she took a step back in surprise. It was as if she was seeing him for the first time. Then she kissed him like she had wanted to do for ages. Her lips tasting his, teasing. He stroked his thumb across her cheek, snubbing away a tear.

How could she have ever doubted this was what she wanted? She stared into his face and it gave her the courage she needed. Yes, she might lose him, but at least if she told him the truth she would put things right. In that moment, it was like a shaft of sunlight shined between a chink in the closed drawn curtains of her mind and she felt lighter and happier than she had in ages, empowered almost. It had started at Arlem and since then her inner strength had been growing apace, almost without her knowing it. She couldn't help smiling. It was like making one of her bad cakes that didn't turn out, not that she'd had many of those. Maybe the sponge was too dry, the filling too sweet, too oozy or not sweet enough. She could plaster it in buttercream icing but when someone bit into it they would know the truth and it would come as a nasty surprise. Sometimes she couldn't hide those mistakes and it was better to go back to basics and start again, find out where it had all gone wrong and even if it was agonizing, maybe amend the recipe and throw the old one in the bin. Trust her to see it in terms of baking.

"So." She patted the cushion next to her. "Now you'd better prop your eyelids open with matchsticks because tonight I have to tell you everything."

"What you mean this complicated tale about your husband? Fine, but how about heating through the Chinese first? Because it sounds like it's going to be a long night."

In the end it wasn't half as bad as she thought. She told him every little detail right from the beginning and he didn't interrupt, just let the conversation flow easily, as easily as buttercream icing. By the time they finished it was the early hours of the morning and the Chinese still lay mostly untouched.

"So that's Carrie Ann's secret?"

"Yes."

He shook his head gently, incredulously. "Know something, I'm so, so proud of you. You're the most amazing woman in the world. You did all that. You realize caring for someone that sick, even a father, takes a very special person?"

She didn't know how to reply to that, she just felt a warm, gooey sensation of relief inside.

"And the competition. You still have the tickets to Paris?"

"Yep and here's the other important thing." She kissed him on the lips. "It's only a weekend. But I can take a guest and I want you to come."

"What like a honeymoon?"

"Don't be that daft, let's don't jump the gun. Not quite yet." She slid the friendship ring between his clenched fist. "Perhaps one day, though, and only if you put this back on my finger."

He laughed. "I think I can do better than that."

He eased the ring on and kissed her hand. "You taste like icing. Why is that? Is Carrie Ann made of icing? Is she a sweet secret? Know what I would like to do with these fingers?"

"I can hazard a guess," she replied. Now all she could think about was the fact he had switched out the lamp and was unfastening the buttons on her dress. As his hands traveled, she floated blissfully.

Of course, there was still one secret Dominic didn't know about and that was her erotic fantasies about Latham. But now she wasn't so sure it mattered. She had a feeling they'd started melting away and her hot daydreams were only going to be reserved for one person in future.

About the Author

Constance is nearly always to be found with a pencil in her hand making notes for a new story. She has led a varied life and done many jobs from cup washer, lecturer, to new age healer but has always written since she was a child.

A major health scare recently though, made her see life differently, and after years as a part-time writer, she turned full-time, because as she says - life is too short not to do what you love. She has literally climbed a mountain and made many sacrifices to pen her novels and now builds on a fund of wonderful encounters with intriguing people, plus her imagination, to write stories with strong characters and determined and adventurous women.

When asked what kind of genre is her favourite, romance is always the answer because to Constance, romance - whether hot and steamy or sweet and emotional is always at the heart of a good story. She hopes her stories reflect all of life's facets from the struggling mother at home who finds a way out of poverty, the ardent and often disappointed dieter, to the girl who triumphs over sickness or has the courage to embrace her rather naughty side.

Constance loves listening to snatched conversations, which often gives her a seed to start a story, taking walks, revelling in the mysteries of life and baking and dancing, when she isn't tapping away at her latest novel, of course.

Constance Munday loves to hear from readers. You can find her contact information, website details and author profile page at http://www.totallybound.com.

Totally Bound Publishing

Home of Erotic Romance